An Arranged Marriage

JAN HAHN

A *Pride & Prejudice* ALTERNATE PATH

Meryton Press

Oysterville, WA

AN ARRANGED MARRIAGE

Copyright © 2011 by Jan Hahn

All rights reserved, including the right to reproduce this book, or portions thereof, in any format whatsoever. For information: P.O. Box 34, Oysterville WA 98641

ISBN: 978-1-936009-14-5

Graphic design by Ellen Pickels

Cover art entitled A Wet Sunday Morning by Edmund Blair Leighton (1896) and Fantasia in White by Albert Ludovici (1854)

Acknowledgments

I owe a great debt of gratitude to the following people who have given me so much aid in writing this book: To Jennifer Padgett and Beth Miller, who helped and supported me through the original manuscript; to *The Derbyshire Writers' Guild, Firthness,* and *Mrs. Darcy's Story Site,* who provided a home for this story on their websites and to all the readers at those sites who offered generous, daily encouragement; to Michele Reed and Ellen Pickels at *Meryton Press,* for their expertise and guidance; to Debbie Styne, my gifted and patient editor; to my friends and family who have cheered me on, and especially to Jane Austen, who created these unforgettable characters who have carved a lasting impression on my heart.

Chapter One

My Aunt Philips, a woman who devoted herself to the affairs of others for as long as I can remember, delighted in quoting proverbs. She also delighted in repeating them on occasions she deemed appropriate. Actually, she delighted in repeating almost everything she heard, whether appropriate or not.

As for proverbs, her favourite was "*Happy is the bride that the sun shines on.*" She echoed it incessantly during the seven days before my wedding, which happened to be the entire length of my engagement. On the morning of said event, when the heavens erupted in a storm of such magnitude the likes of which I cannot describe to this day, she shook her head, rolled her eyes, and tsk-tsked at such length that Mamá finally threatened her with banishment if she did not give over.

That morning, an explosion of thunder awakened our household at dawn with such force that I fully expected to witness Napoleon's cannon aimed at my window. If truth were told, such woe would not have been less welcome than the ceremony awaiting me. I stood at the window, watched the storm clouds unleash their fury, and judged the day perfect for *my* wedding.

At the hour destined for us to walk the short distance to the church, a hard, steady downpour caused Mamá to call for the carriages instead. I am sure it was a festive sight to see — a bevy of black umbrellas bobbing to and fro as the small bridal party hurried from Longbourn Church to the carriages and then back to our house for the wedding breakfast.

And shortly afterwards, if perchance any villagers had ventured out in the storm or peeked through their windows, they would have seen me step

5

quickly to avoid the puddles between the entrance to my childhood home and my new husband's carriage bound for London. What they could not have seen was the turmoil within me, how my reluctant heart yearned to splash through the mud in the opposite direction and to lock myself safely within the house.

I watched the raindrops trickle down the carriage window while the cumbersome vehicle lurched back and forth on the road to Town and my new life. Obviously, the mud increased in depth, for we seemed to reel from rut to rut. The farther we travelled, the greater the storm progressed in strength, as though heaven itself could not help but weep at the travesty of the union I had entered into less than four hours earlier. The man who sat on the opposite seat avoided looking at or speaking to me, choosing to pay as close attention to nature's deluge outside the window as I did.

We had said little to each other since the journey began. Indeed, what was there to say? Ill at ease with nothing in common, thrust into an awkward situation, each one wary of the other, we had ridden in silence for miles.

I smoothed the creases in my skirt, observing that the black bombazine melted into the ebony colour of the fine leather seats. Since I was already skirting propriety by wedding while still in mourning, I suppose I could have worn grey or at least a mixture of black and white, perhaps a stripe, in view of the fact that I was a bride, but I chose the same shade I had worn every day since the funeral. Black shoes, gloves, and cloak, as well as a dark veil over my bonnet caused me to appear in deep mourning, which I considered appropriate for the day.

My eyes swept over the interior of the coach, noting its rich lustre. The upholstery gleamed almost as brightly as my companion's highly polished boots had shone earlier in the day. Now, flecks of mud spoiled the reflection. My eyes travelled from his boots to the long grey coat he wore. It evoked memories of the times I had seen him wear it — at Netherfield Park in the earliest days of our acquaintance, almost a year ago when my sister, Jane, had been taken ill and convalesced there, and most recently, on the morning after I refused his first proposal of marriage. What were those words with which I had rejected him?

I had not known you a month before I felt that you were the last man in the world whom I could ever be prevailed on to marry!

"Are you warm enough?" Mr. Darcy jarred me back to the present. "There is a rug available if you are chilled."

I shook my head.

He turned his face back to the window. "We should reach Town by sundown if this blasted storm does not delay us."

I closed my eyes in dread at the thought and turned my face back to the rain-soaked landscape. Our wedding night awaited, and a more disinclined bride did not exist. Of course, I had been assured intimacy would not be initiated until I desired it, for that was a spoken condition of the marriage if not a written one. I blushed at the remembrance of Mr. Darcy's words.

"You need not fear that I shall demand my conjugal rights. The marriage will not be consummated until you come to my bed willingly."

"It may well be a frigid day in July before I do!" I replied.

"As you like." He raised one eyebrow, piercing my carefully fashioned armour of indignity with his dark, brooding stare. "But I do expect an heir, Miss Bennet. That is one of the terms of this contract. Make sure you have a change of heart before you are past child-bearing years."

"Then you had better withdraw the word *willingly*, Mr. Darcy."

"I shall not. I have never forced my will on any woman, and I shall not begin with you. If you cannot foresee ever having my child, then you must refuse the offer."

"Have I not already? Did I not refuse you six months ago at Hunsford, sir?"

"You did, but your circumstances have changed since then as you are well aware."

I blanched at his words and remembered how carefree I had been in the spring whilst visiting my friend, Charlotte, and her husband, Mr. Collins. That tranquil time had turned turbulent when I dismissed Mr. Darcy's first proposal with all my righteous anger.

I had been correct in doing so. Never had a man proposed in such an insolent manner. Why, he had assumed I would drop to my knees in gratitude for his great condescension in stooping to marry his social inferior! Well, I had put him in his place by refusing him with an equal omission of civility, and from the look on his face, I could tell that my words had penetrated his arrogance.

Only three days later, my light-hearted world had crashed about me. A post arrived at midnight announcing the death of my beloved father in a hunting accident. While lifting his gun to aim, the weapon had discharged, killing him instantly. In April, with new life springing forth all around us, my gentle, kindly father had died a most violent death — a death that should not have happened, a death that had far reaching consequences for my family.

My father's estate was entailed away upon his cousin, Mr. Collins, and he left only the smallest of fortunes to provide for his widow and five daughters. He had never been a man who looked ahead, and with a spendthrift wife who loved to dress her daughters as well as herself in the latest finery, extra funds evaporated before they could be tucked away.

Now, here in this grand carriage, I sighed as I remembered how I had boarded the early coach for Meryton the next morning. I did not even spare time to take leave of Mr. Darcy's noble aunt, Lady Catherine de Bourgh. I arrived home to find my sisters devastated, and I was struck at how small and lost my mother suddenly appeared.

Mr. Darcy looked up at the sound of my sigh, but he said nothing. We continued our journey in silence, a state that suited me. He was such a taciturn man, perhaps we would avoid conversation throughout the marriage, saying as little as possible to each other. I had little desire to talk to him, and I knew he felt the same, for in the whole of our acquaintance, he had rarely carried on a lengthy conversation with me. Instead, he attempted to wither me with his long, steady, disapproving looks. Well, he was mistaken. I refused to wither!

Lightning flashed through the windows, and a volley of thunder shook the carriage. I heard the sound of additional horses and voices and sat forward to look out, observing that we had arrived in a small village. Our vehicle pulled to a stop, and I could hear the shout of men's voices. Mr. Darcy immediately opened the door.

"The bridge is out up ahead, sir," the driver said. "The locals say we can't get through 'til the storm subsides."

"Is there no alternate route?"

"No, sir. This road's the only one passable in this kind of weather."

"Blast!"

"There is an inn, sir. It's not much, but at least it's dry."

Mr. Darcy nodded and closed the door, brushing the water from his coat sleeves. "It seems we do not have a choice. We shall have to spend the night in this God-forsaken place."

"It matters little where I stay."

He pressed his lips together and clenched his jaw.

The inn was small, and if I term it rustic, I speak with generosity. Mr. Darcy's footman had gone ahead and, per orders, informed the owner that his master was a gentleman, and he and his wife required the very best suite of rooms. We walked in to overhear him tell the innkeeper that it was our wedding night. The fat, balding little man laughed coarsely and elbowed his wife in the ribs.

"Their wedding night, eh? They'll have no need of a suite, then, will they, dearie? Just a great big bed! 'Tis a good thing, as we got naught but one room vacant in the whole house. See that other fancy carriage out there? A family of four got here just a'fore you. We let the other two rooms to them."

The footman argued repeatedly, offered more money, and finally resorted to threats, but to no avail. Only one room remained, and the owner could not conjure up another. Mr. Darcy swore and attempted to persuade the innkeeper to find more accommodations, but it was useless. I followed Mr. Darcy and the man up the stairs into the available bedchamber, all the while conscious of his wife's stares and whispers to the barmaid.

"I never seen no bride dressed all in black a'fore."

The room was small but clean. Mr. Darcy stomped around inspecting it while the innkeeper lit the fire. An old chaise that had seen better days sat on the left just inside the door, two straight chairs and a small table were placed near the fireplace, a narrow armoire rested against one wall with a dresser and mirror opposite and, of course, in the most prominent position in the room sat the bed.

"Supper's ready in 'bout an hour, sir, and my missus can assist your lady whenever she's needed. Is there anything else I can fetch for you, Mr. Darcy?"

"A bottle of brandy." His speech was clipped and angry.

"Yes, sir. Right away, sir," the innkeeper repeated several times as he hurried from the room.

I walked to the fireplace, removed my bonnet, and shook the raindrops from it. I stretched out my hands to the warmth of the blaze, and I could not help but smile slightly at the sight of Mr. Darcy pacing back and forth.

"It is not so very bad," I said at last.

He stopped and looked at me. "You think not? No, you would not, for you at least have a bed, while I shall be forced to sleep upright on a hard bench in the common room."

"If you do, it will cause talk."

He gave me an inquisitive look.

"Your servants are aware that this is our wedding night, and it seems they have shared the news with the innkeeper. If we spend the night apart, they will know this marriage is a sham. I have nothing to lose by that revelation, but I would think you wished to avoid such disclosure this early in the game. I recall that you said we were to *act* as though we were married in every respect when in the company of others. Was that not one of your requirements?"

Mr. Darcy stared at me as though measuring my intent in reminding him of his demands. From head to toe and back again, he slowly surveyed my form. I felt a flush creep up my neck to my face, and when I spoke, I was disconcerted that my voice emerged somewhat higher than usual.

"I did not say that, sir, to invite you into my bed. I have no objection, however, if you sleep on the chaise. Perhaps, you might request an additional blanket."

Mr. Darcy looked from the lumpy old chaise — its springs sagging with an obvious sway in the middle — to the bed and back again.

"Very well," he said at last. "If you have no objection, madam."

"None, as long as you afford me privacy to dress for bed and retire while you remain below stairs."

"I would have it no other way," he said and stalked out of the room.

For some reason, his last words stung. Why, I did not know, but it felt as though he rejected me physically, a feeling I did not like. Six months earlier at Hunsford, he had declared that he loved and admired me, that almost from the beginning of our acquaintance he had felt a passionate regard for me. His second proposal did not contain like statements, but I assumed some slight feeling still existed on his part, even though the subsequent offer was more like a business arrangement than any semblance of romantic application.

I drew near a mirror on the far wall and smoothed the slight frizz of my curls caused by the damp outside. Peering at my image, I noted the dark smudges under my eyes and the pinched hollows in my cheeks. I was much thinner than I had been at Hunsford, and I had slept little since this prospect of marriage had been thrust upon me. Did Mr. Darcy now find me unappealing? Had I lost the bloom that had attracted him in the first place? And if so, why should it matter? I disliked the man exceedingly.

A knock at the door preceded the entrance of the innkeeper's wife carrying a china pitcher and bowl. The barmaid followed with towels draped across one arm and a well-worn quilt on the other, and the innkeeper walked in with a tray containing two glasses and a bottle of brandy, which he placed on the small table near the fireplace. The maid spread the multicoloured quilt over the foot of the bed, smoothed it out, and turned it back so that it might be easily pulled up in the night.

"Here's your husband's brandy, ma'am," the man said, "although from the number of drinks he's had downstairs, I doubt he'll need it when he returns to you." He laughed and poked his wife in the ribs once again. Believe me, if he were my husband, I would put a stop to those pokes.

"Go on with you, now," she said, shooing him out, "whilst I help the lady with her toilette. You'll be wantin' to dress for dinner, I suppose, missus, although around these parts it's more of a cold supper."

The maid poured water into the basin and placed the towels on the dresser beside it.

"No," I said, "I shall go as I am."

"As you wish, ma'am," the woman said, but I caught her raising her eyebrows at the maid. "Is there anything you be needin' then?"

I shook my head, and the two women made their exit. I could see little reason to dress for dinner in that place. Surely, Mr. Darcy would not expect it, especially since I wore my best dress already — my best mourning dress.

Once again, I recalled the look of surprise on his face when I had appeared at the altar that morning dressed completely in black. My mother and I were the only ones to be so attired. Even Jane had discontinued her deep mourning clothes and resorted to grey and black stripes some months back. My younger sisters had discarded theirs much sooner and now wore only dark ribbons on their bonnets, Kitty sometimes neglecting even those. At times, I felt that all of them had forgotten our father except for me. My mother rarely wept any more, especially since she was no longer to be expelled from Longbourn. Was I the only one who still felt his loss with such a piercing bite?

Whatever Mr. Darcy felt about my dress had been the least of my concerns when I walked down the aisle. Getting through the marriage vows was the task that had almost caused me to run from the church.

"Wilt thou have this man to thy wedded husband, to live together after God's ordinance in the holy estate of Matrimony? Wilt thou obey him, and serve him, love, honour and keep him in sickness and in health . . ."

I had heard the vicar read the familiar words from the *Book of Common Prayer*, but when he paused and looked up to hear my assent, the lump in my throat ballooned so large that it constricted my breathing. I had to swallow twice before whispering, "I will."

When he continued and I heard Mr. Darcy utter his vows aloud, it sounded like a dull roar to my ears, and I could not have told you one word that he uttered. Then it was my turn to repeat after the minister, but all I could hear was the voice in my head screaming over and over, "You are lying! Lying! Lying!"

Swaying slightly, I had closed my eyes and shaken my head with the tiniest of movements as though I might somehow clear the voices from my mind.

"Miss Bennet?" the vicar had said softly, indicating that it was my turn to respond.

I opened my eyes and searched the old man's kind-looking face. He must have assumed I simply suffered an attack of nerves, and he repeated the words for me to say. That time, I forced myself to listen, and I responded in kind.

"I, Elizabeth, take thee, Fitzwilliam, to my wedded husband, to have and to hold from this day forward, for better, for worse, for richer, for poorer, in sickness and in health, to —" There I faltered, beseeching the vicar for help. Could he not see the desperation in my eyes?

"To love, cherish and to obey, until death us do part," he prodded.

I took a deep breath. I could feel Mr. Darcy's presence beside me, and I turned slightly toward him to see if he would permit me to stand there and lie before God and those witnesses, but his face was turned away from me, his gaze straight ahead, the light in his eyes turned deadly grey.

"To . . . to love." There, I had said it. Now I could continue and repeat the rest of the phrase, but my voice sounded toneless and dead to my ears.

Mr. Darcy must have put a ring on my finger, for I felt it now as I washed my hands and face with the water provided, but I had no memory of him placing it there. I have no recollection of the remainder of the ceremony, the short wedding breakfast thereafter, or the best wishes of the few guests in attendance — my Aunt and Uncle Gardiner, Aunt Philips and, of course, Mamá and my sisters.

Was anyone from Mr. Darcy's family in attendance? I could not remember. Surely, someone had stood up with him, as Jane had done for me. Oh yes, Colonel Fitzwilliam was there. I vaguely remembered him taking my hands before we left Longbourn and the sympathetic look in his eyes as he bade me farewell. Why could he not have been born heir to a fortune and asked for my hand? I did not love him, but I held him in high regard. His kind and pleasing manners were in such contrast to that of his cousin that surely I could be a wife to him with more ease and affection.

Suddenly, a great weariness washed over me, and I sank down upon the bed and closed my eyes for just a moment. Some two hours later, I sensed someone's presence. I opened my eyes to see Mr. Darcy standing by the bed. With a swift motion, he raised his hand to smooth his hair. Had he been about to touch me? I immediately sat up and looked around, observing the darkness outside the window.

"When you are ready, we can go down to supper." Mr. Darcy turned away to stoke the fire. The logs had burned down somewhat. The ashes now threw sparks of blue and orange in response to his prodding.

"I am ready." I glanced in the mirror and patted my hair. I swayed slightly as I stood and reached for the dresser to steady myself.

"Are you ill?"

"No, I must have risen too quickly. That is all."

"Then let us depart." He strode to the door, and I followed him, conscious of the smell of spirits about his person as he held the door open.

The main dish at supper was cold mutton, the fat so heavily congealed that I almost gagged at the sight of it. I picked at the sweetbread pie, but I could not abide any other dish. Mr. Darcy drank more than he ate, bidding the barmaid to fill his glass repeatedly.

I had never before eaten a meal with complete lack of conversation. I grew conscious of the easy chatter among the family members at the table next to us. The girls teased each other, and their mother softly chastised them when they became too boisterous. A wave of loneliness for my sisters, especially Jane, swept over me. The noise of the men in the common room adjoining the small dining area, some of whom were Mr. Darcy's servants, seemed to call even more attention to the silence at our own table.

At last, I gave up the pretence of eating and, placing my knife and fork across the plate, sat back in my chair.

"Do you care for anything more?" Mr. Darcy asked, and when I shook my head, he raised one eyebrow. "You have hardly touched your plate. Are you certain you are not ill?"

"I am perfectly well. I simply have no appetite."

"With what we have been served, I can well understand." He stood and indicated we should leave.

"I can make my way alone, sir, if you prefer to remain here."

"I shall see you to the room."

"It is not necessary."

"I shall see you to the room." His words were hard and insistent.

"Very well." My tone proved equally cold.

I could feel his eyes upon me as I climbed the stairs, knowing he was right behind me. The wooden steps were worn to a dull shine, the handrail likewise a burnished chocolate colour — facts of no importance, but a scene I can still recall to this very day.

Inside the room, Mr. Darcy poured himself a glass of brandy and walked to the window. I dropped my shawl on the bed and stood, waiting. Silently, he nursed his drink and peered out into the dark, wet night.

At last, I spoke. "I shall require at least an hour alone before retiring, and I do not need the maid. I can manage on my own."

He turned and looked at me long and hard, and then, placing his empty glass on the table, he proceeded to the door.

"Mr. Darcy, I would caution you not to drink excessively. The staircase is steep."

He turned, his hand on the doorknob. "Your concern is touching, but if I fall and break my neck, would that not solve your problem? You would be a rich widow." He uttered a laugh, short and mocking, and then closed the door behind him with sudden force.

I took a deep breath and let it out slowly, feeling the animosity in the room envelop me. How had my life come to this? How could I bear the future before me — a future bereft of love or happiness?

Slowly, I unbuttoned my dress and removed it. After washing myself, I slipped out of my chemise and pulled on a long, white nightgown. Mamá had packed it herself, but it was Jane, I knew, who tucked the dried sprigs of lavender between the folds. They both were such optimists, hoping to the end that I should grow to care for my husband. My mother, indeed, could see no reason why I should not be elated and grateful for an offer from such a wealthy man, but Jane, who knew my heart and soul like no other, understood my despair but believed Mr. Darcy would make a good and loving husband after all.

I sighed, closed my eyes, and shook my head slightly at the folly of their hopes. I pulled the pins from my hair and released my curls, reaching for the brush to smooth out the tangles. How I wished Jane were there to brush it for me as she did so many nights of my life. No, what I truly wished was to be home at Longbourn with Jane and not trapped in that dismal little room with a man I did not love.

After folding my chemise and placing it in my trunk, I hung my dress in the armoire and placed my shoes there along with my bonnet and cloak. I stirred the fire and walked to the window one last time. The storm had not lessened. As I passed the table, the bottle of brandy stood there, still containing enough for a full glass. I was not accustomed to drink stronger than wine, but that night I felt the need of warmth and comfort. Perhaps, it would help me sleep. I walked around the room and blew out the candles as I sipped the sweet brandy. I left one taper burning on the mantle for Mr. Darcy's use.

Finally, there was nothing left to do but crawl into bed. I settled down between the sheets, then sighed, and arose once more. Taking the extra quilt from the bottom of the bed and one of the pillows, I tossed them onto the chaise.

A good wife would at least make up the couch for her husband, would she not? No, a good wife would never have banished him from her bed, but I had no wish to be a good wife to Mr. Darcy. With a toss of my curls, I pursed my lips and blew out the remaining candle. Let him find his way in the dark. I then gave myself up to the call of the bed. Even though the sheets were cold and I shivered beneath the quilt, the mattress was fairly plump, and it was not long before I succumbed to the blessed relief of sleep.

Sometime in the night, though, I grew aware of a pleasing, cosy warmth, as though someone cradled me in his arms. I struggled to awaken, but the effects of the brandy and the exhausting strain of the day kept me from conscious thought. I told myself I must be dreaming, and I remember surrendering to the vision, for therein I was comforted. I was safe. I was wanted.

Chapter Two

The morning after my wedding, a slow, steady thump awakened me. A continual rhythmic cadence resonated in my ear, somehow soothing in its perfect repetition. It skipped not a stroke. I felt the pillow under my head move slightly up and down with each beat, in and out, in and out. A beat! That was it — a heartbeat!

Slowly, I opened my eyes, struggled through the fog of sleep, and attempted to focus on the strange room in which I had spent the night. Oh, yes, it was the inn. Now I remembered. But what was that sound, and why did my head rise up and down in that slow, persistent manner?

I raised my eyes, and that is when I saw him — Mr. Darcy!

I lay with my head on his chest, my arm thrown across him, and both his arms around me, clasping my body close to his. How could this have happened? He slept soundly, lying on top of the covers, fully dressed except for his boots. Most of me, fortunately, was under the sheet and counterpane, although I know not how I came to use his chest for a pillow.

I sat up immediately, calling forth his name with sufficient force that he jerked upward in such haste that our heads collided. We both cried out at the shock of the blow, and I shrank back as he grabbed his forehead.

"What? What is it?" he muttered, lost in confusion. A stale smell of spirits permeated his dishevelled clothing, his hair was in disarray, and dark stubble covered his chin.

"Get out!" I cried. "Get out of my bed!"

"Your bed?" He blinked in the radiant sunshine that illuminated the room. "But how — how did I . . . Did you — "

16

"Get out! I do not know what you are about, Mr. Darcy, but I expect you to keep your word!"

"I do keep my word," he muttered, crawling off the bed. When his feet touched the floor, he staggered and grabbed the bedpost to steady himself. He moaned and reached for his head again. "Will you not blow out that blasted candle?"

"What candle? The light is from the sun, and not even you, sir, can order it blown out. Now will you leave this room?"

He blinked again and screwed up his eyes as though they refused to focus. He lurched toward the door, but then turned back once more. "My boots — I need my boots."

They lay beside the bed as though thrown off in a hurry. I crawled across the mattress, picked up first one, then the other, and threw them at him, hitting his stomach with one. He doubled over and glared at me, but he did not cry out. Grabbing the boots and hopping about, he managed to pull them on. With one last bewildered stare in my direction, he opened the door and stumbled forth.

I was in such shock that all I could do was sink down under the sheet, suddenly aware that I had clutched the quilt to my neck, even though my nightgown was sufficiently modest. As I slid back into the warmth of the bed, I felt the heat on the sheets beneath the counterpane where he had lain beside me.

I was angry. More than that, I was furious. How dare he invade my bed! And yet, I had to admit I had slept more soundly that night than any I could remember. I became quite disconcerted when I found myself absently running my arm up and down the sheet, enjoying the warmth he left behind. I ceased that action immediately.

Had Mr. Darcy taken advantage of me in the night? I knew little of such things, but surely he could not have done so and remained fully clothed and outside the bedcovers. And no matter how well I slept, I knew it would have been impossible to sleep through such an encounter with *that* man.

By noon, we were on our way to London. The river had receded, and although the road remained muddy, our horses pulled the carriage through the ruts. Having kept to my room all morning, I had not seen Mr. Darcy until he joined me in the carriage.

How he shaved and cleaned up, I know not, but there he was, looking the impeccable gentleman except for the tired look about his eyes. His clothes were neither rumpled nor smelled of liquor, although I felt certain they were the clothes he had slept in. He must have an invaluable valet in service. I trust he paid him well if the man could work such a miracle.

We said nothing to each other. I did not even grant him the courtesy of a greeting. Instead, I turned my face to the window. No, I turned my entire body to the window and busied myself with an intense perusal of the passing trees, meadows, and grazing sheep. We rode no little distance in this fashion when, suddenly, he cleared his throat and I jumped.

"I beg your pardon," he said. "I did not mean to startle you. Miss Ben — that is, Eliz — " He stopped and blinked as though in search of something. "I do not seem to know how to address you. You are no longer Miss Bennet, but I fear you do not wish to be called Mrs. Darcy. May I call you Elizabeth?"

I worked hard not to smile at his discomfiture. "It is your choice, sir, as long as you do not take the advantage as licence to act in a more familiar manner."

He closed his eyes as though I had struck him. "I would not think of it. But I must be allowed to apologize for my behaviour last evening."

I nodded ever so slightly.

"I do not remember last night. I confess I imbibed far too generously of the innkeeper's ale. How I came to be in your bed, Elizabeth, I am sorry to say, is not possible for me to recall."

"Is this generous intake of spirits a part of your general nature, sir? If it is, you should have warned me, for I have no intention of living with an intemperate man."

"Absolutely not!" He spoke forcefully and leaned forward, a pained expression across his face as he put his hand to his forehead. "I promise you that I do not make a habit of such behaviour."

We said no more for several miles. I returned my attention to the window, but from the corner of my eye, I could see that his headache was severe. Again and again, he closed his eyes to the glare of the out-of-doors. I was glad to see him suffer. His behaviour deserved punishment. I congratulated myself on not feeling any wifely sympathy until I remembered the headache that frequently put me to bed. One did not have to be a loving wife to feel compassion.

"Mr. Darcy, would you prefer the shades be lowered to shield your eyes from the light?"

Surprise covered his countenance at my suggestion. "Do you not wish to observe the scenery?"

"Yes, but I do not suffer a headache."

"Thank you."

He reached up to release the dark shade over his window. I did the same on my side and was astonished at the sudden feeling of closeness within the coach with the absence of light. An intimacy enveloped us that made me self-conscious. I wondered if he felt it, as well. Now I had nowhere to look but at my lap or straight ahead, and then it would appear that I looked at him. Perhaps, compassion had been a mistake.

Nevertheless, had Mr. Darcy not shown compassion in marrying me? Why did he marry me? I remained unsure of the reason and feared I should do so for some time. His first proposal had been so uncivil and arrogant that I heard little argument for marriage and much against it. He openly acknowledged the unsuitability of my family and connections in comparison to his, and yet, he still asked for my hand. He stood in Mr. Collins's parlour at Hunsford, insulting in his manner and words. What had been his reason for marriage? Something about, "You must allow me to tell you how ardently I admire and love you."

I dismissed his words of love as foolishness because his rudeness infuriated me. How could he profess love and treat me as he had?

Moreover, the second proposal six months later could hardly be called that. Arrangement would be a better word. How shocked I had been the day he entered my mother's house at Longbourn with my Aunt and Uncle Gardiner! I could still hear my mother's cry upon greeting her brother.

"Oh, Edward, Edward, you are here at last! Whatever are we to do?"

"There, there, Fanny," he soothed. "Be at ease, Sister. I come with good news."

"Good news? Have you found hidden funds belonging to Mr. Bennet? Are we not to be turned out from Longbourn next week?"

"Not hidden funds, but something better."

Mr. Gardiner looked towards Mr. Darcy. Mamá sniffed as she usually did in his presence. She had not even acknowledged him prior to my uncle's words, for she disliked him intensely since we had first met a year ago at an assembly ball in Meryton. On that occasion, the entire community became acquainted with his arrogant manners. He slighted me when she practically invited him to ask me to dance, and the one thing my mother would never forgive was a man's refusal to dance with one of her five daughters.

I recalled how she had slowly led my aunt, uncle, and Mr. Darcy into my father's study, closing the door behind them.

Jane and I were bewildered, as were Mary and Kitty. What could Mr. Darcy have to do with our mother? Could we trust her to keep a civil tongue in his presence? How much better it would have been if Jane or I had been allowed to be in on the meeting!

"Why is he here?" I asked. "And how did he come to know our uncle?"

"They met this past summer," Jane replied, "when Mr. and Mrs. Gardiner travelled to Derbyshire."

"Oh, yes, they had planned to take me with them."

I had not gone, of course, because of Father's death, for I no longer felt free to go on pleasure trips. Mamá had been totally dependent upon Jane and me, and besides that, we were scrambling to find a means by which to support our family. We knew that our mother's profligate ways would soon exhaust her small fortune, and although we would not be paupers, our manner of living had to be severely reduced. Jane and I both sent out inquiries for governess positions, and I spent May and June searching for a reasonable cottage in which to move our family. I regretted giving up that trip with the Gardiners. We were to tour the Lakes and see some of the grand houses in the North Country.

"But how, Jane? How could they have come into Mr. Darcy's company?"

"Surely you remember that his estate is in Derbyshire. Aunt Gardiner wrote Mamá that they had happened upon him unexpectedly while touring his great house at Pemberley. They had been told he was away from home, but he returned earlier than expected. Our aunt wrote a very pleasing account of his manners in her letter, much different from what we experienced. She said that once he knew of their connection to our family, he overwhelmed them with invitations and civility."

I snorted at the idea.

Jane admonished me. "Lizzy, what a noise! You sound like Lydia!"

I blanched at the thought of being compared to my youngest sister — my wild, irresponsible child of a sister who had only added to our woes in the middle of last summer by running off with a blackguard in the militia, a Mr. Wickham. I recalled with embarrassment that when I first met the gentleman some seven or eight months earlier, I, too, thought him an amiable, pleasant man. Instead, he showed himself to be a cad who preyed on young women of fortune, having even tried his lot with Mr. Darcy's fifteen-year-old sister, Georgiana. Of course, I did not know the truth of his character until after my meeting with Mr. Darcy at Kent.

The morning after Mr. Darcy's first proposal, he gave me a letter outlining his relationship with Mr. Wickham, a far different picture than the one Mr. Wickham had painted.

It seems that Mr. Darcy had not cheated Mr. Wickham of his inheritance as the latter had told far and wide, but rather, Mr. Wickham had refused the living — a curacy in Kympton — in exchange for the sum of three thousand pounds. He later attempted an unsuccessful elopement with Georgiana, a fact shocking to hear and, I am certain, painful for Mr. Darcy to relate.

How I regretted not having warned my own sister about his character before she, too, fell prey to his charms. I fear that if my Uncle Gardiner had not paid out vast sums to Mr. Wickham, he never would have married her but left her a ruined woman deserted in London. For that very reason, our uncle could be of little financial assistance to us, not after he had been so generous with Lydia. We knew that he had given us more than we could ever repay. Our mother, of course, expected him to rescue us, but Jane and I accepted the fact that it was impossible, and we would not allow her to beg him for more.

That was why Jane had taken a governess position in August. I, too, sought such a position, but someone had to remain home and help Mamá and my younger sisters move into new quarters. I had at last found a cottage in Surrey, and we were packing to move before Michaelmas when the strange arrival of Mr. Darcy and my relations occurred without warning.

"Lizzy," Jane said, "perhaps Mr. Darcy has heard of our search for governess positions, and he comes with an offer."

"I think not. Mr. Darcy's sister is well past the age to need a governess. She now has a companion and will soon be out in society."

"Well, if he does want a governess, I shall go. I know how much you dislike him, but I do not feel as strongly. Besides, since I failed miserably at my first post, I should try doubly hard if I am offered another chance."

"Oh, Jane," I cried, "do not talk so. You did not fail, and we all know it."

Kitty and Mary quickly agreed with me. Our oldest sister had chosen the worst possible house in Lancashire in which to be a governess. Even though the master was an earl, he had a lecherous eye, and Jane had not been in residence a week before he invited her to sit on his lap and help him with his figures. When she refused, he persisted with greater advances.

Only a few weeks ago, she had returned home, her beautiful eyes filled with tears, ashamed to admit she could not bear the situation. She even tortured herself that somehow she might have invited the earl's odious behaviour.

I reassured her she had not!

I was so angry I wanted to throttle the man, but that would have only cast me into prison and deprived my family of what little I could earn. After I calmed down, Jane and I once again submitted letters seeking positions, and I was determined this time to accompany Jane and examine the situation with her employer before I left her without recourse.

About an hour after Mamá and our guests had entered Papá's study, she opened the door and motioned for me to come in. Her eyes were aglow, and she positively beamed. I had not seen her thus since before my father's death. In truth, I had seen that look only once before — the day my cousin, Mr. Collins, proposed to me, a match she highly favoured and I refused.

I entered the room and saw Mr. Darcy standing by the window, his tall stature outlined by the reflection of the light from behind. He did not smile. He only stared at me, his expression unreadable. My aunt and uncle did smile, as though they were encouraging me to come in with an accepting manner.

"Your uncle has something to say to you," Mamá said, pushing me forward with a slight nudge.

Mr. Gardiner cleared his throat and asked me to sit, but as everyone else stood, I declined. "Lizzy, Mr. Darcy came to me two days ago with an arrangement that will help your family exceedingly."

"Oh, yes," Mamá said, "exceedingly!"

I glanced at him, but he stared at the floor. "What is it?" I asked.

My uncle looked to Mr. Darcy. "Should you prefer to ask my niece, sir?"

"No — it will probably have more chance of success coming from you, sir."

Well, I thought, that is the truest statement you have ever made. It was evident he had not forgotten our parting. I had scarce thought of the man since I had last seen him in Rosings Park. Oh, I had read his letter and, at the time, found myself much chagrined at how I had misjudged him by heeding Wickham's falsehoods, but his letter did little to curry my favour when I read his defence of his participation in the separation of Mr. Bingley from Jane. And then, my father's death shortly thereafter had caused my life to evolve into a downward spiral of duties and worry. Circumstances caused me to dismiss any further consideration of Mr. Darcy or his letter until that day when his presence filled my father's library at Longbourn.

"Uncle, please tell me what it is."

"Mr. Darcy comes to Longbourn, my dear, to ask for your hand in marriage."

That was when I sat down. Quickly.

I felt as though I had been struck. How was it possible he still wished to marry me? I could not grasp the idea after all the harsh words that had passed between us. The shock deafened me to the remainder of my uncle's statement. I had to ask him to repeat it, and that was when my mother broke in with great impatience.

"Oh, Lizzy, are you not listening? Mr. Darcy wants to marry you! Mr. Darcy! Just think of it. Our problems are over! And he not only will marry you, but he has arranged with Mr. Collins for our family to remain at Longbourn for as long as we wish — for life!"

I turned in amazement to look at him again. "How can you do that, sir? The estate is entailed upon my cousin."

He did not have a chance to speak. Mamá took over once again. "A man of Mr. Darcy's resources can do anything. Mr. Collins is only too willing to forego possession of Longbourn for the remuneration offered, although he does still technically own the estate, I suppose. Is that not correct, Brother?"

My uncle nodded. "Yes, Mr. Collins has agreed to rent Longbourn to your mother, and Mr. Darcy is willing to pay the rental for as long as your family lives here. In addition, he is willing to settle a generous monthly stipend on your mother and establish dowries for your sisters."

Mamá then began to enthuse prodigiously on the benefits of such a transaction. Neither she nor my sisters would have to move to that "horrid little cottage" in Surrey, where her daughters would have absolutely no opportunity to meet suitable young men of fortune — never mind the fact that Lydia's scandal had already prohibited such occurrence — and she could keep her carriage, her servants, and "her place" in Hertfordshire society. She went on and on while I sat there, completely baffled.

At last, my aunt sat beside me. She took my hand in hers. "What say you to this marriage, Lizzy?"

I struggled to control my breathing and keep my lip from trembling. "How can you ask me that, Aunt? And you, Mamá? All of you? Am I nothing more to you than a bargaining piece? Do I not have a say in all of this?"

"Of course you do, my dear," my aunt replied.

"You know this kind of arrangement is made all the time," my uncle added. "It is a most fortunate offer, especially since your father is gone."

"If my father were here, he would not coerce me into such an arrangement! Mr. Darcy is well aware that I do not wish to marry him. He proposed to me six months ago. I refused him then, and I refuse him today."

"Lizzy!" Mamá cried, sinking down on the chaise and vigorously fanning herself with her handkerchief. "Do you mean to say you refused such a man last spring? That we could have been free of worry all these months but for your selfish nature?"

"I do not think I am selfish, Mamá," I pleaded. "I am willing to work to support you. I have searched everywhere for suitable housing that we can afford. I will do anything, but do not ask me to marry where I have no desire to do so."

"I knew it! I knew she would refuse! She has always been headstrong, stubborn — her father coddled her, you know. I knew she would disappoint me again! Mr. Darcy, I have three more daughters, the eldest much prettier than Lizzy, and she possesses a much more compliant nature. Will you not take one of them?"

"Mamá!" I cried, unable to believe what I heard.

Mr. Darcy finally spoke. "Mr. Gardiner, might I be afforded time alone with Miss Bennet?"

"Oh, yes, that is what you need," Mamá cried, "time to plead your case. Come, Brother; come, Madeline, let them talk alone."

"Mamá, there is no need for you to leave. I shall not change my mind."

"You will stay and hear Mr. Darcy, Elizabeth! You can do at least that much for me. I insist upon it!"

Seeing the look on my mother's face, I knew argument was futile. I watched the members of my family leave the room, closing the door behind them.

A good five minutes passed wherein neither of us said a word. I stood when the others left the room, but eventually I sat down, waiting. Mr. Darcy turned and looked out the window for what seemed like forever, and then he walked behind my father's desk, picked up some papers, and put them back down. The man was slower to rouse than waking Kitty in the mornings! At last, I could stand it no longer.

"Mr. Darcy, do you have anything to say? If not, I shall ask you to refrain from wasting my time."

He raised his head with a look that silenced me. I cannot describe it, but the certainty crossed my mind that one could push this man so far and no farther. I closed my mouth and waited. He took the papers, walked around the desk, and sat in the chair next to me.

"Miss Bennet, this marriage contract is the only way to save your family from suffering great disadvantage, both economically and socially. If you would look at the figures, I think you will see that I am prepared to provide generously for all three of your sisters as well as your mother."

"I do not need to look at numbers, sir. I need an answer. Why are you doing this? Why do you want to marry me?"

"You have no other options. You and your sisters cannot attract men of fortune. Your youngest sister's unfortunate escapade will essentially bar all of you from the best of society."

I groaned silently to think he knew of Lydia's marriage. I forgot how fast such news travelled. Mr. Collins must have told Mr. Darcy's aunt, Lady Catherine de Bourgh. What great delight she would have experienced in relaying the gossip, for she gloried in her superiority!

"I would think, sir, that Lydia's marriage would certainly bar *you* from the slightest consideration of making any connection with my family. Do not forget that if we marry, Mr. Wickham shall be your relation."

He winced at my words, but he did not back down. "Mr. Wickham shall never, of course, be permitted to visit Pemberley or my house in London, but your sister is welcome, as is the rest of your family."

"You say I have no other options, but you are wrong, Mr. Darcy. As soon as I see my mother and sisters settled in their new place, I shall secure a position as governess, as will Jane. We thank you for your offer, but we are quite able to provide for ourselves and our family."

"Are you? Come now, Miss Bennet. Governesses make hardly enough to keep themselves alive. There will be precious little to spare to send home to your family and, knowing the habits of your mother, frugality is not in her nature. Besides that, Miss Bennet is far too fine for the governess trade . . . as are you."

I could not think of a reply. I never had a head for figures, and I feared he was right about governess salaries. Still, how could I enter into such a marriage?

"As you know, I have a younger sister. She is in need of someone like you. Since her . . . mistreatment by Wickham, of which we never speak and which I insist shall not be mentioned in her presence, Georgiana has been withdrawn and melancholy. It has been more than a year, and still she is timid and shy of everything and everyone."

"Then, could not Jane or I be employed as her companion?"

"You could, although she has a fine companion in Mrs. Annesley, but I want someone permanent in her life, someone full of wit and vitality, able to tease and enjoy life as you do. Georgiana needs a sister."

"And you would ask me to marry you just to give your sister a lively companion? Really, Mr. Darcy, I find that hard to believe. No one is that unselfish when it comes to family members."

He bristled at my remarks. I could see a cold anger descend upon his countenance. "Perhaps *you* are not that unselfish, but *I* take my family responsibilities seriously."

"So now you agree with my mother and say that I am selfish because I shall not sell myself to you! There are many other women with wit and vitality and love of life that you could marry who would assist your sister. Why must it be me? Why do you want to marry me?"

He rose and walked to the window and back. "I have my reasons, Miss Bennet."

"And they are?"

"*My* reasons."

When he could see that I was not impressed by his lack of candour, he went on to tell me expressly what he would require. In public, I was to act as though we were perfectly amiable. I was to serve as hostess and mistress of his houses; however, he would not impose upon me privately until I was ready. That was when I turned on him like a cat, and he answered with like anger, a conversation I have already related.

I rose, ready to flee the room, when he stopped me by catching my hand. "Miss Bennet, do not refuse me today. You have much on which to think. Consider it overnight at least, and give me your answer on the morrow. If your answer remains in the negative, it will silence me. I will never ask you again."

My first thought was to cry out that I did not need time to ponder my answer, but something about his eyes, the look in them, a sort of softness I had never seen before, caused me reluctantly to agree to sleep on my decision. The relief on his face at my answer almost made me ashamed, and when he released my hand, I could still feel its warmth.

That night my mind was too weary to think clearly. Mamá had lectured me for what seemed like hours. My uncle and aunt each took me aside privately to persuade me that the match would be beneficial to all concerned. At length, even Jane entreated me to consider the union's benefits. That broke me — the look in Jane's eyes. What she had endured during her brief sojourn in Lancashire had scarred her. She truly feared for either of us to go into service.

"I wish I was the one Mr. Darcy wanted. I would go in your place if I could."

"How can you say that when in your heart you know it is Mr. Bingley you love? How could you give yourself to another?"

She stopped plaiting her hair and looked away for a moment. It was after midnight, and we sat on my bed, spending our last waking moments of the day sharing confidences as we had done almost every night since childhood.

"Mr. Bingley does not love me. I have accepted that, and I am determined to be sensible from now on. I shall marry the first kind, respectable man who asks me. I no longer look for a love match."

"But, I know love is what you desire."

Her eyes filled with tears. "Not with any other man, Lizzy. I shall love Mr. Bingley the rest of my life."

"Oh, Jane," I cried, pulling her close and kissing her hair.

And that was what made me do it. For some reason, I felt certain that Mr. Bingley still loved Jane in spite of his apparent disinterest. I suspected he had ceased his attentions to her only because of the influence of his sisters and Mr. Darcy. I did not have power over Mr. Bingley's sisters, but I could make it a condition of marriage that Mr. Darcy right the wrong he had committed upon my sister. At least one of us should be happy in marriage.

The next morning my bed looked like the remains of a wrestler's match, but I was resigned to my fate. Mr. Darcy, surprisingly, did not object to my regulation concerning Mr. Bingley and even asked if I wanted it to be added to the marriage contract. Although I believed that he would do it without such, I asked for it in writing, perhaps because I wished him to know with whom he struck a bargain — not some gullible chit, but a woman of understanding who would not allow him to take advantage of her.

So, one might say that I married for purely noble reasons, putting the welfare of my family before my own pleasure. Deep within, though, and even hidden at the time from my own acknowledgement, there was another reason for the marriage — a reason I was not yet able to put into words, envision, or admit to myself.

Something in me wanted to know Mr. Darcy in his entirety, to put to rest the curiosity excited by his intriguing masculinity. I wanted to understand why my senses quickened in his presence, why I felt every part of life more keenly around him — and what it was that made him want to marry me.

"Elizabeth," Mr. Darcy said, shocking me back to the reality of our journey, "I do not want Georgiana to know the truth of our conjugal arrangement. I trust that you will honour our contract with discretion."

"If the *truth* of our conjugal arrangement were the opposite, do you think that I would be so indiscreet as to share that with your sister or any other member of your family?" I was insulted that he should think I needed cautioning.

"I should hope not, but seeing that you have been reared in circumstances quite different from my own, I thought it prudent to admonish you with this warning."

Oh, the man was an absolute churl! Could he insult my family to any greater degree? Did he think I was a child? With a quick flick of my wrist, I reached over and jerked up the shade on my window.

May your head burst, Mr. Darcy!

Chapter Three

We arrived at Mr. Darcy's townhouse in London by late afternoon. From the moment we first reached the outskirts, the city's parade of sights and sounds entertained me. I had not been in Town for some time, and the intensity of the noise, odours, colours, confusion, and general uproar proved a welcome diversion to the silence that had ensued during the past hour and a half of our carriage ride.

I was not surprised at the stately grandeur of the house, for the Gardiners had described the richness of Mr. Darcy's estate in Derbyshire, and I expected no less in London. I was relieved to see upon entering the house that it was tastefully furnished, quietly elegant, and without evidence of the need to impress. Although I did not pretend to know him well, his house reflected the man I thought him to be — a gentleman long used to the best in life, without posturing or affected manner, with a certain assumption that this was how life was to be. I supposed it had always been that way for him, and now it was to be my way of life. That would take adjustment on my part.

In the foyer, the butler, Adams, and the housekeeper, Mrs. James, met us. If they were surprised to see a new mistress, their manners were circumspect and unrevealing. Adams informed us that Miss Georgiana was entertaining callers in the salon, and I saw Mr. Darcy frown at the news.

"Did not Colonel Fitzwilliam fetch her last night and take her to the Earl of Matlock's residence?"

"No, sir, the colonel arrived just a short while ago, and by that time, Mrs. Hurst and Miss Bingley attended Miss Darcy. He has gone above stairs to freshen up before joining them, sir." Adams indicated the direction of the salon. Mr. Darcy groaned, and I almost rolled my eyes at the thought of a visit with my least favourite people.

As he and his butler continued their conversation regarding general news of the household, I ventured a few steps farther so that I might observe the inhabitants of the salon without their knowledge. I wished to have a look at my new sister before that relationship was thrust upon us.

I saw a young girl, slender and pale, the opposite in colour to her brother, sitting across from her guests. With what appeared to be caution and some trepidation, Georgiana Darcy poured tea into china cups for her guests. She seemed uneasy with the practice, which surprised me, for I assumed she had served as hostess for her brother numerous times in the past, but the presence of Miss Bingley and Mrs. Hurst could contribute to the discomfiture of even the most accomplished hostess. How well I knew that!

"You say that you expected your brother to return last night, Miss Darcy?"

"Yes, Miss Bingley." She extended the cup and saucer with a slightly shaky hand.

"Perhaps the storm caused the delay," Mrs. Hurst offered. "The lightning was quite severe at our townhouse."

"Quite," Caroline Bingley agreed. "The thunder disturbed my slumber several times."

"I feel certain they spent the night on the road," Georgiana said. "At least I hope they did. I would not have them caught in the rain somewhere without aid."

Caroline laughed. "Oh, you need not worry, my dear. Your brother is well able to take care of himself. He is so strong and capable. I have not the least fear that he could withstand last night's storm with no harm whatsoever."

"Yes, I am sure that Wills could make his way, but with his bride, I — "

Caroline snorted, coughed, and sloshed her tea into the saucer. She quickly placed it on the table and grabbed frantically for a napkin to mop up the liquid dribbling down her chin. "What did you say, Miss Darcy? I must have misunderstood you!"

"Yes," Mrs. Hurst interjected, casting a horrified glance at her sister, "surely you did not say Mr. Darcy had a bride, my dear, did you?"

Georgiana nodded. "My brother married yesterday at Hertfordshire."

Caroline appeared almost in a swoon; her eyes rolled back in her head in a most unappealing manner. She turned to her sister with a frantic look, and Mrs. Hurst took over the conversation.

"He married at Hertfordshire, you say? To anyone we might know?"

"I do not know whether you are acquainted with the lady. I have never met her."

"And . . . and her name, my dear? Would you happen to know her name?"

"Elizabeth Bennet."

Both of Mr. Bingley's sisters now gasped in unison, Caroline grabbing her throat as though she had been shot. Georgiana's eyes grew large as she observed their obvious shock and disbelief.

"Do either of you know Miss Bennet?"

"Yes," Mrs. Hurst answered, recovering somewhat, "a little. We met her sister, Jane, when we were last at Netherfield. Her family has a small estate nearby."

"What is she like? My brother has told me little, other than he feels certain I shall like her."

"She is very different from us," Caroline said, having completed her mopping up. "I cannot believe Charles did not tell us of the wedding."

"I do not know if Wills told your brother. It all happened rather quickly."

"It must have," Mrs. Hurst said, "not to invite us. Mr. Darcy is an intimate friend of ours." Caroline gave her a quizzical look, and her sister explained. "That is, of our brother, and consequently, of us as well. I know my husband thinks highly of him. I truly cannot understand why your brother would not have at least asked Charles to stand up with him."

Caroline's eyebrows shot up as though she had just become privy to a shocking idea. "Surely there was no *need* for a quick wedding, was there, Miss Darcy?" She and Mrs. Hurst both leaned forward in anticipation.

"I do not know what you mean," Georgiana answered.

Just then, Colonel Fitzwilliam walked into the salon from an adjoining door on the far side of the room. Georgiana rose to greet him as he swept into the room, the shine on his boots less than sparkling, and his cloak heavy with moisture. He kissed her hand and smiled, and it seemed to me that he searched her eyes to determine how she fared.

"Richard! I am glad to see you!"

"My sweet Georgie! You must excuse my appearance. Since dawn, I rode through mud thicker than pudding. Ah, I see you have guests, and I intrude."

"No, not at all. You remember Mrs. Hurst and Miss Bingley. They are Mr. Bingley's sisters."

The colonel bowed to each of the ladies. "Yes, of course. I believe we met once before."

"We did," Mrs. Hurst agreed, "at Lord Dalrymple's ball last winter."

"Yes, how could I forget? As I recall, your brother was sick with love for some young thing, and my cousin and the two of you worked together all evening attempting to convince him to forget her by introducing him to every eligible young woman at the dance. What was it Darcy kept saying? 'There are some very strong objections against the lady, Bingley. Surely, you can do better.' Yes, that was it! I think he felt quite pleased with himself when he succeeded in thwarting Mr. Bingley's plans."

I felt a flush creep up my neck to my cheeks, and I had to bite my lip to keep from crying out, "You speak of my sister!" Fortunately, I restrained myself, and looking back to see Mr. Darcy still in earnest discussion with the servants, I moved a little closer to the room so that I might have a better view.

Georgiana offered the colonel a cup of tea, with which he busied himself. He added sugar and cream and stirred the cup with more effort than it seemed to need. Caroline watched him intently. I suspected that she was about to shower him with questions about my marriage, and I was soon proven correct.

"Colonel, we have just heard the most surprising news. Miss Darcy told us that her brother was married yesterday and to Miss Elizabeth Bennet. Can this be true?"

"Ah, yes, most definitely. I, myself, stood up with Darcy, and he performed his vows admirably."

"But this is so sudden. We did not even know they were engaged," Mrs. Hurst said.

"I believe it was a short betrothal, or at least a rather private one. You may not have heard that Miss Bennet's father passed away some six months ago. That may be why they elected to have a quiet wedding. There was no one in attendance but family."

Mrs. Hurst continued to sip her tea. Caroline sank back against the cushioned settee, her face falling like a pillow robbed of its feathers. Conversation lagged until Georgiana asked that her cousin provide them with more details of the event.

There was not that much to tell, he admitted. The wedding had been brief, the wedding breakfast almost as much so, and the couple had left in a heavy downpour. Darcy had requested that the colonel return to London immediately and take Georgiana to his parents' estate just outside of Town. The colonel had been delayed by the storm, and he had taken refuge, at last, in a small inn and then rose at daybreak to reach London before the newly married couple. Since he had travelled by a different route than Mr. and Mrs. Darcy, he assumed they had also spent the night on the road and would arrive soon.

Just then, Mr. Darcy startled me by clearing his throat. Although my eavesdropping was apparent, he did not censure me for it. He indicated the way to the salon, and we proceeded therein. Georgiana rose, a picture of surprise on her face that turned to pleasure, I assumed, at the recognition of her brother, for she rushed to his side.

"Mr. Darcy!" Miss Bingley crowed. Her eyes lit up at his presence but then narrowed at the sight of me.

"And Miss Bennet," Mrs. Hurst cooed. "We have just heard the news."

We all spoke in acknowledgement, and then Mr. Darcy introduced me to Georgiana. We bowed to each other, and I searched for something credible to say. "I am very glad to make your acquaintance."

"And I, yours," she replied. "I have heard much of you."

That was another time I could have rolled my eyes, but I did not. "I hope you will not hold whatever information you have heard against me, for I know your brother's critiques can be quite harsh."

"Oh, no! My brother has not spoken ill of you but rather praised you. He said you play and sing beautifully."

"I fear he is teasing, needless to say, for some playful reason known only to him."

"I do not think so, for my brother always tells the absolute truth." There was no mistaking the love and regard she held for him.

I did not know what to say, so I changed the subject. "I have heard that you are a music lover and that you play exceptionally well."

"She does," Mrs. Hurst cut in. "My brother says he has never heard anyone play with such spirit as Miss Darcy. Perhaps we may all have an opportunity to hear her during your stay in Town. But you must tell us of your wedding! Colonel Fitzwilliam has just this very moment informed us of the event." She continued to utter silly, meaningless phrases that I knew to be untrue and then added, "How delightful and yet shocking, Mr. Darcy! When did this happen, and how could you have kept it from us? Does Charles know?"

Before he could reply, she went on. "And *where* did you marry? Surely, you did not whisk her off to Gretna Green, sir!"

How could she ask that, I wondered, when I had just overheard Colonel Fitzwilliam tell them we were married in Hertfordshire?

"Louisa!" Caroline cried. "How can you even suggest such a thing? Mr. Darcy would never consent to an elopement, even if Miss Bennet would."

I was seething by that time. "We did not elope. Why ever would you suggest that *I* should do so?"

As only she could do, Caroline smiled but did not really smile. "Well, we heard news of your youngest sister and Mr. Wickham. Did they not run off to Scotland to marry this past summer?"

I felt Mr. Darcy stiffen — I did not even have to look at him — and I heard Georgiana's quick intake of breath. What surprised me was the look of ferocity that descended upon Colonel Fitzwilliam's countenance. Mr. Darcy had told me to look to the colonel for verification of his account of Wickham's misdeeds with Georgiana, but I had never discussed the matter with him. Obviously, he shared his cousin's feelings in the matter and was aghast at the impact of Miss Bingley's words on the young girl. Did the woman have no idea how she hurt the child? Georgiana sat down on the sofa, her hands trembling. I walked across the room and sat beside my new sister before answering.

"You are mistaken, Miss Bingley. Lydia married in London two months ago."

"My, my, how strange this must be for you, Mr. Darcy," Caroline continued.

He strode to his sister's side and stood behind the couch, placing one hand on her shoulder. "In what way?" he replied, his tone deadly.

"Why, you are now brother to the son of your former servant. Shall we look forward to seeing him at Pemberley?"

I could sense Mr. Darcy's anger, but before he could speak, Colonel Fitzwilliam came to his rescue. "As much as I would love to continue this visit, I am much in need of returning home, and I would suggest we give

Mr. and Mrs. Darcy some time to themselves. Georgiana, Mamá looks forward to your visit. Shall I ask the servant to pack your trunk?"

"No," she said quickly, "I shall arrange it. If you will excuse me, Miss Bingley, Mrs. Hurst . . . Mrs. Darcy."

"Georgiana — " Mr. Darcy began, but she escaped the room before he could say more.

Caroline and her sister rose and made their farewells. They could hardly do otherwise since the person they came to visit had just fled their presence. Mrs. Hurst was effusive in her congratulations and offer to have us visit at her house in Grosvenor Square, but Caroline did nothing more than nod curtly. Poor Miss Bingley! Her worst nightmare had come true. The man at whom she had literally thrown herself for years was now removed from the marriage market. Little did she know I gladly would have changed places with her.

As soon as the guests left, Mr. Darcy took the stairs two at a time, heading for his sister's room, I presumed. That left the colonel and me alone. We had never been at a disadvantage for conversation, but neither of us said much of anything. We spoke of the weather again and of how tedious our journeys had been, but little else. I wondered if Mr. Darcy had confided in his cousin, had told him of our marriage arrangement, or whether he sensed innately that all was not right between us.

I remembered how he had looked upon me at the wedding with an expression of sympathy. I did not want his sympathy. The last thing I desired was pity. I had made this decision to marry for my own reasons. I would not be the object of anyone's commiseration. Perhaps that was why I acted as I did when we heard Mr. Darcy and Georgiana descend the stairs together. Colonel Fitzwilliam left to join them, but I lagged behind, remaining in the salon, although I did move toward the door where I could see the three of them talking together.

Georgiana had forgotten a favourite book, and instead of calling a servant, Mr. Darcy ran up the stairs to retrieve it. I could just make out the conversation between Georgiana and Colonel Fitzwilliam.

"No, Sprout," he said, "it is Darcy's wish that you stay with my parents for at least two weeks, and Mother looks forward to your visit. You have always been her favourite, you know, even though I have no idea why." The last words were said in a teasing manner, and it was obvious that he was fond of her.

"But Richard, how will it look to Mrs. Darcy if I run off like this? She will think I do not like her."

"Little one, you are talking about a newly married couple. They are thinking of no one but each other right now. She will have plenty of time later to acquaint herself with you. For now, let them have their honeymoon."

Georgiana blushed and ducked her head. "Oh, you must think me a silly goose."

"No, just an innocent one." He smiled and lifted her chin with his forefinger. "Do not turn your head away from me, little cousin. You are much too pretty to hide your face."

"I pray you do not tease me. You know that I am not innocent — just stupid." She turned away from him and appeared adamant in her refusal to face him, but he placed his hands on her shoulders and turned her around.

"I do not want to ever hear you say that again, Georgiana. Nothing could be farther from the truth."

"But after what happened last year — "

"That is behind you now, my dear — far, far behind you." He gathered her into his arms, cradled her head against his chest, and smoothed her blonde curls as he held her close. "If only you could forget that it ever happened."

"If only it had never happened."

He held her for some time, and finally she lifted her face. "Do not be concerned, Richard. Truly, I shall be well."

When she offered him a tentative smile, the colonel's face broke into a relieved grin, and I felt almost embarrassed to be privy to their conversation. There was an intimacy there I knew nothing about, and I wondered if Mr. Darcy did. For some reason I felt almost envious. How pleasant it would be to have a protector like Colonel Fitzwilliam — to have someone who cared as much for me.

At the sound of Mr. Darcy descending the stairs, they looked up. I decided to make my presence known and joined them. I still do not know why I did it, but I tucked my hand into Mr. Darcy's arm as though we were married in all respects. I felt him stiffen and imagined his surprise, but I did not even glance in his direction. Instead, I gave my warmest smile to his sister.

"I look forward to your return, Georgiana. I hope we shall become good friends."

She curtseyed in reply but did not echo my sentiment. I could see the wary expression in her eyes, and after she and the colonel departed, I felt a great weariness descend upon me. The situation would not be easy. This young girl would not welcome me with any degree of warmth. How could she after learning that I was a sister to Wickham?

"You may stop the pretence now, Elizabeth," Mr. Darcy said, straightening his arm.

I withdrew my hand with haste, bristling at his cold tone. Did my touch fill him with such distaste that he must rid himself of it at the first chance? Well and good! I had no desire ever to touch him again. If he did not appreciate my efforts at presenting the picture of domestic happiness, then I would be all too glad to oblige him.

"I am tired, Mr. Darcy. Will you call a servant to show me to my apartment?"

"I shall take you there. I planned on giving you a tour of the house, but we can defer that until tomorrow."

He indicated that I should climb the wide staircase, and I noted the rich gleam of the highly polished balustrade. It was made of the finest mahogany, and the intricately curved spindles complemented the dark wine carpet on the stairs. No wonder he had objected to the rough inn we had been forced to stay in the night before. When a man was accustomed to such splendour, it must be hard to adjust to less.

Upon reaching the third floor, he led me down the hallway to the second door on the left. Inside was a beautiful, spacious bedroom, artfully decorated in blues and greens. I was happy to see it contained four narrow, floor-to-ceiling windows facing the east so that I would awaken to the warmth of the sun. They opened upon a small, verdant garden. The trees were turning red and gold, and the hawthorn shrubs sprouted the beginnings of red berries. This spot had been designed to please the eye in all seasons with various plantings of flowering bushes.

"These shall be your rooms," Mr. Darcy said. "Your maid has unpacked for you, but if you desire anything further, do not hesitate to ring for her. Dinner is served at half-past eight, so there should be time for you to rest before then." With a slight bow, he walked out the door, closing it behind him.

I spent no little time exploring the bedroom. I peeked into the armoires, for there were two. I opened drawers and noted how little space my nightgowns and underclothes occupied. There was ample room for a much better dressed woman to live in these quarters. I sat on the sofa before the fireplace and leaned against its ample cushions. From there, I moved to the large four-poster bed and was pleased to feel its comforting depth — neither too soft, nor too hard. Well, I expected no less from a man of Mr. Darcy's means.

On the north wall, a small writing desk contained two pots of ink, quills, and a box of the finest writing paper. Beside it, a door opened to a combination dressing room and bath. I had never before enjoyed the luxury of my own bath, and I inspected it with great thoroughness, anticipating the pleasure of a long soak.

On the south wall, I fingered the small china dogs nestled beneath a vase of autumn's last roses sitting on the bureau. Next to it, I saw another large door, hooded with ornate cream-coloured moulding that continued around the room, crowned the walls, and separated them from the high ceiling. I wondered what further personal extravagance awaited me on the other side, and so I promptly turned the brass doorknob.

What astonishment I felt at the sight before me! I saw another completely furnished chamber, as warm and inviting as mine, but decidedly darker. Rich chocolate colours mixed with smoky greens covered the walls, furniture, and linens.

At first, I drew back, afraid that I had stumbled into someone's bedroom, but since there was an adjoining door to mine, I dismissed that idea, believing instead that perhaps it was a sort of study or personal library for my use, for two walls were lined with bookshelves filled to capacity. I saw another desk, larger than the first and fitted out with even more writing materials. I delighted in it and anticipated writing to Jane that very night. The only strange thing about the room was that it contained another bed, a great handsome bed furnished with warmth and taste.

"What need shall I have for two beds?" I wondered aloud, and then thought how perfect it would be for Jane when she came to visit, how we would enjoy the benefit of being next to each other. Yes, that was it! The room must be a combination study for me and guest chamber for my most intimate friends.

My, I thought, the very rich certainly do have advantages of which I have never dreamt. However, at that moment, the door from the room to the hall opened, and a completely unexpected visitor walked in.

"Madam?" Mr. Darcy raised one eyebrow in a sardonic expression. "May I presume that you seek my presence, seeing that you have invaded my bedroom?"

I was aghast! "Your bedroom? But — but it connects with mine!"

"It does, indeed." A faint smile crossed his lips — actually, more of a smirk than smile.

I whirled around and marched back to my room, slamming the door between us. I turned to reach for the lock, when the door itself was snatched from my hands and pulled open by Mr. Darcy.

"I am not accustomed to having doors slammed in my face," he said, advancing into the room as I backed away from him.

"And I am not accustomed to such high-handed treatment."

"I fail to comprehend your meaning."

"Why does your room connect to mine? How dare you put me in such a situation?"

"Such a situation? Mrs. Darcy, these two rooms belonged to my parents, and after their deaths, I naturally took my father's chamber as master of the house. You are now to preside as mistress. Thus, I placed you in the very best suite which, obviously, happens to adjoin mine." He enjoyed this. It was evident by the continued smirk on his face.

"Well," I sputtered, "well . . . I shall require a lock on this door. It does possess one, does it not?"

With what appeared to be a deliberate, tedious turning of his head, Mr. Darcy looked at the knob and then back at me. "It does not."

"Will you see that one is installed this very night?"

"I will not."

"Mr. Darcy! I protest! You assured me that, according to the terms of our arrangement, our marriage would be in name only until I wished differently. Are you going back on your word?"

"I am not. That is why you have no need for a lock. I do not open doors where I am not wanted."

"And how can I believe that after your behaviour last night? I insist upon having a lock."

"I have apologized for my actions last night. I shall not do so again. But do heed what I am about to say: If you think a blasted lock will keep me from your room, you are mistaken." His eyes turned darker than night, and the look on his countenance provoked an awakening within me that I had never experienced before.

Before I could think of an answer, he turned and strode from the room, closing the door firmly behind him. Oh, I could not think clearly for the shock of his statement! How could he speak to me so? I gasped for air and paced the floor ten minutes or longer.

Had his performance last night been an indicator of what was to come? Need I fear a repetition of it? If so, I would leave the house, no matter that I had agreed to the arrangement. I would not live in fear of his coming through that door at any moment.

I fumed and muttered to myself. I even cried a little, but when my emotions were spent and my anger subsided, I sank down upon the sofa, clasped my arms together and hugged them close to my body. Each time I looked at that door, gooseflesh ran up and down my arms. Gradually, I began to realize that neither fear nor even anger caused that reaction, but a sensation I was unable to name, a sensation that made me extremely uncomfortable.

It welled up from somewhere deep within, spurred by the memory of awakening in Mr. Darcy's arms.

Chapter Four

Dinner that evening was a strained affair.

I was surprised at the intimacy of the dining room when first I entered until Mrs. James explained that, since it was just the two of us, Mr. Darcy had ordered our meal held in the smaller dining room.

Naturally! I should have known he had two dining rooms — did he not have two or more of everything?

I tried not to look at him, but it was next to impossible when there was little else on which to place my eyes. The crystal and china gleamed in the candlelight, and I tried to keep my eyes on both for some time. The food was delicious — perfect in every detail — and if I had not been tormented by a headache, I would have eaten with more appetite.

I had thought to decline dinner, begging off with the excuse of my ailment, but then I recalled how servants talk. If they knew that Mr. Darcy had a headache and I complained of one, too, would not such ills so early in a marriage alert them to the unhappiness of our arrangement? They would know soon enough — how could the fact that we slept in separate beds be avoided? I knew little of marital intimacies, but it was a well-known fact that husbands and wives shared a bed early in their marriage.

After dinner, Mr. Darcy escorted me into the music room and asked me to play and sing for him. I started to refuse until he spoke again.

"My headache continues to plague me. Some soft music might soothe it."

"I shall play, sir, but do not ask me to sing. I am not in the mood."

"As you like." He sat down on a sofa opposite the pianoforte.

I chose to play a Beethoven sonata in F minor, feeling his eyes upon me the entire time. Fortunately, the piece required that I watch the keys or music and not meet his gaze. If I had done so, I felt sure he would have had a critical expression thereon, as I misfingered several of the sombre chords.

At the end of the song, I looked up and saw that he had leaned his head against the sofa back and closed his eyes. Assuming I had put him to sleep, I rose and attempted to quietly slip out of the room and escape to my bedchamber, but he spoke before I could reach the door.

"Thank you, Elizabeth; that was lovely. Will you have some wine?"

"I thank you, no," I said, seating myself on a small chair. "And I hope you do not intend to imbibe tonight, sir. You said in the carriage that you were not in the habit of consuming much strong drink."

He smiled slightly. "Do not fear a repeat of last evening. Even if I wanted to drink, my headache prevents it."

We sat quietly for some time, neither of us even attempting to converse. I may as well get used to this silence, I thought. At last, he rose and walked to the window, pushed aside the heavy drapery, and looked out. "I see that the rain has returned."

"Then I shall sleep well. The sound of raindrops against the window has always soothed me."

"Except for last night."

"Yes," I replied, somewhat disconcerted that he should speak of it again. "But even with the storm, I did sleep well."

"Did you?" He turned to look upon me with an expression in his eyes that made me feel suddenly weak, almost trembling. I could do nothing but nod slightly. What possessed me? Why should his gaze affect me so? He walked toward me and held out his hand. "Shall we retire early tonight?"

I am sure my wide eyes caused him to realize my discomfort at such a proposal.

"I meant no untoward suggestion, Elizabeth. I have a headache. I am tired. And I assume the day has been long for you as well. Shall we proceed above stairs — you to your chamber and I to mine?"

"Actually, sir, I would beg leave to select a book from your library before I retire."

"Of course. I shall show you the way."

"There is no need. I can summon a servant."

The coolness of my tone must have succeeded in discouraging him, for he bowed slightly and with a simple, "Good-night, then," he strode up the stairs after having summoned the butler to lead me into the large, well-stocked library.

I delighted in canvassing the room as I explored the volumes upon volumes of books. I took my time in doing so, not merely for the pleasure it afforded me, but also to insure that Mr. Darcy might be safely ensconced in his bedchamber by the time I retired to mine.

At last, I chose a new novel and hurried up the staircase. Closing the door once I reached my room and holding my breath, I leaned against it and listened for the sound of footsteps. When I heard none, I ventured into the room and noted the warmth of the fire already laid and waiting for me. I spread my hands before it and then, completely unbidden, my eyes could not help but travel to the door between my suite and that of Mr. Darcy. I felt quite unnerved that we should sleep with only a wall between us.

Suddenly, I heard footsteps behind me and turned, covering my mouth to stifle a gasp.

"Ma'am?" A young maid walked through the doorway from my dressing room. "I didn't mean to startle you. I'm Fiona. Does Madam require a bath tonight?"

"Fiona," I said, so relieved I had to sit down on the sofa. "I would. I would, indeed. A bath would be the very thing to wash away the weariness of the road."

"I'll attend to it immediately, ma'am," she said, but instead of returning to the dressing room, she opened the door to the hallway.

"Fiona, where are you going?"

She blushed and then stammered, "To inform Master Darcy's valet that you'll require additional time before you are . . . ready."

"Ready? I do not understand."

"For the master's visit, ma'am," she said softly, obviously embarrassed to meet my eyes.

I closed mine, amazed at my ignorance. Of course, she and Mr. Darcy's servant expected us to spend the night together. I must adjust to this. I was married, and I must act the married woman at least until the servants realized we did not sleep together.

"There is no need," I said. "Mr. Darcy has . . . tasks awaiting him. There will be adequate time for my bath before his visit."

She nodded, returned to the dressing room, and readied the tub with steaming hot water. I proceeded to the dressing table and began to unpin my hair. How luxurious it felt to have her brush it and then pin it up loosely, just enough to keep from getting wet. She helped me to disrobe, and I sighed with pleasure when I stepped in, slipped down into the hot water, and laid my head back against the tub. Fiona had poured sweet-smelling salts into the water, and the incense and heat combined to make me feel at ease at last.

"Oh, I've forgotten the lotions, ma'am." She pulled drawers open while she searched throughout the room. "One moment, please. I'll return with great haste."

"Do not hurry. I will soak for a while."

I heard the click of her heels as she left the dressing room and walked through my bedchamber and out into the hall. I sighed again, for I could not believe how much I needed this respite. The worries and cares of the last days seemed to slide off me as I slipped my shoulders under the water. I closed my eyes and inhaled the pleasing scent. I wriggled my toes, pulled my leg up and stretched it toward the ceiling, running a soapy cloth down the calf.

I heard footsteps behind me again and realized I should allow the maid to wash me, as that was her job, and so I sat up. When the steps ceased and she did not appear, I turned to glance over my shoulder and caught my breath. There, just inside the doorway between the dressing room and my bedchamber, stood Mr. Darcy!

I was too shocked to say or do anything other than sit there, my mouth agape. He, likewise, appeared stunned, but he did not turn and leave immediately as one would have expected. He stared as though transfixed. He opened his mouth, but remained silent. At last, he turned and vanished. I heard the door to the hallway close firmly behind him.

I gasped for air, realizing suddenly that I had held my breath the entire time we had stared at each other. Why had he entered my room? Had he not promised to honour my privacy? And to think that he had seen me in my bath! I looked around, realizing that since the doorway was behind me, he had seen nothing more than my exposed back and shoulders, but still — we both knew that I was unclothed. Oh, what mortification! How could I ever face him again?

Just then, I heard the door to the hall open, and I reached for the towel draped across the front of the tub. The sound of voices could be heard, one of them, which I recognized as Mr. Darcy's, loud and insistent. The door then closed, and Fiona hurried into the room, carrying the lotion.

"I beg your pardon, ma'am," she said, obviously flustered. "I didn't mean to be so long."

"Is something amiss, Fiona?"

"Yes, ma'am, it's my little one. He has a toothache, and he cries for me even though Betty tends him. Children always want their mothers when they're sick."

"You have a son?"

"Yes, ma'am. His name's William, but I call him Willie."

"But how can you be in service and care for a child?"

"The master — he gave me special permission, ma'am. I know it's unusual, but the master's the kindest of men, although he's quite unhappy with me just now."

"The master? Was that his voice I heard raised in the hall?"

"Yes, ma'am. He came in search of me when he was told that the child was crying, and he said I had left the door to your chamber open, for which I beg your pardon most heartily, ma'am. I pray you won't hold it against me. We're quite lucky it was only the master who discovered it, aren't we?" She smiled and winked at me, as though to say she understood the intimacies of marriage. Well, of course, she would; she had a child.

"Yes, quite," I murmured. She then proceeded to wash my back and helped me dry off and get dressed for bed. She rubbed my arms, hands and neck with the lotion. After unpinning my hair, she brushed it again, the steaming bath having caused my curls to misbehave in their own wayward manner.

"So, this Betty tends your son while you are working, Fiona? Is that correct?"

"Yes, she's grown old now, but once she worked in the kitchen at Pemberley like I did."

"Oh, you work at Pemberley also?"

"Not any more. I worked there in the kitchen when I was much younger until — until I had Willie. With his birth, the master moved me to London, and I trained to be an upstairs maid. The master's so good. He could have banished me when I became with child, but instead, he moved me here, and he kept Betty on so she could help me. Master Darcy's truly the best of men."

"And your husband? Does he work in the house also?"

She blushed, and she would not meet my eyes. "'Tis shameful to admit, ma'am, but I've never married."

"I see."

Now, I was embarrassed but surprised at the news. Why should Mr. Darcy, who prided himself upon his propriety, show kindness to a fallen woman and keep her in his employment — not only keep her employed, but elevate her to ladies' maid?

"I had Willie five years ago, ma'am, when I was naught but fifteen years old. The year before, I left Scotland to come live with my uncle and aunt who are in service at Pemberley, and when I learnt I was going to have the child, I had nowhere to go. They're all the family I have left. The master was most understanding. He couldn't have me remain at Pemberley because of Miss Georgiana. She was so young at the time, and he's very protective over her, but he found a place for me here in Town. I'm much obliged."

"I can see how you would be," I said, rising. "Go back to your child, now. I do not need anything else this evening." One last time she plumped the pillows on the bed she had turned down and then curtseyed and departed.

I was glad to be alone. Not only did I suffer a headache, but now my thoughts reeled with what had happened earlier. Mr. Darcy had entered my room uninvited and invaded my privacy once again. Was he a man I should fear? Would he burst through the door adjoining our chambers in the middle of the night, demanding his conjugal rights? That image was in complete opposition to the picture just painted by the servant — that of a merciful, kind, and compassionate master. Who was the real Mr. Darcy?

A knock at the inner door caused me to jump! It could be no one other than him. My first thought was to barricade myself inside the dressing room, an idea I quickly abandoned upon remembering his warning that not even a lock would bar him if he wanted to enter. I took a deep breath and opened the door, although I must admit that my hand shook as I reached for the doorknob.

There he stood, still completely dressed, which I took as a reassuring sign. I realized that I was dressed for bed and drew my robe a little closer. It was the one exception to my dark wardrobe that I had allowed — a beautiful champagne-coloured silk robe given to me by Aunt Gardiner. I knew she had envisioned me in it on my wedding night, wearing it for my new husband. I could tell it flattered me by the way Mr. Darcy looked me up and down, but I refused to cower and met his eyes with fierceness.

"Sir?"

"May I come in, Elizabeth?"

"For what reason?"

"I brought you some books. I thought they might prove diverting. And . . . to apologize."

The look of contrition in his eyes seemed genuine, and so I stepped back, allowing him entrance. I returned to the fireplace, and he followed me but maintained an acceptable distance from my person.

"Forgive me, Elizabeth, for barging in earlier. I had not the least idea you were bathing."

I said nothing, giving him not the slightest assistance.

"My valet said Fee's child was ill, and when he could not find her, I thought she must be preparing your room. With the door left ajar, I assumed you were still in the library and that she had not heard my knocking. I did knock."

"I did not hear a knock."

"But I did. You must believe me. I entered only to find the maid."

His apology sounded sincere, but I was not in a mood to make things easier for him, so I did not reply and, instead, settled myself upon the sofa.

"I know that you like to read, so I selected a couple of books for you." He handed me a collection of Dunne's sonnets and a novel by Richard Graves.

"Thank you." I flipped through the pages.

"I hope you found something of interest below stairs, but I picked these two from among my favourites, which I keep on the shelves inside my room."

"You have a great many favourites." I recalled the walls of bookshelves I had seen earlier.

He nodded, and I could not keep myself from adding, "I do like books, Mr. Darcy, and I shall endeavour most heartily to improve my mind by extensive reading."

He winced at my words, both of us aware that I made reference to a sharp retort he had made last winter about a refined woman needing to be an extensive reader if she were to entertain his fancy of *an accomplished woman*. For some cause, I had a brief glimmer of remorse at teasing him, for it was plain to see that he knew not how to take it, and so I changed the subject.

"Fiona told me of your kindness toward her."

He did not answer but frowned in response.

"How you allowed her to remain in your employ after her unfortunate situation."

"Aye, well, she had nowhere to go, and I could not see turning her out. She was very young and ignorant."

"I assume the man could not be forced to take responsibility."

He shook his head. "I felt it was my responsibility."

"Yours? But why? Do you know who the father is?"

"I do." He turned and started for the door. "But that is all I care to say about the matter. I bid you good-night."

As he closed the door behind him, a suspicion began to nag at my mind — an ugly, worrisome thought. Why had he voiced his reply like that? His responsibility? Surely not! Oh, surely not!

I AWOKE THE NEXT MORNING to blessed sunshine streaming through the windows. There was not even a hint of fog. How I rejoiced at the sight, for I did not think I could abide another dark, dreary day. If I were in charge of rain, I would have it do so only at night at the accustomed hours of slumber, and every day would be as beautiful as that morning promised. It lightened my mood considerably, and when I recalled the distasteful thought with which I had ended the prior evening, I determined to dismiss it as nothing more than a foolish fancy on my part.

From my earliest childhood, I had been blessed with a sanguine nature, and although it had been sorely tried in the last six months and the past two days in particular, I decided to think more positively, to try my best to be optimistic. A great longing to leave the house and walk in the garden came over me, and I planned to do so as soon as I had breakfasted. I even resolved to hold my tongue in Mr. Darcy's presence. I would attempt to be more compliant, to overlook his disagreeableness, and to enjoy the day.

My resolve lasted a good half-hour.

We had just sat down to a breakfast that included a steaming cup of freshly brewed coffee, which I dearly loved and was enjoying thoroughly, when Mr. Darcy announced that I must have new gowns made as soon as possible.

"I do not mean to disparage your wardrobe," he said. "It is perfectly suitable for the sphere in which you were brought up, but you will need more extensive selections as my wife."

His tone grated on me, perhaps because all that had transpired the night before had not truly been put to rest in spite of my efforts, and so with the greatest of ease, my cheerful resolve flew right up the chimney.

"I have never been one to put on airs, Mr. Darcy, in either my manners or my dress."

"I am well aware of that. I would not have you do so, but you must see that we shall attend concerts and assemblies as well as balls during the upcoming Season, and I want you to feel at ease. You must take advantage of the time we are in Town to order new gowns. Having grown up with a sister, I know how important clothes are to a woman. And besides that, I think it is time that you soften the severity of your attire."

Severity! What did he mean? When I raised my eyebrows in reply, he went on. "Pray, do not think I am insensitive to the loss of your father, Elizabeth, but more than six months has gone by since his passing. One rarely sees anyone completely garbed in black as you are for this length of time."

"Perhaps that is because you have never seen anyone who mourns the loss as deeply as I do, sir. How can you possibly know the depth of my grief?"

His voice softened when next he spoke. "I, too, have grieved for my parents. Although it occurred years ago, I still feel their absence."

His words shamed me. How could I have forgotten that he had also suffered such a loss? Still, my ire was raised at the thought that he would tell me when to cease my own observance.

"Shall you not visit the dressmakers and milliners later in the week and at least select some fabrics and patterns or whatever it is that women require in something other than black? I shall allow you to choose the time you actually make the change."

"That *is* generous of you, sir. At least I shall be permitted the freedom to choose when I quit mourning!"

I rose and stormed out of the dining room. Just before I reached the staircase, Mr. Darcy, having followed me, grabbed my hand.

"Must you make a scene out of our every conversation?"

"A scene! I cannot see that I am making a scene. I simply expressed my opinion, sir, and if I am to refrain from doing so, that should have been made a clause in our marriage contract!"

Two servants could be heard approaching the staircase above stairs, and so he said nothing, but with a nod of his head, indicated that I must return to the dining room. I complied but only because I, too, did not care to air our differences in front of the staff. Behind the doors that he closed firmly, Mr. Darcy's scowl deepened. He escorted me to the chair on which I had previously sat and stood so close by that I had no choice but to sit down.

"You and I must come to a truce, Elizabeth. You are behaving like a child, and I expect much more of you."

"I am behaving like a child? And why not, when you persist in treating me like one?"

He clenched his fist and put it to his mouth the way I had seen him do before when he was angry. Pacing back and forth before the fireplace, he said nothing for several minutes. At last, he seemed to have gained his composure.

"If I have treated you as less than you are, I ask your forgiveness. You must acknowledge that being a husband is as foreign to me as the role of wife is to you. I have been master in this house for five years, and Georgiana has been my responsibility for as long. I am accustomed to say what I will, and it is done."

"I shall acknowledge that, if you will accept that I am not a servant, a dependent child, or a younger sister. Whether we like it or not, you have made me your wife, and I intend to be treated with the honour and respect such position merits. I will not be talked down to, scolded, or ordered. If you have not already discovered it — I hope you soon do so — I am not your property!"

There must have been fire in my eyes, for I was as deadly earnest as I had been when he had insulted me at Hunsford six months previous. When I saw a slight smile flicker about his mouth, it did nothing to abate my anger.

"What statement have I made that you deem humorous, sir?"

"Only that I marvel at how quickly you forget your marriage vows."

"I do not understand your meaning."

"Did you not but two days ago in the presence of God and witnesses promise to obey me?"

I closed my eyes in dismay. How could he bring up that sham of a wedding ceremony and the words I had been forced to utter?

"Or was your pledge of obedience as false as your vow of love?"

There was no need for me to answer, for he knew the truth as well as I. This time Mr. Darcy was the one to turn and stride out of the room.

We did not speak of our disagreement again; instead, we separated for much of the day. Late that afternoon, he sent Fiona to my sitting room with a request.

"If you'd like to see a bit of the city, ma'am, the master says it's his particular wish that you meet him in the front hall. He's going out, and he desires that you accompany him."

I wasted no time in readying myself and joined him there. It was not an apology, per se, but it would do for now. Besides, I had grown tired of being indoors all day and longed to go out — at least, that was the excuse I made to myself.

The remainder of our so-called wedding week and the next, as well, passed more rapidly than I anticipated. There were no more intrusions on my privacy or events that sparked controversy. On the contrary, Mr. Darcy could not have been more of a gentleman.

He assembled the entire staff and introduced me. I was allowed sufficient time with Mrs. James to go over the household accounts and acquaint myself with everything involved in running the townhouse. I felt quite certain that it could run itself with little input on my part, but it gratified me to learn that Mr. Darcy publicly acknowledged me as mistress of the house, no matter what situation existed privately.

It was as though both of us were making a valiant attempt to get along, and I must admit that Mr. Darcy proved to be an interesting and stimulating companion. He knew much more than I about London and its society. In years past, I had visited my relatives near Cheapside, of course, but we had rarely ventured far from the area in which they lived. Mr. Darcy introduced me to a grander side of Town, and I did enjoy exploring a world I had never dreamed of inhabiting.

He conducted me on a tour of the city, showing me the best neighbourhoods, shops, and parks. I saw St. James's Palace from the outside, at least, and learned that he frequented it but little, as he found himself bored with the hangers-on that populated royal society. Still, I planned to write to Mamá and tell her that her son had been in the presence of the king. Would that not be a feather in her cap! Now she would have a rejoinder for Sir William Lucas' many references to such.

He pointed out St. George's Church, a grand stone edifice, and then named many more churches we passed by. We also drove along the Thames for some distance, but he cautioned me not to stray past a particular bend of it, for it was not a safe part of the city from thereon. Once the rain, which had returned, let up in the middle of the week, I particularly enjoyed our strolls through the park across the street from his home.

Among the trees and well-tended lawns, I felt that I could breathe deeply. Even though the noise of the city could be heard in the background, it seemed more like Hertfordshire as we ambled through the fallen leaves of red and brown. We watched children chase their kites close to the pond and throw bread to the family of ducks hovering on the bank, while parents or nannies sitting nearby kept a watchful eye upon them. Mr. Darcy introduced me to several couples we met there, and they promised to call.

It was in the park that we both seemed more at ease with one another. We talked of books and music, and I was surprised to discover that our tastes were similar. In fact, his favourite authors were the same as my father's, which pleased me. I had thought Mr. Darcy a man who laughed rarely, but he told me he enjoyed the sly wit of Dr. Johnson. He asked my opinion of certain artists, but I was forced to plead ignorance, for I was woefully uneducated in the world of art.

"We shall have to remedy that," he announced. "A trip to Montagu House in Bloomsbury seems to be in order. Shall we go on the morrow?"

I readily agreed, and we spent Friday surveying the great works found therein. I learned much from him and felt myself quite educated by the end of the day. It would take more tours before I would feel at ease discussing the Rosetta Stone and other Egyptian antiquities or Mr. Townley's collection of classical sculpture.

I marvelled at Mr. Darcy's knowledge of the world, and when he imparted it — almost as a teacher with a student — we enjoyed perfect amiability. It was only when personal subjects intruded into our conversations that our familiar masks once again slipped back into place.

At the end of the second week, he announced that we were invited to a ball at the Earl of Matlock's mansion on Saturday next. The invitation caused a mixture of anticipation and hesitation within me. I had always loved balls and dancing, but I would know hardly anyone, and I remembered what a disaster my one and only dance with Mr. Darcy had been at

Netherfield almost a year before.

"Shall I know anyone in attendance other than Colonel Fitzwilliam?" I asked.

"I feel certain Bingley and his sister will attend as well as Mr. and Mrs. Hurst."

Since he had introduced the subject of Mr. Bingley, I felt this as good a time as any to question him about our pre-marital agreement. "I wonder, sir, have you had opportunity to speak to Mr. Bingley about Jane?"

He frowned before speaking. "In what way?"

In what way! Was he purposefully forgetting our bargain? "You promised to right the wrong you committed upon my sister in regard to your influence upon Mr. Bingley."

"Oh, that," he said in a dismissive tone. "No, the time has not yet been right."

"And may I ask when it shall be right?"

We sat at the dinner table, and it seemed to me that he took more than adequate time in answering me, choosing to cut his roast beef carefully, chew it thoroughly, and slowly wash it down with a long swallow of wine. At this rate, I thought, Jane shall die an old maid before he finished the meal!

He wiped his mouth with his napkin, then rose and started for the door. "Trust me, Elizabeth," he said, as he reached for the doorknob. "I shall speak to Bingley when *I* deem the time is right."

Oh, the man was pompous! Why must everything be done on his timetable? I threw down my napkin and stormed from the room, unable to eat another bite. I was too angry to search him out and confront him further, afraid of what I might say. Instead, I ran up the stairs to my chamber.

Once again, I spent the evening regretting that I had ever entered into marriage with the man. Where was his agreeable nature that I had come to enjoy in the last few days? Had he abandoned it in the carriage as carelessly as one leaves behind an umbrella? And what had happened to our newly found but tenuous cordiality? Had I merely imagined a slight crack in the shells in which we both sought protection? Was I the only one who had been fooled into thinking we might possibly tear apart those shells?

Well, no more! Mr. Darcy had sealed up the crack with his own particular impenetrable paste.

Chapter Five

At the end of dinner on the following Sunday evening, when we had been married a total of sixteen days, Mr. Darcy announced that Georgiana would return on the morrow from her stay at her uncle's home. I received the news with pleasure and yet, a degree or two of trepidation. During our brief marriage, neither Mr. Darcy nor I had discussed his sister except in passing, but I had many questions on my mind, not the least of which involved my maid.

"I wonder, sir, exactly why you chose to place Fiona in my service?"

He looked up from his plate with a strange expression about his eyes. "What do you mean?"

"She informed me that you removed her from Pemberley because of Georgiana, yet you stationed her above stairs where she is sure to come in frequent contact with your sister."

"When I moved Fee to London five years ago, Georgiana was very young, far too young to understand the circumstances of an unmarried girl giving birth to someone's *natural* child."

"And I take it you feel she is mature enough now to have that understanding."

"I do." Scowling and tossing his napkin aside, he rose from the table. "Georgiana is no longer a naïve school-girl, not after her experience with George Wickham."

I could tell he did not want to discuss the subject, but I persisted. "We must have some conversation about that fact, Mr. Darcy. I fail to understand why you did not inform your sister before we married that Mr. Wickham is now my brother."

"Frankly, I take no pleasure in relating that fact to anyone. But as for Georgiana, the answer is simple. When I left her to travel to Hertfordshire with the Gardiners, I did not know whether you would accept my proposal. I prepared her with that truth — I would seek your hand in marriage, but I was unsure of the outcome. In the event that you declined, I saw no reason to alarm her as to your connections. If truth be told, I was somewhat surprised when you did agree."

I looked up to meet his eyes, but he had turned away with those words and walked to the fireplace. Had he asked me to marry, hoping I would say no? I could not believe that, for he had appeared far too persuasive at Longbourn.

Or had he? I remembered his stern, cold expression when my uncle had first voiced the idea of such a marriage. When he asked to see me alone, Mr. Darcy had not declared his love as he had done before his first proposal. It had all seemed more of a business arrangement, but why would he even make the offer if he did not want me? I had nothing to bring to the union, for my paltry dowry was almost nonexistent. He would not profit from such a marriage.

Suddenly, I felt plain and undesirable, and the feeling hurt — why, I knew not. I did not desire the man, did I? The very thought filled me with such turmoil that I resolved not to think on it.

"I fear that your decision may cause your sister great distress. Pray, do enlighten me on your conversation with her wherein she learned of my connection to Mr. Wickham."

"She was troubled somewhat, but I assured her that we will not see Wickham, that she has nothing to fear in that regard. I trust that you will do all you can to alleviate her worries."

"Certainly, but is it not possible we will see Lydia sometime in the future — if not at either of your homes, perhaps at Longbourn? You will allow me to visit my family, will you not?"

"Of course. I shall not prevent your seeing any of your sisters. I would think, however, that it shall be some time before Mrs. Wickham travels from her new home, being as great a distance as Newcastle is from either Longbourn or Derbyshire."

"Oh, I was not aware that you were privy to the site of the Wickhams' relocation."

"Yes," he muttered, averting his face as he strode toward the door that led to the hall. "I knew that they moved there and that Wickham had joined the regulars. Pray excuse me."

He exited the room, and I was left to wonder who had told him of that news. Probably Mamá. She seemed as proud of Lydia's marriage as she was of mine, even though a more worthless man in England than Lydia's husband could not be found.

I sighed as I rose from the table. I had made little progress in discussing Georgiana with her brother, and my feelings were hurt at the way he had dismissed my apprehension. Did he think I worked miracles — that I could transform that shy, young girl into a poised, lively woman when I knew little about her? He could at least discuss her likes and dislikes with me.

Furthermore, I tired of the man running off every time he did not care to continue a conversation with me. I resolved to question him further and quit the room in search of him. I supposed he would partake of an after-dinner drink, but when I did not find him in any of the public rooms, I asked a servant for his whereabouts, and he directed me to a large room that I remembered on my tour of the townhouse as the game room.

Sure enough, when I entered the doorway, Mr. Darcy stood poised to make a shot at the billiards table. Upon seeing me, he straightened and bowed slightly. Our formality with each other seemed pretentious. I wondered if we would ever be at ease with one another. After all, we had been together every day for over two weeks, and we were married — and yet *not* married.

"Do not interrupt your game." I advanced into the room. "I will sit quietly until you finish."

"As you like."

He bent over the table once more and made a shot that I assumed to be correct, as it hit another ball into the side pocket. I knew little of the game and watched with interest as he walked around the table, positioned his cue stick with studied precision, and evidently executed perfect shots from the sound the balls made as they smacked into each other and then dropped into the pockets around the table.

He had removed his coat, and I could not help but notice his excellent form. He was handsome — there was no denying it — and through the long sleeves of his white shirt, I could see the span of his shoulders and the manner in which his strong arms filled out his clothing. I wondered what it would feel like to touch those arms, to experience their strength. While I mused upon such idle thoughts, he stopped playing and stood watching me. Upon becoming aware of his gaze, I started visibly. Could he read my mind? Surely not! Then why did I feel guilty and exposed? I spoke quickly to conceal my consternation.

"Do you enjoy other games, sir?"

"When in town, I engage in fencing at least twice a week."

I could think of nothing to say in reply, and nodding, I turned away from his gaze.

"Have you ever played billiards, Elizabeth?"

I raised my eyebrows at such a question. "Hardly, sir. It is a gentleman's game."

"Would you like to learn?"

"Pardon?"

"We are quite alone. Are you not at all curious to try your hand?"

I was intrigued by the suggestion, and yes, I did want to try. I rose and took the cue stick from his outstretched hand. He took my right hand, placed the stick between my fingers and then told me where to position my left hand.

"Now place your hand upon the table and aim at the white ball nearest the red one."

I attempted to do so, but I felt awkward.

"You must bend over the table in order to aim. Here, let me show you."

He took the stick from me and demonstrated the correct posture. We stood quite close, near enough that I could have reached out and touched him, touched that arm that proved so attractive. Such distraction limited my power of concentration, so much so that, when I attempted to copy his position, he stopped me once again.

"No, no, you must bend over closer to the table."

I leaned over further, suddenly cognizant that the neckline of my gown proved far too revealing. I was thankful that Mr. Darcy stood behind me and not on the opposite side of the table, but then I thought of how the shape of my derriere must be exposed from the back. No wonder women did not play that game!

"You still do not have it right. Let me help you," he said, and to my utter amazement, I felt him lean over me, his left arm circling round my shoulder. He clasped my left hand and moved it further back, while his right arm surrounded mine, and he covered my hand with his. I could feel the warmth of his body, his breath upon my cheek, and the scent of his skin — heady and pleasing — filling my senses until I found it hard not to tremble.

"Now pull the cue stick through your fingers like this," he said, pulling it back and forth through our interlocked fingers. "Keep your eyes on the ball and shoot."

With a deft movement, we sent the white ball rolling across the table, where it hit a red ball neatly into the corner pocket.

"There! See with what ease you made the shot!" he said as we both straightened up together. Was he as aware as I that his arms still encircled me?

"Yes," I managed to say, "easy, indeed, with your guidance."

I turned my face toward him, and there was hardly any space at all between his face and mine. We gazed into each other's eyes for what seemed like minutes to me, but surely could not have been more than an instant before he released me and stepped aside. I felt my colour rise, and I averted my face, busying myself with replacing the cue stick in its holder.

"Shall you not try your hand again?"

"No, sir, I believe I have tried enough for now. Perhaps another night."

"Yes, perhaps," he said, keeping his gaze upon me. I looked up, met his eyes, and wondered if it was billiards of which we spoke.

I excused myself and left the room, all too shaken by the feelings that engulfed me. I found my way into a small parlour where I had left some needlework. How grateful I was to find something with which to occupy my hands, but how disconcerting to discover my fingers trembled too much to make a straight stitch!

I had never experienced such feelings before, such attraction to any man, not even to the young swains who had courted me in earlier times. I liked dancing with handsome men well enough, even flirting with them at balls and assemblies, but not one of them had ever affected me the way Mr. Darcy had. In one way, the sentiment filled me with anticipation and, in another, with great dismay. Could such sensations occur with someone I professed to dislike, with someone I could not possibly love?

My thoughts were interrupted when he entered the room. I applied myself to my embroidery with a renewed focus while he poured himself a glass of Madeira. He offered me one, but I declined. I needed nothing more to cause my head to swim. I determined to discuss his sister with him once again; not only did we need that discussion, it was also the safest subject I could devise.

"Sir, I would importune upon you to speak more of Georgiana. You have instructed me not to talk with her about Mr. Wickham, but I fear he is the object she most needs to discuss with me."

His brows knit together in a frown. "I fail to comprehend your meaning."

"Your sister was heartily misused by my new brother. Can you possibly think that she will not resent me?"

"Why should she? You had nothing to do with it. Your sister married the scoundrel without your sanction, did she not?"

"She did not, sir. By the time Lydia and Mr. Wickham wed, I was all too relieved that he married her."

"That is not what I meant. Let me rephrase my words. You would never have desired your sister to elope with Wickham, would you?"

"Of course not, but Georgiana is unaware of that."

"But she is, for I told her that very truth on the day she departed with Fitzwilliam. The entire subject is one that causes her great pain, and I do not want the issue even mentioned in her presence."

"Are you sure that her feelings correspond with yours? Could it be that she might benefit from talking of her fears and anxieties about the matter?"

"Absolutely not. I do not see wisdom in such an approach. My wishes and directions remain as they were, Elizabeth. Do not ever mention Wickham to Georgiana, other than to assure her she need have no contact with him."

I glared at him. How could he be so infuriating in his demands, so insensible in his discernment? How did he know what Georgiana needed to talk about? For that matter, how did I? Once again, I thought of the morrow with diffidence.

THE NEXT DAY I AROSE late, my sleep disturbed for much of the night by strange dreams. At times some unseen menace chased me, and then without explanation, I turned willingly to embrace that same fearful, faceless person. I had not the slightest idea what it all meant and awoke exhausted.

Added to my fatigue was the fact that, before I went to bed, I had spent nigh onto two hours rummaging through my books and correspondence, searching out the letter Mr. Darcy had given me last April at Rosings Park. My efforts proved in vain. I longed to read the letter anew, to review once again the history between the writer and Mr. Wickham. It was my belief that much was gained by reading between the lines, and I wondered if that letter might enlighten me as to Mr. Darcy's character, for I certainly needed no further enlightenment as to Wickham's nature.

I recalled the anger that had beset me upon reading it the first time. Oh yes, I had been ashamed that I had ever believed Mr. Wickham's lies, but I confess that Mr. Darcy's further admission that he had willingly kept Mr. Bingley and Jane apart had so infuriated me that I had thrown the letter aside after only one reading. Instead of carefully weighing his words, I had dismissed them, and evidently, I had done an effective job of discarding the letter.

I wondered if I had forgotten it at Longbourn or, even worse, left it at Hunsford parsonage. I vowed to write Jane that morning and ask her to make a thorough inspection of my room and, upon finding the missive, dispatch it to me immediately. I should like to do the same with Charlotte, but I feared she might read it or that the letter might fall into the hands of Mr. Collins. I would begin with Jane, for I knew I could trust her to send it unread.

As for the present, I was in great need of a cup of coffee, and so I descended the stairs to the sound of voices within the breakfast room. I assumed Mr. Darcy's sister must have already returned. What must she think of me still abed at that hour? With a determined straightening of my shoulders and a forced smile, I raised my head and resolved to face my new responsibility — that of winning over Georgiana.

I entered the room only to be calmed by the welcome sight of Mr. Bingley. How relieved I was to see him instead of Mr. Darcy's sister!

"Miss Bennet!" he exclaimed. "That is, I should say Mrs. Darcy! How good it is to see you! Let me be the first to wish you joy on the occasion of your marriage to this dull fellow here."

"Thank you, sir. I am very glad to see you as well."

"Only yesterday I returned to Town, and I could not believe the two of you married without letting me know. I have upbraided Darcy for the past half-hour. Tell me, were all your sisters present at the wedding?"

"All but one, sir."

"Ah," he said, and I felt certain he was fishing for information about Jane.

"My youngest sister is lately married, Mr. Bingley, and has moved to Newcastle with her husband. It was too far a distance to travel for my wedding, and in fact, I have not seen her since her marriage."

The relief on his face shone through in his eyes and even broader smile. "I see. And so all of your other sisters are well, I trust, and still reside at Longbourn?"

"Yes," I assured him.

I shot a glance at Mr. Darcy, wondering if he had yet deigned the time appropriate to inform Mr. Bingley of his part in preventing him from seeing Jane when she was in London last winter. From the easy camaraderie between them, it did not appear that he had, for I felt certain Mr. Bingley would at least countenance some anger toward his friend at such deceit. Oh, how I hoped that discussion might occur between them today! But at present, I discovered they were making plans to attend a concert together on Wednesday evening.

"Shall you not enjoy such an outing, Mrs. Darcy?" Mr. Bingley asked.

"I do not know, sir. I have never been to a concert in London, but I look forward to it."

"Excellent."

Just then, a commotion in the hall signalled the return of Georgiana, accompanied by Colonel Fitzwilliam. They were greeted and offered refreshment, but it appeared all had eaten except for me. I decided to forego the meal and made do with coffee. Mr. Darcy and Mr. Bingley made much of Miss Darcy, and brother and sister were soon engrossed in conversation.

I observed Mr. Bingley to see if his attentions to her were apropos of a man in love — as Caroline had insisted that he was — but I could ascertain no special attention other than that he paid to any other woman. Certainly, it did not compare to the interest he had shown my sister when at Hertfordshire.

"And so, Mrs. Darcy," Colonel Fitzwilliam said, joining me by taking a cup of coffee, "how do you like married life by now?"

I blushed at the question and tried to smile. "I am much intrigued by London, sir. I have never been so excessively diverted. There is much to see and do. One is quite bewildered by all the choices."

He agreed with me, and I hoped that he did not wonder why I had answered his question by changing the subject. If he did, thankfully, he was too much of a gentleman to pursue it, and we passed no little time in casual conversation. Three-quarters of an hour later, he arose and announced that he must return to his unit.

"Come and walk me to the door, Georgie," he said, holding out his hand to her.

"And why should I? Just so you can lecture me once again?"

"Lecture?" Mr. Darcy asked. "Has she needed lecturing?"

"You would not believe how often, Darcy! I have spent two weeks trying to make a lady out of her, but I fear the task is impossible."

"Richard! You will have Mrs. Darcy think I am a hoyden!" She turned to me. "Truly, I have not needed lectures. He simply enjoys having someone to harangue. I fear he has been away from his troops far too long, and I have borne the brunt of their absence."

"Go along with you now, Sprout," the colonel said, laughing as he escorted her out of the breakfast room. We could hear their gentle banter continue down the hall. Once again, I found myself envying their easy spirit with one another.

It was not long after the colonel left the house that Mr. Bingley and Mr. Darcy made plans to depart for their men's club. Out in the hall, Mr. Darcy kissed his sister's cheek, telling her how glad he was that she had returned.

"Then why do you leave almost as soon as I arrive, Wills?"

"Appointments, my dear. Besides, this will give you time to acquaint yourself with Elizabeth."

As soon as the door closed behind the men, however, she turned for the stairs, and I could see that she was poised to flee my presence.

"Georgiana, might you accompany me to the music room? I found a fugue by Bach that I am unable to play. Will you not take pity and assist me with the fingering?"

I could see the hesitation in her manner, but the enticement of Bach proved to win her over. We sat down at the pianoforte together, and she demonstrated the correct manner in which to play the selection.

"I fear I have not practiced near enough," I said. "It is evident you have progressed much further in your mastery of the technique required for this difficult a piece. Pray, tell me how many hours you devote to your art."

"It depends upon the day. When I am alone, as is often the case, I seem to lose myself in the music. At times, a half-day has gone by before I rise from this instrument."

I shook my head. "I am impressed, my dear. You are even more dedicated than my sister."

She stiffened at my remark, and I wondered what I had said to cause her response. "Your sister who married recently? Is that the one to whom you refer?"

"Lydia? Oh, no, Lydia has neither an ear for music nor the patience to practice. I refer to my sister, Mary. She is the one who loves to play."

"So you have two sisters then? I should have liked to have a sister."

"I have four sisters . . . and now, it appears I have five."

When she looked at me with a question in her eyes, I said, "You, Georgiana, are now my sister, are you not?"

"Oh, I had not thought of that. I am afraid I do not know how to act with a sister."

"Well, it is not difficult, believe me. I hope that you and I shall be friends, as that is what the best of sisters become."

"I have never had many friends, Mrs. Darcy."

"Oh? And why is that? I do not understand."

"Most of the year I live at Pemberley with my companion, Mrs. Annesley. I have had a succession of companions, but never many friends my own age. I am rarely in London, for my brother prefers that I stay in the country, and when in Town, I see only his friends who are all much older than I."

"That is abominable! The house should be filled with young people your age. Why does your brother not see to it?"

"Wills is very protective. I . . . I have been taken advantage of in the past, and he is careful that it should not occur again."

"I understand protection, but Georgiana, you must not be forced to live a solitary life."

"Oh, I am not complaining," she said quickly, rising from the piano stool and walking to a chair near the fireplace. "I love my brother."

"That is well and good," I said, following her, "but he cannot be your only companion."

"My mother died shortly after I was born, and I fear my father did not know what to do with a daughter. He loved me dearly, but I think he and

Wills have always been afraid something would happen to me, perhaps because of the loss of my mother. Thus, I have seen little outside of our home in Derbyshire and this house in London."

"But who did you play with when you were little?"

"As I said, I had a number of companions and governesses, all much older women who were more like mothers than friends. About six years ago, however, I did make friends with one of the servants. I know that sounds strange, for such an attachment is not usually sanctioned, but we had a common affliction, having both lost our mothers when very young. She was a few years older than I was, and for some reason, we took to each other immediately, and I loved her. When she could steal away from her duties, we would run and play in the orchard at Pemberley. She taught me to climb trees and wade in the shallow end of the pond — things that scandalized my governess."

I smiled with her at the memory, gratified that she would confide in me. "And is she still at Pemberley?"

"No, she is here. In fact, Wills said he was giving her to you as your personal maid."

"Fiona?"

"Yes. Do you find her work satisfactory? If not, I should be glad to have Fee transferred to my service."

"She is quite satisfactory." This turn in the conversation surprised me. *"Fee"* seemed to be a favourite of both brother and sister, it would seem.

"I hope that you do not object to the fact that she has a child." She blushed slightly and looked at her hands in her lap.

"As long as the child does not interfere with her duties, I can see no reason to object."

"She is not married, you know." Georgiana pressed her lips together and kept her face averted.

"Yes. She informed me of that fact, and your brother confirmed it."

"He did?" she said quickly, her eyes searching mine. "Did he tell you who the father is?"

I shook my head. "Do you know, Georgiana?"

"No," she answered, looking away, "although I have my suspicions."

Neither of us said anything for a while, and she soon excused herself, retreating to her room. I pondered our conversation no little time. My new sister did not appear to be as innocent of the world as Mr. Darcy would have her. I wondered how far Mr. Wickham had gone in his betrayal of her, and then, although I did not wish it, my mind wandered back to my questions about Fiona. Surely Georgiana could not possibly suspect that the maid's little William was named for his father.

I did not care for that distasteful thought and its attempt to overtake me. In order to divert my attention, I picked up a book and walked out into the garden. An abundance of clouds hid the sun that day, but rain had not yet arrived, and so I relished the solitary time among the fragrant shrubs and blooming plants. I wandered down the narrow walk that wound in and around the greenery. Coming upon a stone bench hidden away in an alcove that backed up to a hedge over eight feet tall, I seated myself and opened my novel. It was light and entertaining, and I anticipated a good read.

Naught but a few moments passed, however, before my reverie was interrupted by what I presumed to be servants on the other side of the giant, dense hedges behind me. They obviously toiled at planting bulbs in the flower beds below. I could not see the men, nor could they see me, for from their conversation, it was evident they thought they were alone.

I attempted to disregard their talk and even stood up in search of a quieter nook until the nature of their conversation caught my complete attention. One man complained repeatedly that he, a house servant, had been relegated to the duties of an under-gardener, while the other reminded him that it was his own fault that had caused his descent in position.

"How can you say that," the first man replied, "when I looked far more of a dandy in my tails and wig than Duffy?"

"Ah, the only reason you be put in as footman in the first place were because you and Duffy matched in size," the other man said. "You never were no great shakes at your job, Johnny, my lad, and the master taken no account with your looks. A few weeks doing grunt work inside and out, and maybe if your luck holds, Master Darcy will relent and put you back in your fancy uniform."

"The master — hah! He's as unfair as they come, and he thinks hisself so far above us. Well, I heard a thing or two about him what brings him right back down even with me."

"Careful, lad, you don't go talkin' bad 'bout the master too loud. Someone might hear you other than me, and he's thought highly of by ever other man 'bout the place."

"And every gal," Johnny said, snickering.

"Aye, they all think he's a looker, that's for sure."

"I can't see that he's a beauty, but I reckon he does more than look at the girls. That Scottish girly, the one with the by-blow — I heard talk the child might be the master's. Why else would he bring her to London and bide the brat? And what made her so grand that warranted makin' a lady's maid out of her?"

"Ah, don't be spreadin' your filthy talk 'round, Johnny. Just 'cause the girl won't let you have your way with her don't mean you ought to talk so."

"It's not just me what's sayin' it. I swear I heard it from one of the lads in the stable."

"Well, if you did, you're mighty sorry to repeat it is all I got to say. Now, get on with your work a'fore I call the steward."

The man called 'Johnny' muttered something under his breath, but I heard nothing more. I sat frozen in place as they worked their way down the long hedge.

The suspicions I had been unable even to utter had just been spoken aloud and in the vilest of terms. The man's ugly words harrowed up fears within me, fears that I had refused to indulge. Until that moment, I had not even recognized that such thoughts might possibly take root within my heart, and the awareness overwhelmed me with shame. To listen to servants' talk and give it credence was beneath me.

I will not have this — I almost spoke the words aloud. He might have his faults, but Mr. Darcy could not be that kind of man. I refused to believe it — absolutely, completely! I would put it out of my mind as though I never heard it.

There, it was gone!

And with a valiant, intrepid determination, I rose from the bench and marched into the house, absolutely resolved at the time that I would never believe such rumours. No matter what my intentions, however, my heart was troubled, deeply troubled, and that night an affliction beset me — an affliction I had suffered since childhood whenever profoundly distressed.

I began walking in my sleep, and the next morning I awakened to find myself lying in Mr. Darcy's arms.

Chapter Six

The first thing I saw was his smile. I screwed up my eyes, certain I was still asleep and dreaming, but then allowed myself to peek through my lashes, for one does not inhale the pleasing scent of a man's skin in a dream, and Mr. Darcy's scent not only filled my senses, it seemed to permeate every pore on my body.

I opened my eyes wider. His fine lawn nightshirt fell open at the neck, and there in the hollow I could see the slight shadow of his beating pulse. That was the moment I became conscious that I lay in his arms, those very arms that only yesterday I had bemused myself with the thought of touching.

"Good morning, Elizabeth." His voice was barely more than a low whisper, deep and full of gravel from early morning sleepiness.

I could not respond. In truth, I felt such shock that I wondered if I could recall *how* to talk. I could not take it in — his face so near to mine, my head upon his shoulder, his dark curls mussed and falling across his forehead in the most provocative manner, the dark shadow of his beard outlining his face. How had this happened?

Slowly — very, very slowly — I sat up, clutching the sheet to my throat. I dared a frantic peek below the cover to assure myself that I was still clothed and closed my eyes in relief to see my gown.

"Where . . . where am I?"

"In my bed," he replied as though it were the most natural thing in the world.

I opened my mouth to speak, but he put his finger against my lips. "Now, before you attack me with accusations, hear what I have to say. Sometime

67

during the night, I awoke and found you right here, cuddled up against me. You came willingly, Elizabeth," he said, the smile continuing upon his countenance. "I did not coerce you in any way."

"But — how — why would I — did we? Help me! I cannot remember anything!"

"My, my, you certainly know how to flatter a man. Share his bed and not remember a bit of it!"

I searched his face, mine evidently reflecting horror, but that same tantalizing smile continued to grace his. Then slowly, I realized he had made the last statement in jest. Mr. Darcy was teasing me!

"Sir, I pray you be serious and tell me what happened."

He took pity on me then and began to explain. "I confess I was as surprised to find you in my bed last night as you are this morning. I attempted to talk to you, but I soon discerned you were sound asleep. I had an uncle who was a somnambulist. His physician cautioned us never to awaken him as it might cause irreparable damage, so what else could I do other than allow you to share my bed?"

He reached over and patted my hand. "Quit your fretting, Elizabeth, and be assured that nothing untoward happened between us, for I am not a man who takes advantage of an unconscious woman. Have you ever walked in your sleep before?"

I nodded and then sighed with relief, a sigh so heavy and obvious that I saw him struggle not to laugh. It *was* humorous. Even I could acknowledge that, and as I saw him press his lips together to restrain his mirth, I began to giggle, softly at first, and then when he joined me, we both erupted in laughter. I had never seen him laugh before. In truth, I had never allowed myself such unbridled liberty in his presence. We both laughed until I almost cried. When our amusement eventually slowed, I became all too aware of the intimacy of our postures, for there we sat, still facing each other right in the middle of Mr. Darcy's bed.

Suddenly, I blushed anew and began to look around me, searching for a way I could escape his chamber without exposing myself. He startled me by reaching out and gently touching my face, turning it back toward him.

"What is it, Elizabeth? What do you need?"

"A graceful way out of this predicament, I confess. Will you leave, sir, so that I might return to my room?"

"And expose myself in my nightshirt, madam? Oh, I think not. You are the invader; it is up to you to leave."

"But I am not dressed properly."

"So I see." He smiled once more as his eyes wandered over me, lazily surveying my dishabille.

"Really, Mr. Darcy, you might take pity on me and act in a gentleman-like manner."

He folded his arms across his chest and nodded. "Aye, I might, and then again I might demand that you get out of my bed immediately. Were not those the words in which you addressed me when I inadvertently wandered into your bed in that wretched little inn where we spent our wedding night?"

"But you, sir, were drunk!"

"Yes, I was and consequently unaware of my actions just as you were last night. Shall we not forgive each other these lapses and admit that neither of us is perfect?"

I was unsure whether he was serious or still teasing me, but I took advantage of the offer and agreed with him. In turn, he pulled the counterpane loose from the bottom of the bed and suggested that I make use of it as a temporary robe. I wasted no time in wrapping it around my shoulders, slipping from the bed, and hurriedly walking through the open door between our chambers. I did turn and catch one last glimpse of him over my shoulder. He sat there, watching my retreat with that same beguiling smile playing about his lips.

Goodness, but he was incredibly fine to look upon first thing in the morning!

After I returned to my rooms, I stewed and fretted for some time about what I had done. The last time I had walked in my sleep occurred during the wee hours of the morning after my father's burial. That morning I had awakened lying on the ground beside his new grave. From then on, Mamá ordered the doors at Longbourn locked at night.

Would that I had a lock on the door between my chamber and that of Mr. Darcy! But then my heart raced at the memory of waking up beside him. New and exciting sensations overwhelmed me until my head felt completely muddled.

LATER THAT DAY, MY NEW gown arrived that had been ordered for Lord Matlock's ball. I welcomed the diversion and opened the box at once. A pearl grey silk, it was finer than any I had ever owned. I had prevailed and insisted that it be trimmed in black lace, but even so, the ornamentation seemed to make it more festive rather than sombre as I had desired. When I tried it on, I gasped at my reflection in the glass. I no longer appeared as one in mourning, and the change shocked even me. My maid was delighted and could not contain her excitement.

"Oh, ma'am, you're truly lovely in that dress! Won't the master be pleased!"

Again, my pulse beat faster as I wondered at his reaction.

"And here are the black feathers for your hair. Aren't they beautiful? And with these silver combs, you'll be outstanding."

"No feathers, Fiona."

"But, ma'am, they come with the dress."

"You heard me. I do not wear feathers."

"Not even to a ball, ma'am?"

I silenced her with a look, and she quietly returned the feathers to the box in which they had come.

"Help me get out of this." Realizing I had spoken in irritation, I softened my voice as she unfastened the back of the gown. "I will use the silver combs."

That seemed to satisfy her. "Yes, ma'am, and I'll fix your hair in ring-lets. Fancy up-dos are my speciality, you know. I used to practice on Miss Georgiana when she was a child, and I'm quite skilled, if I do say so, myself, ma'am. The master would laugh so at our shows."

"Your shows?"

"Yes, ma'am. Back at Pemberley I'd spend hours fixing up the little miss's hairdos, and she had to run into the master's study for his approval of each one. She called it putting on a show, but it wasn't, really. It was just her way of begging his attention."

Once again, I noted the tone of intimacy in the maid's voice as she spoke of Mr. Darcy and Georgiana. It was almost as though she were a member of the family. Just last evening I happened upon the three of them all smiles and talking together in the great hall. It ceased when I appeared, and with a nod from Mr. Darcy, Fiona vanished to the back stairs. For some reason, I felt left out, excluded from their shared affinity.

I watched her now as she carefully hung my gown, smoothing the creases from the skirt. We were the same age. She was a pretty lass, red-haired with green eyes and fair, fair skin. Bearing a child had done nothing to hurt her figure, and I could see how appealing she might be to any man.

Suddenly, the hateful gossip I had heard the servant utter about her in the garden rushed up, from where I do not know, almost smothering me with its intensity. I thought I had rid my heart of such ugliness, but now I felt an urgent need to meet her child. I wished to see for myself if he had inherited his mother's red hair.

After dressing in my familiar black bombazine, I told Fiona she was free to go, but on second thought, I decided to follow her out of the room and toward the servant's back staircase. "Do you have other duties now, or will you return to your child, Fiona?"

"I was just going to check on him, ma'am," she said, uncertainty evident in her voice. "Was there something you needed?"

"Actually, I am curious about your son. May I accompany you?"

"Oh, no, ma'am! That wouldn't be proper and all — you such a fine lady going to my quarters. But I'll be glad to show him to you, ma'am. Just let me run fetch him."

I nodded in agreement. "Bring him to the small parlour on the second floor."

I found a book I had left on the table near the fireplace and settled myself to read, thinking it would be some time before she brought the child. I had not long to wait, however, as I had scarce read two pages before she entered the door, a sturdy little boy clasping her hand.

"Mrs. Darcy, this is my Willie," she said. "Willie, do your bow like I learned you."

I smiled to see him pull his thumb out of his mouth and putting his hand to his waist, make an exaggerated bow before me.

"I am pleased to meet you, Willie."

He immediately popped his thumb back into his pink little mouth although his mother tried her best to keep him from it. As she bent over him, a strand of light auburn hair escaped from her bun, and I watched it fall over his dark curls. He had beautiful large eyes, but they were not green. They were as dark brown as his hair, and Willie looked nothing like his mother. His face struck me with its familiarity and yet to whom, I could not bring myself to acknowledge.

"He is a fine boy, Fiona. Take him to the kitchen and give him a treat, and have Adams summon the carriage for me. I have a call to make."

I returned to my room, donned my bonnet, and grabbed my shawl. I had suddenly been taken by a great longing to see my own family, to find comfort in the familiar world from which I had been thrust. I instructed the driver to take me directly to Gracechurch Street.

My Aunt Gardiner met me at the door, for she was about to go out. She cancelled her excursion when she correctly ascertained that I was in great need of her company. We embraced and sat together on the sofa for no little time as she peppered me with questions about the weeks of marriage I had endured so far.

We talked of my mother and sisters, and I was gratified when she shared a recent letter she had received from Jane. I described Mr. Darcy's townhouse in great detail, and I talked of Georgiana — how shy and reticent she was — and the inadequacy I felt in fulfilling Mr. Darcy's wishes to be her friend. I avoided any reference to the intimate side of my union with Mr. Darcy. Indeed, my aunt would never presume to intrude upon such private matters, but I could not conceal my troubled mood from her, no matter how brave my endeavours.

"Lizzy, tell me true now. Is this marriage as dreadful as you feared?"

"I am not mistreated, Aunt."

"You are not happy, though, are you?"

"I did not expect to be, and there are moments —"

"Your mother had such hopes for you, and I confess I entertained them as well. You must know that your uncle and I encouraged this union only because we thought it would be best, not only for your family but for you."

"I know that is what you wished, but I had always hoped to marry for love."

The maid brought in a tea tray just then, and my aunt stopped to pour us both a cup. She stirred in sugar cubes until the servant left us alone.

"Many people marry without love, Lizzy. I hope that you will eventually come to have a high regard for Mr. Darcy. When we were in Derbyshire, his behaviour to us was pleasing in every respect, as well as his understanding and opinions. He lacks nothing but a little more liveliness, and I hoped you might teach him that. Believe me; your uncle never would have entertained his proposal if he had not known him to be an honourable man."

"And how, may I ask, does my uncle know Mr. Darcy's character? Hospitality and pleasant ways do not always reflect the truth of a man. He is quite taciturn, you know, and unrevealing, certainly not an easy person to grasp.

What assurance does my uncle have that Mr. Darcy is an honourable man?"

The look on my aunt's face told me I had said more than I should have. I had no intention of repeating idle gossip about Mr. Darcy and my maid or allowing my fears to be spoken aloud. How could I have blurted out such a doubt? Surely she would now question me about things I must not reveal. Oh, why had I gone there? I had allowed my need for comforting familiarity to lead me to a place where I could not afford to be candid, for I refused to accuse Mr. Darcy of a deed I hoped most desperately to be untrue.

"Elizabeth, I want to tell you something. Mr. Darcy and your uncle had an occasion to enter into an agreement. Has he never spoken to you about it?"

When I answered that he had not, she looked surprised and somewhat troubled. "Then I am not at liberty to speak of it, but be assured that Mr. Darcy acted every bit the gentleman in all of his dealings with your uncle. It was this very occurrence that elevated him to great esteem in our eyes and provided the means by which we were receptive to his marriage proposal to you."

I was baffled by the news. "Pray, tell me to what you refer. What possible business could my uncle have with Mr. Darcy?"

"I cannot, Lizzy." She rose, and placing her cup and saucer on the table, she walked to the window that looked down on the busy street outside, avoiding my inquiring stare. "I am sworn to secrecy, but my dearest, do believe me. Mr. Darcy is a good man, no matter what vile things Mr. Wickham said about him."

I rolled my eyes. "Oh, I know very well about his dealings with Mr. Wickham."

"You do?" An expression of relief seemed to light up her eyes.

"How wrong I was to believe his lies about Mr. Darcy. He explained all of that to me in a letter last spring at Rosings Park, and I have rued the day I ever believed Mr. Wickham's tale of woe. I know what a rogue he truly is. We have discussed this before, Aunt. What I do not understand is any further intercourse between Mr. Darcy and my uncle and your need to keep it from me."

That same worried look descended once more upon my aunt's countenance as I spoke, and she turned back to the window.

"Please do not ask me about it, my dear. If it were up to me, I would tell you all that I know, but I am bound by my oath. I will say this: I refuse to believe Mr. Darcy would do anything less than that which is admirable and worthy."

A moment later, two of my young cousins escaped their nanny and descended upon us, and we were prohibited from further serious conversation. I enjoyed the hilarity the children provided, and by the time I took my leave, my heart was eased. Perhaps my aunt was right about Mr. Darcy, and my fears were senseless fancy. After all, I trusted the Gardiners, and if they thought highly of him, then they must be correct in their assessment. I repeated that idea over and over during the carriage ride, vowing to believe it and hoping repetition would cause it to be true.

As I entered the townhouse, a servant informed me that Mr. Darcy desired my presence in the garden. It was almost dusk, so I kept my shawl but discarded my bonnet. The early November air grew cooler with each day, but fortunately, the breeze had died down that evening.

As I followed the servant through the side door that led into the small yard directly below the window of my bedchamber, I heard voices — those of Mr. Darcy and a child. We rounded the shrubbery, and there I saw Mr. Darcy and Willie engaged in tossing a ball back and forth. The child delighted in his attention and eagerly ran and retrieved the object each time he missed a catch.

"Mrs. Darcy, sir," the servant announced.

Mr. Darcy looked me up and down as he usually did. "Willie, stop and greet your mistress."

The child attempted to obey, but he dropped the ball just as he tried to bow and naturally ran off after it instead of greeting me. What child would not? I smiled, and Mr. Darcy did, too — a pleasant sight, indeed. He was a handsome man — it could not be denied — but when he smiled, he was almost beautiful.

"Fee, come and take Willie in," Mr. Darcy said, and from around a bend in the walk emerged Fiona, a pair of shears in her hand and a basket of freshly cut blossoms on her arm. She curtseyed to Mr. Darcy and to me and hurried her child inside.

Now why was he out there alone with Fiona and her son? I wondered. She was collecting cuttings — that was obvious — and why should Mr. Darcy not enjoy his garden? I silently chided myself at the thought of any other conclusion.

Mr. Darcy watched the little boy drop his ball once more on his way into the house, and then he invited me to take a turn about the garden with him. Most of the anemone blossoms had faded only to be replaced by woolly-looking fruits that resembled clusters of snow. I loved the blending of white mixed with the dark green of the holly shrubs. The autumn mums were in full bloom, nestled in a bed below the finely clipped hedges. All of it provided a beautiful, serene haven from the noise of the street heard in the background.

If only I had never walked this walk before and heard the hateful gossip from the other side of the tall hedge. That memory insisted upon intruding into the present idyll like a slithering snake, hissing with the threat of its poisonous venom. Try as I might, I could not restrain my thoughts; and consequently, they intruded on my conversation.

"You appear to take great delight in Fiona's child," I heard myself say.

"He is a fine boy."

"I have rarely seen a master so interested in a servant's child."

"It is not that rare. My own father, as you know, cared deeply for his steward's son."

"Like father, like son," I murmured.

Mr. Darcy stopped abruptly. "What are you saying?"

"I only wonder if you intend to educate and provide a living for Willie, as your father did for Mr. Wickham."

"He shall learn to read and write, yes, and I shall provide him with a position in my service when he is of age; but no, I shall not send him to Cambridge along with my son as my father did."

"And why not?"

"For one reason, we can well see what little good that did Wickham. Elizabeth, I am not in the habit of sponsoring all of my servants' children, nor do I intend to begin doing so."

"But Fiona's child is not like all of your servants' children, is he? Do you not show him particular favour, as you do toward his mother?"

"Perhaps I do, but only because I feel a . . . well, a partiality toward Fee."

"Partiality?" My agitation increased.

"Georgiana has always loved her, and it is hard not to appreciate one who makes my sister happy. The two of them together remind me of more pleasant times — days gone by when George Wickham and I were boyhood friends. And as for Willie, he certainly bears no responsibility for the circumstances of his birth. He is a fine boy."

"Yes, you said that earlier."

"Did I? Well, let us change the subject." I did not trust myself to say any more, and so we walked in silence for a bit before he spoke again. "You went out this afternoon, did you not?"

"I did."

"You told no one where you were going. Why?"

"Who should I have told? I was unaware that I am required to report the destination of my outings before leaving the house. I am a grown woman."

"It is only common courtesy."

"A courtesy you fail to perform."

"I beg to differ. Either Adams or my valet is apprised of my comings and goings, with rare exception."

"And how should I have known that? You have often left the house, and I had no idea where you were. You might have told me before now that you leave such information with particular servants so I would not need to canvass the entire household as to your whereabouts. That, sir, would be common courtesy as I see it."

He stopped again and stared at me. Had I gone too far? Would he now unleash his temper upon me? I might have feared such, except that my own self-justification was in full mode, fuelled by an emotion I had not yet acknowledged. We stood there, returning each other's gaze without flinching, and suddenly, right there on the garden walk, I realized for the first time what I felt — I was jealous of Fiona! When I found her and Willie in the garden alone with Mr. Darcy, I did not like it. I did not like it at all!

The thought so alarmed me that I had retreated to a much more familiar sensibility. I could handle anger. Anger felt good and right and just, and so I stood my ground. This time, however, Mr. Darcy would not respond to my baiting. Instead, I saw a slight twitch about his mouth.

"*Touché*," he said with just the tiniest hint of a smile. "I shall attempt to mend my ways if you will mend yours."

I opened my mouth to make a retort, but he silenced me. "And before you announce you have none to mend, I shall call upon you to exercise discretion. Since we have agreed to live under the same roof for the rest of our lives and, I might add, even share the same bed at times, shall we endeavour to practice the niceties of polite society? Will it not make things more pleasant?"

I closed my eyes at the reminder of that morning's mortification, my head beginning to ache with the strain of tension.

"Very well," I said flatly and let it go at that.

We walked on a bit farther, and coming upon a bench placed beneath a large deciduous tree that had already lost most of its leaves, he indicated we should sit. From there, we could see the evening sky, the reds, oranges, and blues of the setting sun streaking across in magnificent display. London's houses were so close that I rarely caught a glimpse of the sky, and I missed the sunsets at Hertfordshire. How pleasant it would be if we could just sit there quietly for a while, but no, he *would* speak.

"Will you tell me where you went?"

"To Gracechurch Street."

"To visit the Gardiners? How did you find them?"

"Well." I looked at him, surprised that he should take any interest in my connections.

"Mr. and Mrs. Gardiner are fine people. We should include them when next we entertain."

Although shocked, I tried not to reveal it. "And when might that be?"

"Sometime next week after the earl's ball. I think we should host a small dinner party. Will you see to it?"

"Of course, but shall my aunt and uncle be the only guests?"

"No, we shall invite Bingley and his sister, the Hursts, and Lord and Lady Matlock and Fitzwilliam, as well."

I truly could not believe my ears. "You wish to include the Gardiners in such a gathering?"

"Yes, I do."

"Shall it not embarrass you, having such low connections? My uncle is in trade, you know."

"The Gardiners should never embarrass you or me. I shall be glad to have them in my house."

I gave thanks that I was sitting when Mr. Darcy relayed that bit of news. What had happened to the censure he was sure to endure at the hands of society upon marrying a woman with such low relations? Had he not listed my family's improprieties last Easter when he proposed to me at Hunsford and clearly pointed out that I could not expect him to rejoice in the inferiority of my connections whose condition in life is so decidedly beneath his own?

"Mr. Darcy, my aunt told me you had business with my uncle in the recent past."

He stood up abruptly, turned his back, and I could not see his face. "What else did she tell you?"

"She refused to relate the particulars of your transaction because she said it was of a confidential nature. It is only natural that I am curious. Will you tell me of it?"

"No." He turned and offered his hand, indicating that we should go. "It was a private affair and not worth repeating."

"She said because of that occurrence my uncle regards you as an honourable man."

Mr. Darcy smiled slightly. "Does he now? An honourable man, hmm? Well, I shall say the same in return. I esteem your uncle an honourable man as well and one I shall be ever glad to have present at my table and among my guests. Now, shall we go in? The light is failing."

I followed him inside, more confused than ever. The man was an enigma — raising so many questions with precious few answers.

That night after I had done with Fiona's services and before I climbed into bed, I pushed and pulled a large chair across the room, stationing it squarely in front of the door between Mr. Darcy's chamber and mine. I then retired for the night, quite tired, yet unable to sleep. I turned from side to side. I plumped my pillows not once, but twice. I turned back the top cover and then pulled it back up around me. At last, I arose and tugged at the chair until I had returned it to its rightful place.

After all, I could not be held responsible for where I awakened when walking in my sleep.

Chapter Seven

On Wednesday evening, we attended a concert at the assembly rooms in Drury Lane. A large company attended, among whom was Lady Jersey, whom Caroline Bingley pointedly informed me was a viscountess. She was granted, of course, the choicest of seats while the rest of us filed in behind her party. Caroline pushed her way forward so that she might sit directly behind the viscount's wife. She manoeuvred Georgiana along with her and insisted that she sit between her brother and herself, whereupon she fawned over the poor girl excessively. I could see her suffer at such oppressive attentions, but Mr. Darcy and I were situated in the row behind, and I was at a loss to rescue her.

Caroline remained frosty in her attentions to me, except to enlighten me on rank and privilege and to note how pale — "almost to the point of illness" — my complexion appeared contrasted with my black gown. I doubted, however, that her feigned concern for my health fooled anyone.

She flirted with Mr. Darcy before we went in and again while the musicians tuned their instruments, turning around in her seat to bestow adoring looks upon him as she talked and laughed far too loudly. I saw Mr. Bingley give her several pertinent frowns, as she persisted in calling attention to herself. I thought of how she had sneered in disdain when Lydia had acted untoward with some of the officers at the Netherfield ball, and that night she exhibited almost the same behaviour.

The beginning of the concert and the quieting of the entire audience afforded us relief from Caroline's attentions. I was much impressed with the artistry of the soloist. Her Italian art songs and arias were exquisite, and I discovered that Mr. Darcy was so well versed in the language that he offered to interpret the verse for me while she sang. Naturally, I accepted, and in order to do so, it was necessary for him to lean his head quite close to mine so that his soft words would not detract from the performance.

The woman sang in a clear, vibrant soprano, "*Sento nel core certo dolore, che la mia pace turbando va, splende una face che l'alma accende, se non e amore, amor sara.*"

I listened closely as Mr. Darcy whispered, "I feel in my heart a certain sorrow, which goes on disturbing my peace; there shines a torch which inflames my soul . . . if it is not love, it will be love soon."

I was unsettled at first by such intimate words, his breath warm upon my ear, and the essence of his scent all about me, but I did not object. I found myself almost bewitched by the tender, romantic verses of the songs, a meaning I would have missed if not for his translation. His voice was as low and resonant as the diva's was high and clear, and I thought how lovely it would be to hear such words on his lips if we truly cared for each other.

"*Caro mio ben, credimi almen, senza di te languisce il cor.*"

"My dear beloved, believe me at least, without you my heart languishes."

With that last phrase, I turned and found him gazing directly into my eyes as he spoke. That proved far too intense an encounter, and I immediately refrained from looking at him. A flush swept over my body. I feared my rosy countenance exposed my consternation.

After the concert, we mingled with Mr. and Mrs. Hurst and Mr. Bingley at the tables filled with light refreshments. While I was engrossed in conversation with Mr. Bingley, Caroline renewed her attention upon Mr. Darcy by insisting that he and Georgiana meet Lady Jersey's niece, whom Caroline evidently knew slightly. She linked an arm in each of theirs and actually pulled them away from our party and across the great room to the throng surrounding the nobility. It was a direct snub toward me, evident to all, and I suppose I should have been angry, but in my opinion, it was of little consequence.

I almost felt sorry for Caroline. She had been out in society for some time, I felt sure, and the threat of spinsterhood loomed over her as it would for any woman her age. Now that Mr. Darcy was no longer available, she needed to broaden her vision and encourage other men who might be induced by her fortune to seek her hand. What possible motivation could she have in continuing her interest in Mr. Darcy? Did she envision my early death? I would have experienced a chill at the thought except for the fact that I was a healthy woman. And if she hoped for the event to happen in childbirth, how disappointed she would be to know such a possibility did not exist — for one must suffer exposure before contracting the condition.

Mr. Darcy's requirement that I eventually present him with an heir intruded upon my thoughts, and I felt myself again grow flushed at the thought of what that would entail. Three weeks ago the very idea would have alarmed me, but now I felt the lock upon my heart slightly, oh so slightly, loosened. I certainly would not welcome such an event, but I no longer cringed at the thought.

No, that is incorrect, for I had never cringed at the thought. I had been far too immersed in my anger. And now with memories of his touch still alive in my heart, and at times like this evening with his head inclined close to mine, and his warm, caressing voice repeating words of love in my ear, I found it difficult to remember exactly why I ever disliked him.

GEORGIANA AND I BOTH SLEPT late Friday morning, descending the stairs together for breakfast. We had taken but two or three steps before the sound of forceful argument caused us to halt. It emanated from the drawing room below. One voice definitely belonged to Mr. Darcy, and the other filled me with familiar apprehension and drove Georgiana to turn and flee in the opposite direction. Lady Catherine de Bourgh's imperiously demanding tone was unmistakable.

"Where are you going, Georgiana?" I cried.

"Shh! Do not let my aunt hear. I shall have Cook send breakfast to my room." With an urgent expression pleading for my cooperation, she vanished down the hall.

I sighed and proceeded toward the lion's den, or should I say lioness, for from what I could hear, Lady Catherine was already attempting to preside over this house just as she did every house into which she entered. I halted outside the open door and listened, for neither party had yet seen me, although I had a clear picture of their confrontation.

"It is insufferable!" she cried. "The son of my late sister aligning himself with such an upstart is unbelievable! When Mr. Collins told me of this arrangement, I imagined it a scandalous falsehood, and now you have the gall to say it is true. You have actually married the girl?"

"I have," Mr. Darcy said.

"How can you stand there and make such an announcement without a sign of remorse? Surely, you were tricked into the agreement. Her arts and allurements may have made you, in a moment of infatuation, forget what you owe yourself and all your family. She must have drawn you in."

"I assure you, Aunt; that is not the case. There was no trickery, no infatuation, no practicing of *arts*, as you put it. And if there has been any allurement, it is only that of her own good character and suitability to be my wife."

Mr. Darcy stood at the fireplace, his hands behind him, but when he turned, I could see how tightly he clenched his fists.

Lady Catherine stood opposite him beside a small table on which she tapped her forefinger as she continued to list her objections to me. "But she has no family, no connections or fortune! Is this to be endured? It must not; it shall not! You must secure an annulment at once, Darcy! I absolutely insist upon it!"

"And I respectfully insist that you discontinue giving orders in my house, Lady Catherine. I am a man full grown, beholden to no one, and I shall marry whomever I please. I have already married, and I shall not make any provision to end the union. I must beg you, therefore, not to importune me any further on the subject." He then offered her his arm as though he would escort her from the room.

"Not so hasty if you please. I am by no means done. To all the objections I have already urged, I have still another to add. I am no stranger to the particulars of the infamous elopement of Miss Bennet's younger sister. I know it all — that the young man's marrying her was a patched-up business at the expense of her uncle. Is such a girl to be your sister? Is her husband, the son of your father's servant, to be your brother? Heaven and earth! Of what are you thinking, Nephew? Are the shades of Pemberley to be thus polluted?"

"You have said quite enough." Mr. Darcy's eyes were black and narrowed. "I shall hear no more of this. I beg your leave, ma'am."

He started toward the door and saw me standing there, knowing I had heard the terrible accusations. He opened his mouth to speak, but before he did, Lady Catherine also became aware of my presence.

"Aha! So she shows herself! Eavesdropping at the door on a private conversation!"

"It can hardly be considered private, when the pitch and volume of your voice can be heard throughout the house," Mr. Darcy said. "We can have nothing further to say to each other. Good day."

He strode toward me and taking my arm, hastened me from the room, but his aunt was not so easily deterred, for she followed, pointing her umbrella in our direction as though she would physically stop us.

"This will not do, Darcy! I shall not have Georgiana brought up in that girl's presence and under her influence! I shall take steps to have her removed to Rosings and my care. It is the least I can do for your poor mother."

Mr. Darcy turned and faced her once again. "And just how do you propose to do that, Lady Catherine? I am my sister's legal guardian."

"But you are not the sole guardian. Fitzwilliam shares your responsibility, and once I meet with him, he and I shall journey to my solicitors and petition the court to have you declared unfit."

"Unfit?" Mr. Darcy was incredulous. "You would attempt to denigrate *my* character, Aunt?"

She blinked several times and modified her tone slightly, making it more placating. "Darcy, you know how dear you are to me. Can you think this is my desire? Why, it was the wish of your mother from your birth that you would one day become my own son, wedded to my dear Anne. But if you persist in this ill-judged alliance, I cannot in good conscience allow Georgiana to remain in this house, exposed to this unfeeling, selfish girl's lack of character. Duty and honour forbid it. And I am sure Fitzwilliam will be in agreement with me, as well as the Earl of Matlock."

"Then with all due respect, madam, go to it," Mr. Darcy said evenly, indicating with an outstretched arm that she should exit through the door from which she had entered. With an obvious sniff in my direction, Lady Catherine raised her head and turned for the door. Mr. Darcy, however, had one more thing to say. "Be advised, however, that Colonel Fitzwilliam stood up with me at our wedding. He congratulated both of us on our union, and his parents have already called upon us, expressing their joy. In fact, they have invited us to a ball to be held at Eden Park tomorrow evening."

Lady Catherine's eyes bulged, and her mouth flew open, but she could not speak. Truly, I feared for a moment she suffered from apoplexy — but only for a moment.

"And this is your final resolve, Darcy! Very well. I shall now know how to act. Do not imagine, Miss Bennet, that your ambition will ever be gratified at Rosings. Neither you nor Darcy will be welcome there again until my nephew recovers his senses! I take no leave of either of you. You deserve no such attention. I am seriously displeased!"

And with head held high and nose even higher, she stalked out the door.

Mr. Darcy was seething. I knew not what to say, and so I waited. He watched his aunt's retreat and at last said, "I apologize for the ill-treatment Lady Catherine has rendered you, Elizabeth. I shall make it a point from this time forward to refrain from criticism of your family. None of them can begin to exhibit such abominable behaviour as my aunt portrayed."

He bowed stiffly and strode briskly up the staircase.

A flood of emotions fought their way through my being, and I did not know whether to feel relief or anguish. I made my way into the breakfast room and sank down upon a chair, grateful for the cup of coffee the servant placed before me. I had supposed Lady Catherine would be ill pleased at the news of Mr. Darcy's marriage to me, but I never dreamt it would cause her to break relations with him, or that in such a rift, he would choose in my favour and defend me with such fervour.

It would seem I had a champion!

THE NEXT DAY, SATURDAY MORNING, presented the first occasion for Georgiana to begin to warm toward me. All week she had pestered her brother, in her own gentle and unassuming manner, for permission to attend Lord Matlock's ball, but Mr. Darcy refused, adamant that she was far too young.

"But I am almost seventeen, Wills," she said that morning at the breakfast table for what seemed the hundredth time. "My birthday is less than two months away."

"You have not yet come out, and I shall not have you endure the scrutiny of the *ton* until you have."

I was surprised the young girl wished to attend the dance as she had proved far too reticent to enter into any other social obligation with alacrity, but for some reason she would not give over about that evening's entertainment.

"I shall be out after Easter. You and Lady Matlock have already settled upon the date I am to be presented. That is scarce six or seven months from now. What harm would come from my attending tonight's ball?"

"I shall not have every fortune hunter in Town eyeing you before it is necessary!" Mr. Darcy slammed down his teacup with such emphasis that it sloshed out upon the tablecloth. "You will not go, Georgiana."

"Even if I promise to dance with no one other than the earl or Richard?"

"Once you dance with *anyone*, you shall be fair game for every young blade in the city."

"I fear there will be a scarcity of 'young blades' in attendance tonight," Colonel Fitzwilliam said, entering the dining room at that very moment without waiting to be announced. "Good morning, Mrs. Darcy, Georgiana, and you, my overwrought and highly agitated cousin." He smiled with the last remark, as I did. "I am not accustomed to seeing your colour so high this early in the morning. Pray, tell me what all the racket is about."

"Come in, Fitzwilliam." Mr. Darcy's tone sounded less inviting than his words.

"Will you not join us in some breakfast?" I offered.

"A cup of tea will suffice, but someone take pity and explain what has my cousins at each other's throats. No, let me guess. Georgie wants to attend my parents' ball, and you do not want her to, Darcy. Am I correct?"

"You are." I spoke quickly before either of the two resumed their carping.

"Wills is being somewhat stubborn, Richard. He says I am too young to go, and I am almost seventeen!"

"The fact is you are now sixteen," Mr. Darcy said, "and too young to attend a ball. That is all there is to it."

But his sister would not let it rest. Her obstinacy truly surprised me, for I had never seen this side of her. "I have even promised to dance with no one other than the earl or you, Richard, and still my brother will not relent. Pray, talk to him."

"Ah," the colonel said, "and what makes you think I wish to spend the evening dancing with the likes of you?"

Her only reply was to make a face at him, and I could not refrain from laughing. Mr. Darcy, however, did not.

"If she dances with anyone, she will be available to any who ask," he repeated. "You know that as well as I do."

"Well, that may be, but I have it on very good authority that tonight's ball shall be quite intimate. The majority of society has not yet returned to Town, what with this being the season for grouse and pheasant as well as partridge. Almost every so-called young blade remains in the country in search of game they can shoot rather than dance with."

"I fail to see why your parents are even hosting this ball then," Mr. Darcy said.

"Well, it happens to be in honour of your new wife."

I was surprised to hear this and evidently so was Mr. Darcy. We looked at each other as though to ask why. Fortunately, we remembered that we were a newly married couple and recovered in time to make the appropriate responses of gratitude.

"My mother knows that Elizabeth will be unable to meet the majority of our friends because they remain in the country, but after all, she is a new bride, and we must make her feel welcome."

"Thank you, Colonel," I said. "That is most kind."

That provided even more impetus for Georgiana's argument. "And if I stay at home, think what impression that will give, Wills. People will say I do not welcome my new sister."

"They will say nothing of the sort." He rose from the table and headed for the door, and I could see that he was not open to any more discussion.

"Mr. Darcy," I said just before he left the room, "might I offer a compromise?" When his response was nothing more than a frown, I ventured on. "If Georgiana agrees not to dance at all and to remain in my company, would you allow her to attend?"

"That would limit you. Shall you give up dancing the entire evening just so she can go?"

"I shall. I am not inclined to dance, and as we both are well acquainted with your abhorrence of the art, we may be quite content remaining at her side."

"Well," Colonel Fitzwilliam said, "I trust the two of you will concede and at least lead the first dance, as is the custom when the ball is held in your honour. And if you do, I suppose I might sacrifice myself and tend the child during your absence." Once again, Georgiana screwed up her face at him, but he only laughed.

Mr. Darcy sighed. "Very well. If you are sure about this, Elizabeth, I shall agree."

"I am sure." Our eyes met, transmitting an unspoken understanding between us that united us in our solicitude for Georgiana. He turned away at last and departed the room with Colonel Fitzwilliam following.

"And now, young lady," I said, turning to my sister, "whatever shall you wear at this late date?"

She smiled the biggest smile I had yet seen on her pretty face. "My aunt has already taken me shopping, Elizabeth. I returned from my visit at Eden Park in possession of a beautiful, blue ball gown. Shall we go up and see it?"

I agreed, of course — thrilled that she had called me by name — and we spent the morning selecting gloves and shoes and ribbons for her hair from the vast array she had purchased with Lady Matlock. We actually giggled at times during our visit, and I felt my heart lighten almost as it had when at home with my younger sisters.

That evening Fiona did her best with my unruly curls, and when she was through, I was surprised to see how well she had succeeded in taming my tresses into a pleasing display. The silver combs provided just enough sheen in my dark hair to suit me.

When I stepped into the silver grey gown and she fastened up the back, I caught my breath at my image in the floor-length mirror. The touch of black lace inside the silk neckline proved much more provocative than demure, and it appeared to me that the décolletage was cut even lower than I remembered. Lady Catherine's angry accusation that I had won her nephew by my "arts and allurements" suddenly echoed in my ears. If Fiona had not been there, I think I would have immediately changed the dress for my familiar black. I longed for the safety of its dark concealment, but the maid was far too excited, and I could not think of an excuse for such action.

"Oh, ma'am, you'll turn every head in the place tonight, you will!"

I dismissed her remark and sent her into the dressing room in search of my wrap, but only so that I might quell the tremor I felt upon seeing my image in the mirror. Why had I ever consented to leave off my mourning clothes? And why did I feel so exposed having done so?

She had just returned with the shawl when we heard a knock at the interior door between Mr. Darcy's chamber and mine.

"That'll be the master," Fiona said, smiling, as she hurried to turn the knob. Sure enough, when she opened the door, there he stood, dressed in formal evening clothes and more handsome than ever. "Here she is, sir. All ready for the ball."

"Thank you, Fee," he said, keeping his eyes on me. "That will be all."

I suppose that she curtseyed before departing, but in truth, I could not tell, for I was not conscious of anyone other than Mr. Darcy. His presence filled the room until the walls suddenly seemed much too close. He walked toward me, his eyes sweeping up and down my form. I waited. Was he displeased? I could not tell, for he did not smile or frown. He just looked and looked and looked.

At last, I broke his gaze and lowered my head. I knew I blushed at his inspection, and if he were to reprimand me for my choice of gown, then let him do so at once so that I might change back into my familiar dress and be done with it.

I closed my eyes in anticipation of his rebuke, but they flew open when, instead, I felt his hands at the nape of my neck. He stood very close behind me and encircled my neck with a delicate gold chain containing a perfect black pearl quite large in size, encrusted with diamonds on either side. I gasped at the beauty of the rare pearl that appeared to match my gown in colour, a luminous silver grey.

"I am glad I chose this trinket now that I see your choice of gowns. Perhaps our tastes are more alike than we first thought."

"It is a beautiful necklace." I fingered the pearl as it lay against my bosom. "Thank you."

"You are welcome, and thank you for wearing something other than that blasted black."

No compliment. No kind words about my appearance. Not one solitary word of approval other than I was not wearing black. Well, why should I have expected more? This is Mr. Darcy, after all, I reminded myself. I gathered my shawl from the bed and swept out the door he held open, my head up and my teeth clenched tightly together.

Lord, give me strength to get through the night without throttling him!

Georgiana chattered throughout the carriage ride to Eden Park, an unusual amount of conversation on her part, for which I was grateful. She talked because of nerves while I remained silent for fear I would say more than I should. Mr. Darcy answered in one-word responses, except when he reminded her more than once of her agreement to remain on the sides of the room within my view at all times. Even his dour mood could not dampen her excitement, though, and I was glad to see that at least one of us looked forward to the evening.

When Lady Matlock had called earlier in the week with the earl, I was relieved to discover that she was nothing like Lady Catherine, and Mr. Darcy had said privately that her thoughtful demeanour reminded him of his late mother. She was kind and welcoming, although somewhat curious as to my background. The earl seemed much like Colonel Fitzwilliam with his genial manner, and I soon felt at ease around him.

Their estate, just outside London, reflected their status in society, for it was grand enough for any lord and lady. Tonight it shone with candles and crystal, elaborate autumn floral arrangements graced each table, and a polished inlaid walnut floor in the huge ballroom awaited dancers made up from the throng of richly dressed people who filled the room. If that was considered an intimate gathering, I wondered at the size of a grand ball. Before the first dance began, I had met more persons than I would ever be able to remember. If Mamá could see me now, would she not be undone by such finery? It would take her a full two days just to describe the lace on the ladies' gowns to my Aunt Philips.

I rejoiced to see Mr. Bingley stride across the large room, a smile stretching his countenance from ear to ear.

"Mrs. Darcy, I say, you look exceptionally well tonight," he said, bowing over my hand. "And you, as well, Miss Georgiana," he added upon seeing her.

"Thank you, Mr. Bingley," I said. "Are your sisters and Mr. Hurst not with you tonight?"

He looked around and nodded across the room at Caroline, who I happened to know had seen me when I first entered the room but had not as yet bothered to speak to us. She could not escape now, and so she and Mrs. Hurst made their way through the throng and greeted us.

Caroline was in her usual feathers and satin, and Mrs. Hurst's ample bosom almost fell out of her low-cut velvet dress. Well, at least these people and their clothing were familiar to me. I endured the sisters' false compliments as well as I could, and when Caroline stood far too close to Mr. Darcy than any single woman should, I simply turned my head. That night I would have given him to her in a heartbeat.

"She is tolerable, but not handsome enough to tempt me." Unexpectedly, the memory of those words from a year ago reverberated in my ears. I recalled Mr. Darcy's utterance of that contemptuous statement as clearly as if he had said it again. I turned to look at him out of the corner of my eye, but he was deep in conversation with Colonel Fitzwilliam. Would I ever be able to forget his rudeness? And did he still consider me only tolerable? That would explain his earlier lack of praise. Suddenly, I felt out of place, wondering when I would ever measure up to his standards.

Just then, the musicians finished tuning their instruments, and the first dance of the evening began. The earl motioned for Mr. Darcy and me to lead the way, and I took a deep breath as he held out his hand to me. We circled the room and then lined up with the other couples following. As the sprightly tune began, we moved together in a semi-embrace before parting to move back into position. I held my breath when his arm encircled my waist, but fortunately, we had only to look into each other's eyes but a moment. The song was lengthy, and I held hands with many men, making my way down the line opposite Mr. Darcy. Each time I met my temporary partner's smile with one of my own, only to have it vanish upon facing Mr. Darcy's sombre countenance. Did the man never smile when dancing? Could he not at least pretend some enjoyment when performing with his wife?

At the end of the tune, we both let out relieved sighs. Neither of us had said one word to the other during the entire half-hour of the dance. He returned me to Georgiana's side while he went in search of the punch bowl. I politely begged off invitations from several gentlemen who presented themselves before me and guided Georgiana to the far side of the room where we might sit for a moment. Mr. Darcy soon found us with cups of punch, and naturally, his presence brought more guests to engage us in conversation.

We went into dinner at the appointed hour, and Lady Matlock's table was laden with the season's bounty — turkey, venison, and lamb along with white soup, of course, autumn vegetables, and at least three different puddings. Iced cakes were served for dessert as well as platters heaped high with squares of marzipan.

Caroline Bingley managed to sit upon Mr. Darcy's right, and she attempted to monopolize his attention throughout the courses. I found myself at Lord Matlock's left and was fascinated at his knowledge of Hertfordshire. He spent a great part of his youth there on hunting expeditions, and he was well acquainted with the countryside. We spent no little time extolling its virtues.

"Hertfordshire may be a hunter's delight," Caroline interjected, "but it cannot compare in beauty with Derbyshire and Pemberley, in particular. Is that not correct, Mr. Darcy?"

"I am somewhat prejudiced," he said, "so it will not do to ask my opinion."

"And I suppose you will answer in the opposite," Caroline said, directing the supposition to me. "Or have you even seen Pemberley as of yet?"

I knew she was hoping to learn more of my history with Mr. Darcy. "I have not, Miss Bingley, but some of my family have, and they assure me Mr. Darcy does not exaggerate its beauty."

"Your family has visited Pemberley?" She lifted an eyebrow in doubt. "Pray, let me guess which of all your sisters has been so fortunate? Surely not the youngest."

Before I could answer, Mr. Darcy did so. "My wife's aunt and uncle visited the estate last summer, Miss Bingley. Do you not remember? You were there at the time."

"No, I do not, sir."

"Mr. and Mrs. Gardiner dined with us two, perhaps three times, I believe."

"Mr. and Mrs. Gardiner? The people who reside near Cheapside were your guests at Pemberley?"

"They were. Yes, now I recall. You and your sister made a trip to Ashbourne that week to visit your aunt. Forgive me; you were not there after all, so how could I expect you to remember? 'Tis a shame, for they are delightful people. You must meet them sometime."

Caroline's mouth remained agape much longer than it should have before she was able to respond. "I have met Mrs. Gardiner," she finally said and returned to her plate. She was noticeably quieter for the remainder of the meal.

The evening progressed with little more to report except that I could not help but notice Georgiana's toe tapping to the rhythm of each song. The child wished to dance ever so much as my younger sisters, and I thought it harsh of her brother to forbid it.

Toward the end of the evening, he wandered from our presence and was in deep conversation with several acquaintances. Colonel Fitzwilliam had joined Georgiana and me, and he spent no little time teasing her as to how popular she should be once she was out. He often whispered in her ear and caused her to laugh. Once again, I envied their gentle camaraderie.

"Elizabeth," Georgiana said, "will you release me to freshen up?"

I nodded and turned back to the crowd to converse with Lady Matlock and yet another of her friends she wished me to meet. When I glanced around sometime later, neither my sister nor the colonel could be seen. I knew sufficient time had elapsed for her to return, and so I began searching the room for her blonde curls. It would not do for Mr. Darcy to discover her absent from my company. I made my way around the perimeter of the ballroom, but she was nowhere to be found.

At last I exited the room into the large gallery outside where I stopped in surprise at the sight before me, for there was Georgiana dancing with Colonel Fitzwilliam, the two of them all alone. I could not help but smile, for they made a pretty couple, and the colonel was quite adept at manoeuvring the steps so that there was no need to change partners as was the custom among the dancers inside. Neither of them saw me, and I slipped back inside the doorway so that I would not spoil their fun.

When the music ended, Fitzwilliam bowed over her hand and kissed it. She laughed gaily, and I rejoiced to see her pleasure.

"Oh, Richard, what fun! May we do it again?"

"As long as we are not found out, Sprout."

He looked up and down the great hall. I pulled back even farther so they would not see me, and when the next air began, he embraced her and began the dance. I turned back to the inside room and prayed that Mr. Darcy might still be engrossed in conversation, but it was not to be, for there he came striding across the room straight toward me.

"Where is Georgiana?" he asked immediately.

"She excused herself for the moment." I moved to stand between him and the entry to the hallway.

"Well, shall we take the opportunity and dance this set? I believe it to be the last of the evening."

Although surprised at his invitation, I nodded quickly, and with an anxious glance over my shoulder, I allowed him to lead me once more to the floor. This time he appeared at ease, perhaps because the ball was nearly over. He even smiled slightly, and his touch was gentle, almost like a caress. I found myself caught up in the beauty of the music, for I dearly loved to dance, and however much he disliked the art, he was skilled in its performance. Suddenly, I wished the dance would never end. Although we did not talk, there was no need for we seemed in harmony, complementing the other perfectly, our bodies in tune with both the music and each other.

Upon returning home, Georgiana kissed her brother's cheek and thanked him again for allowing her to attend the ball. She then squeezed my hand and ran up the great staircase to her bedchamber.

"I am glad you persuaded me to change my mind about Georgiana attending the ball," Mr. Darcy said, as we stood before the fireplace in the drawing room. "I have not seen so much colour in her cheeks in months, nor such sparkle in her eyes. One would think she had danced the evening away instead of watching from the side. I did not know it took so little to make her happy."

He poured glasses of wine for both of us, and I accepted mine without response. What could I say? That I had gone against his wishes and allowed her to dance with Fitzwilliam? Truly, there had been no allowance on my part; they had simply done it, but I had not moved to halt its occurrence. Why should I? It was innocent in my opinion, no matter what Mr. Darcy thought, and yet I felt a twinge of conscience at deceiving him. When I felt his gaze upon me, I wondered if he could read my guilt. Instead, I was surprised by his remark.

"I was right about you. You are good for Georgiana."

We stood close to each other. I could see gratitude in his eyes and yet, something more, a sort of ease between us that I had not witnessed prior. I resolved not to tell him of Georgiana's dance, for I did not wish his good will or that look in his eyes to vanish or for anything to break the mood.

He took my hand in his. "I failed to tell you how beautiful you are tonight, Elizabeth. Forgive me."

His eyes travelled to my lips and to my eyes and then back again. I could not say a word. I could not even think. He stood so near. I felt enthralled by his presence and yet intensely alive, conscious only of the intimacy of the moment. How long we remained thus, I know not, but at last he spoke again.

"Will you not content yourself with mourning ribbons from this day forward?"

I almost gasped, searching for breath with which to speak. "I shall," I said softly. "I shall."

He smiled and kissed my hand before releasing it. We then retired for the night, each to our separate rooms, and I was even more aware than usual that we lay sleeping with only a wall and an unlocked heart between us.

Did I say heart? I meant door. Truly, I did. Indeed, I meant door.

Chapter Eight

Preparations for the dinner party we were to host the following Thursday night consumed much of the coming days. I spent considerable time with Cook in planning the menu. I gave the housekeeper a list of every room that needed to be in pristine condition. I met with the gardener an entire morning, examining and choosing the plants that were still in bloom, and I ordered the best silver polished once again as well as the re-washing of the finest china in the house. Mr. Darcy's home was kept in perfect order, but still I persisted in directing extra care and attention as I found myself nervous and yet excited at the prospect of presiding over my first table. I truly desired Mr. Darcy's good opinion of me in this endeavour, a desire I found surprising, uncomfortable, and disquieting. I even went to him for approval of the seating plan I had worked out.

"Shall Lady Matlock take offense at having Mr. Gardiner seated so nearby? Shall I place my aunt and uncle in lower positions at the table?"

"Hmm," Mr. Darcy said, "I see nothing wrong with your plan, other than the fact that Miss Bingley sits next to Fitzwilliam. That may cause offense on his part."

He said these words with a smile, and I joined him with one of my own. I immediately moved Miss Bingley next to Mr. Gardiner, and we both burst out laughing at the thought of her reaction to such a slight.

"No, no, you must not inflict her on Mr. Gardiner. I think too highly of the man. Here, move her next to Hurst, for he is far too occupied with his plate and drink to be aware of who sits next to him."

We laughed again at the absurdity of it all, and I felt enjoyment in his presence I rarely experienced. This newly found atmosphere persisted throughout the week, and it spilled over into every occasion when we were together. I discovered that Mr. Darcy could charm when he wished. We spent at least two evenings listening to Georgiana play and sing for us, and on another night, Mr. Darcy read to us from his latest acquisition, a copy of Coleridge's lectures on literature and philosophy. I was amazed that not a single word of dissension had passed between us since the night of Lord Matlock's ball.

What had caused this transformation? Surely it could not be just the absence of my mourning clothes, could it? No, that would afford my appearance far too great a power. However, I was surprised to find that when I donned lighter colours, my entire mood lightened, and I flattered myself that perchance *my* outlook influenced that of my husband as well, at least a little.

I followed through on my resolve not to reveal to her brother Georgiana's transgression at the ball, for I did not wish to cause any conflict between them or draw his wrath upon me for concealing it. I did confess to my sister, however, that I had seen her dance with her cousin in the great hall at Eden Park.

Her eyes grew large with fear at my words. "And have you told Wills?"

I shook my head and could see the relief upon her face. "That does not mean that I condone your disobedience, Georgiana."

"I suppose it was wrong of me to go against Wills, but I so wanted to dance, and Colonel Fitzwilliam is my guardian, also. I cannot see that I behaved so badly if he approved."

"You are very close to the colonel, are you not?"

"I adore him," she answered, her eyes aglow. "I always have. He is the kindest of men. Next to Wills, I think I love him more than anyone else in the world."

"You are fortunate."

"Yes, I am, but you are as well, Elizabeth."

"Oh? Do I enjoy Colonel Fitzwilliam's favour?"

"Of course you do, but you mistake my meaning. You are married to my brother, and he is the best of men. I am sure you could not find a better husband in the land."

"Ah, yes." I turned away and busied myself with rearranging a vase of already perfectly arranged flowers.

Nevertheless, Georgiana persisted. "Tell me, what is it like to be married? Is it so different from one's solitary state?"

I felt myself blush and kept my face averted. "I fear that I do not understand your question."

"I mean . . . do you feel different?"

"Feel different?"

"Yes, once you were married, did you feel more sure of yourself? Did you develop more confidence, or have you always possessed such a nature?"

I let out a sigh, closing my eyes with relief that Georgiana was not asking me the personal question I had presumed. "Actually, my feelings are not that altered. I suppose I have been cursed with too much confidence all my life. At least, that is what my mother would tell you."

"Oh, no, I should never call it cursed, but rather, blessed. I would give anything to be as self-assured as you are, never to fear others' judgment or censure, to know in myself that I am correct in whatever I do."

I walked to her side and sat beside her on the couch. "Oh, my dear, believe me, I am not that confident. I, too, have fears and doubts about my abilities."

"But you never allow them to show, Elizabeth. You appear in control."

"It is a good performance, one I have perfected. Consider this dinner party I am planning. I am quite concerned that I do it properly, that I do not embarrass Mr. Darcy in any way."

"You could never do that, for he has the highest regard for you."

"Does he?" I looked into her eyes, searching for the assurance she felt.

"Of course, he does. Wills never would have married you if he did not."

I looked away then, reflecting on my sister's simple conclusion, her total ignorance of the facts. Had she known the true nature of our arrangement, she would not have spoken of her brother's regard with such certainty. She would have wondered about the truth of his feelings for me, but not nearly as much as I did.

ON WEDNESDAY, THE DAY BEFORE the anticipated party, I did not see Mr. Darcy at all. Adams informed me that he had left the house before breakfast and would be at his solicitor's office for much of the day. I thought nothing of it, as Mr. Darcy did not discuss his business affairs with me, and I had a long list of duties awaiting my attention.

Georgiana accompanied me on my morning calls. During the afternoon while I checked with the steward on the wines to be served, I heard her practice the pianoforte, for she had agreed to play for our guests after dinner.

The day was full, and I did not notice Mr. Darcy's absence until the hour arrived for our evening meal, and yet he still had not returned. That did surprise me, for it was quite unusual. Georgiana and I eventually sat down to eat without him and passed the evening reading. We both looked up several times, anticipating his arrival, but when the clock chimed ten bells, we retired to our chambers.

Fiona had just unpinned my hair and brushed through the curls when he knocked on the door adjoining our rooms. She opened the door and then vanished with the wave of his hand. I watched him walk into the room, my surprise evident. He was still dressed in daytime garb, obviously just arrived, having shed only his coat and hat. I stood in greeting and pulled my robe close around my figure.

"Elizabeth, forgive me for intruding so late in the evening."

"Of course. Will you not sit down?"

"No." He strode across the room and paced back and forth. "I have a pressing task for you. Cancel the dinner party for tomorrow night. Write to each of our invited guests this very evening and inform them of our regrets. Say that urgent matters call you to Pemberley. Then see that Fiona packs your trunks so that you and Georgiana may leave by first light. I have already directed my sister's maid to prepare her things."

"But why? I do not understand."

"I do not have time for explanations. Just do as I say and with all haste. Do you understand, Elizabeth? I demand that you carry out my orders with strict compliance."

I felt vexation rise up in my throat. "And are you coming with us?"

"No." Without further word or allowance of questions, Mr. Darcy strode from the room, firmly closing the door between us.

I was speechless! How dare he demand this of me — cancel all my carefully laid plans with a curt word of dismissal and deem me unworthy of an explanation! Did I not merit any more value in his eyes than a servant?

With his evacuation of my bedchamber, all of the recent goodwill between us disappeared like a cup of water poured out on parched ground.

I paced the floor in the exact pattern he used not five minutes before, my previous doubts and fears descending upon me with a vengeance. How could he treat me in such a manner? He was as arrogant, uncivil, and brash in his conduct as he had ever been.

How long my anger persisted, I know not, but Fiona interrupted by lightly tapping at the door opening into the hallway. When I granted her entrance, she quietly went about her duties, hauling out my trunks and emptying the drawers and armoires of my belongings. Obviously, Mr. Darcy had already informed her that we were leaving. My first inclination was to question her and ascertain whether she knew the reason for our banishment from London, but I thought better of it, not wishing a servant to know how angry I was nor how humiliated I felt by a man who professed to be my husband.

I sat down and began to write the notes of regret to my aunt and uncle, Lord and Lady Matlock, the Bingleys, Hursts, and Colonel Fitzwilliam. I confess that I had to discard the first two notes because tears of rage smeared the words. I balled them up and threw them into the fire. Digging my fists into my eyes, I willed myself to cease crying, for I did not want Fiona to witness my distress.

All my work had been for nothing, all my plans a needless exercise. What could be so important that our departure for Pemberley could not be delayed by at least one day? And why could Mr. Darcy not confide the reason to me?

No, I was not his confidante. How could I ever have dreamt I might be? In truth, I was not his wife but only a figurehead. I played the part — hostess when he desired it and exiled non-entity when it struck his fancy. His tender words the night of Lord Matlock's ball must have been nothing more than pretence, his affability this week a sham, for now he discarded me by a single command without the barest courtesy of any qualifying justification.

"Will there be anything more, ma'am?"

I turned from my writing and saw the trunks lined up against the wall.

"I left your travelling clothes in the armoire, ma'am, and I'll pack your toiletries in the morning after you're dressed."

"Very well. That will be all for tonight."

Fiona curtseyed and left the room, and not five minutes later, I regretted having dismissed her. I should have sent the notes with her to be placed downstairs for delivery first thing on the morrow. It was bad form to cancel a dinner party, but to do so on the very day it was to be held must be considered a grievous breach of manners.

I finished the last note and resolved to take them downstairs myself. Perhaps I would slip into the library while there and find some dull book to help lull me, for I knew in my present mood sleep would be difficult to come by.

It was after midnight, so I felt safe in leaving my room dressed in gown and robe, for surely everyone had retired by then. At the bottom of the great staircase, I laid the notes on the silver salver where all outgoing messages were left and walked across the gallery toward the library. I was surprised to see a light coming from the room next to it, Mr. Darcy's study. The door was open, and I wondered if the servant had failed to extinguish the candles. I walked softly; my slippers barely made a sound.

I peered through the entry and saw Mr. Darcy sitting there with his elbows leaning on the desk, his head in his hands. He had discarded his coat and neckcloth. His waistcoat hung open, and his shirt was partially unbuttoned. His hair appeared mussed as though he had raked his hands through it over and over again. As I watched, he raised his head and leaned back against the chair, closed his eyes, and sighed. A deep frown knit his brows together, and I was astonished at the amount of pain I saw revealed in his face.

I started to turn away and go about my first inclination of searching the library shelves for a book, but the haunting look upon his countenance drew me into the room like a siren's song. I cleared my throat, and he looked up, surprise evident in his eyes.

"Pardon me, sir, but you appear ill. Shall I call the servant to summon a physician?"

"No, no."

"Truly, you are not well. Is there nothing you could take to give you present relief? A glass of wine? Shall I get you one?

He shook his head and waved his hand in dismissal. "I am not ill, Elizabeth. Do not concern yourself."

I ventured closer and sat on the edge of a chair near the desk. "Will you tell me what is troubling you? May I not be of some assistance?"

"There is nothing you can do. Indeed, you must leave me, for there is nothing anyone can do tonight."

He rose from the desk and walked around it to stand before me, but instead of assisting me to my feet, he chose to sit down on the chair next to me. I could see the worry and concern in his eyes, the anguish so apparent on his face, and I sensed that he did not wish me to go, in spite of his words to the contrary.

We sat quietly for a while, but at last I could not keep from speaking. "Mr. Darcy, will you confide in me? Can you not tell me what is causing you such discontent?"

"I would not burden you."

I did something quite daring then. I reached out and took his hand in mine. I held it between my palms and forced him to meet my eyes. "I am your wife, sir. I know that we are not partners in the truest sense, but can we not attempt a beginning? Will you trust me enough to share whatever it is that disturbs you so?"

His eyes looked like deep pools of black, tortured with agony, and yet lightened somewhat at my boldness. He made no reply at first but gazed into my eyes for the longest time.

"It is Georgiana," he said at last. "She — I fear she may be in danger and must be removed from Town immediately."

His news alarmed me. "Danger? From whom?"

He rose, took a letter from his desk, and held it out to me. "This is a blackmail notice. From whom, I do not know, but the author knows our family and knows it well. This blackguard threatens to tell Lady Catherine of Wickham's designs on Georgiana, how he almost succeeded in seducing her and eloping to Scotland. You heard my aunt's threats last week. This will surely give her fuel for legal action to remove Georgiana from my guardianship. This provides fodder for the idea that I am unfit and remiss in my duties toward my sister."

I hastily read the note and was shocked at its contents. How could anyone be so cruel, so hateful as to separate a brother and sister who were devoted to each other? And yes, I could well imagine Lady Catherine using the knowledge to have her way in the matter. She did not take defeat with grace, and her venom would only be enflamed at such a revelation.

"Who has knowledge of this occurrence?"

"The only people who know are the parties involved, along with Colonel Fitzwilliam, you and me, and, of course, Mrs. Younge."

"Could she have written the note?"

"She could, but why? She knows nothing of Lady Catherine's desire to take Georgiana from me. How could she be privy to that intelligence?"

My heart went out to him. What a heavy burden he bore! How foolish I had been to let my anger erupt when he was laden with care.

"What shall you do?"

"Remain here and search out the person or persons who have made the threat. As you can see from the note, I am to leave the funds they demand at the designated location on Saturday next."

"And shall you pay them, sir? I cannot fathom rewarding such scoundrels!"

"I have little choice right now. I met with my barrister most of the day along with a trusted detective he recommended. We arranged to have the meeting place watched and hope to discover the blackmailer. What I do not know is how to find the informant. I suspect it may be someone here in my own house, a suspicion I find most alarming."

I gasped. "In your own house? But why?"

"Because of the anger and pitch of her voice, Lady Catherine's threats were heard throughout the house last week. I have not the slightest doubt every servant in the place knows of her fury. I must find out who would use that knowledge to betray us."

He began to pace again. I watched him for some time, my own thoughts in a whirl. Who could it be? Mr. Darcy treated his servants well. How could any one of them turn against him in such a traitorous manner? And yet, throughout history the lure of silver has corrupted many a man or woman. My thoughts darted back and forth, searching for any means of discovering a malcontent among the household, when all of a sudden the recollection struck me. The memory I had tried so hard to forget washed over me.

"Sir, I must tell you something. Some weeks ago, I overheard two of the servants talk, gossip actually, and one of them exhibited anger towards you. I do not want to accuse anyone unduly, but you might begin your investigation with him."

"Tell me exactly what you heard."

I blanched at repeating the ugly words spoken against him and chewed my bottom lip.

"Elizabeth? It is vital that you tell what you remember."

I nodded, and taking a deep breath, I repeated the under-gardener's scurrilous remarks about Mr. Darcy and Fiona. He began to pace again, placing his hand at his mouth, knitting his brows into an even fiercer scowl than before. "And do you know who the man was that said these things?"

I shook my head. "No, sir, for I did not see him. All I know is that the other servant called him Johnny."

"Johnny? We have more than one servant by that name. What about the stable hand who supposedly told Johnny in the first place? Did you learn his name?"

"No." I felt sad to see his disappointment. I watched him retrace his steps back and forth until I wondered if the carpet would be permanently indented from his desperate walk. I finally rose and, placing my hand on Mr. Darcy's arm, I restrained him. "What else can I do to assist you, sir? Is there not some way I might help?"

"You can help me by doing as I ask, Elizabeth. Take Georgiana to Pemberley where she will be safe. I have asked Fitzwilliam to accompany you, and I have not the slightest doubt that he will protect her on the journey. I trust my staff in the country implicitly, for they have been in my service for years. I shall feel much relief to have my sister tucked away in Derbyshire, rather than here in Town. And pray, do not tell her of this threat. I do not want her frightened."

"But what reason have you given her for this sudden trip?"

"I told her I had changed my mind and wanted both of you out of the city, what with winter coming on and disease rampant during the cold weather, which is not an untruth."

"And she accepted this without further explanation?"

"My sister is accustomed to obeying me." He smiled slightly. "You could learn from her example, and if you will do so in this regard, I shall rest easier."

I blushed, wondering if he had read my mind earlier. Did he know how angry I had become when ordered about? "I confess obedience does not come easily to me, especially when I am given commands without a reason." We stared at each other, and by the turn of his countenance, it appeared that he understood my application, and so I did not allow my earlier disappointment further rein.

"In this matter, however," I said softly, "I shall do as you say. I only regret that I cannot do more, for I do not like to see you consumed with anguish."

He closed his eyes and turned away, but then returned his gaze to me, and when he spoke, his voice was tender and low. "Your compassion does you credit. I am not in the habit of being so cared for. I find I quite like it."

We stood very close to each other, and I suddenly remembered that I was in a state of undress when I saw his eyes roam over my figure. He took my hand and my skin burned at the warmth of his touch. This time he was the one to enclose my hand within both of his, and I found that I liked the way his large hands completely covered mine, making it feel small and protected. With his thumb, he began to rub circles around and around my palm, and I suddenly found my breathing somewhat constricted.

"Elizabeth," he said in a husky whisper.

"Yes," I murmured, never taking my eyes from his.

"You should go to bed. It is late."

"Yes, I should."

"You must arise early."

"Very early."

Neither of us moved to act upon our words. His gaze travelled from my eyes to my mouth and back to my eyes, as they had done the night of the ball. I felt a longing well up deep within me with a force I had never felt before, a quickening within the pit of my stomach that only added fuel to that yearning. I wanted him to kiss me — oh, how I wanted him to kiss me — and I wondered if that was the desire I saw reflected in his dark eyes.

"Leave me," he pleaded, his voice utterly ragged, but still he neither moved nor released my hand.

"Yes," I whispered, and then without thought, I reached up and touched his face. I felt its flushed heat and drew my fingers along his jaw. And then I kissed his cheek. It was the most natural impulse I had ever experienced. When I drew back, he searched my eyes, his breath coming short and hard. And then he placed his lips upon mine, slowly, softly searching his way until my lips parted, and I tasted heaven for the first time in my life.

I felt the room whirl around me and my whole body tremble as I clung to him. At last he gently released my lips. Neither of us moved. Our eyes gazed at each other, both of us too filled with emotion to move or speak. I could not even think, for my senses flooded my entire being. He still held my hand — I knew that much, for I could feel the pressure of his thumb tracing circles in that same maddening, probing pattern — and finally he looked down at it.

"Such a little hand," he whispered, and placing the palm to his lips, he kissed it tenderly while once again gazing into my eyes. "Go," he said softly and released me.

I nodded and turned woodenly. Somehow I found my way to the door and up the stairs to my chamber.

If I said that I slept much that night, it would be a lie, for my thoughts, my feelings, my senses, every nerve in my body was so intensely alive that I could find ease in neither bed nor pillow. I could not fathom all that had happened that evening. My emotions had run the gamut from fierce anger to . . . to what? Was this feeling of unbearable excitement and joy actually love for Mr. Darcy? I did not know; I truly did not know. I just knew that the last thing I wanted was to be sent to Pemberley, to be out of his sight, unable to see his face, hear his voice, and give him comfort. Was that love?

And what about Georgiana? Who could wish to harm her? Who would want to cause Mr. Darcy such distress? Over and over again, I reflected on the details of the blackmail note, searching for any clue that might stand out, that might enable me to assist my husband in solving this terrifying riddle. *My husband* — I had come to think of him as my husband for the first time.

And then those delicious memories of his kiss flooded my body once again, and I relived the sensation. I pondered how and why it had happened and wondered when and if it ever would again.

FIONA AWAKENED ME BEFORE DAWN by lighting a candle and laying the fire. I shivered in the cold morning as I washed my face with the water she poured into the china basin. She helped me dress, and while I sat down to fasten my buttons, she began to brush my hair and pin it up with the skill she possessed.

Another knock at the door caused me to turn in expectation, hoping against hope that it was Mr. Darcy, but I was disappointed to see only another servant enter, bearing a tray containing my breakfast. She said the master had ordered light meals for Georgiana and me to be served in our rooms. I looked at her closely and wondered if that girl from the kitchen perhaps might be the spy in our employ, the one who had assisted Mr.

Darcy's blackmailer with news of Lady Catherine's threats. But she was a simple girl, dull of manner and wit, and one I would never suspect clever enough to carry out such a scheme. Ashamed of my suspicions, I spoke kindly and thanked her for the meal.

After eating and gathering a few books Fiona had failed to pack the night before, I was ready to don my coat and bonnet.

"Here, ma'am," she said, holding out my coat for me. "The master bid me have you ready to go by six o'clock, and it's nigh onto it."

"Yes, Fiona, call the footman and have him gather my bags. Then you must hurry and get your things together so that you and your child will not be late, either. I am sure the servants' coach will travel right behind that of Miss Georgiana and myself."

"I beg your pardon, ma'am?" The maid looked at me as though I spoke French.

"Your bags, Fiona, yours and Willie's. You cannot travel to Derbyshire without your things. Come, hurry! Do not wait for me. I can manage from here."

"But ma'am, I'm not going to Derbyshire with you."

I stopped tying the ribbons of my bonnet. "What? Are you not moving to Pemberley as my maid?"

"Eventually, ma'am, when it's the master's wish. But for now, he bid me stay here in London 'til he's ready to leave the city. I'll travel when the master does."

The footman knocked at the door, and she turned her attention to assist him in carrying my trunks below stairs. As they left the room, I allowed myself to sink down onto the bed.

What possible reason could Mr. Darcy have to keep Fiona here with him? She was *my* maid, after all. And then the old fears crowded into my mind. I could see Willie's dark eyes and hair, the soft look about Mr. Darcy's expression when he played with him in the garden, and his refusal to reveal the identity of the child's father. I suddenly recalled that when I had repeated the servant's hateful gossip last night, it had angered Mr. Darcy, but he had never denied it.

I felt sick to my stomach, and it was all that I could do not to lose the breakfast I had just eaten. What kind of man had I married, and what sort of game was he playing? Sending me off with the memory of his tender kiss and yet keeping his mistress and child here with him?

I walked down the stairs with a heart as heavy as the trunks carried before me. Just outside the entry, I saw Colonel Fitzwilliam mounted on his horse, ready to ride escort while Mr. Darcy assisted Georgiana into the carriage. I steeled myself not to show any emotion, not to give him the satisfaction of seeing how much he had hurt me.

"Elizabeth." He held out his hand to help me into the carriage.

I refused to look at him and ignored his outstretched hand. Instead, I reached for the side of the coach and climbed the steps without assistance.

"Good morning, Georgiana," I said, seating myself on the far side of the carriage and turning my face to the opposite window.

"Good-bye, Wills," Georgiana cried. "Come soon."

"Yes . . . yes, I will come as soon as possible."

I could hear the confusion in his voice, but I did nothing to alleviate it. I gave him no greeting. I took no leave of him. I refused to even glance his way as I heard him say to the driver, "Walk on," his voice cracking somewhat. I felt little sympathy for him, for I could feel my own heart breaking, shattering into a million tiny pieces.

Chapter Nine

Fortunately, Georgiana slept through the first hours of the journey. I was relieved to be spared the agony of making conversation when all I wished to do was weep. The reprieve allowed me to wallow in my misery, and wallow I did. How could I have allowed myself to let down my guard, to permit Mr. Darcy entrance into my heart when even yet I did not know the depth of his character?

I brooded over Fiona's words — "I will travel when the master does."

What reason could he have to send me off and yet keep her with him other than the vile, ugly thought now breaking my heart? She was his mistress after all and Willie his child! I had to become reconciled to that truth no matter how much I hated it. And yet it went against every single thing I had learned about Mr. Darcy in the short time we had been married. Indeed, it ran contrary to what I knew of him even before our marriage. Had he not condemned Wickham for his dissolute ways and for attempting to meddle with his own sister? Could he, in turn, be as false and low? Was he nothing more than a hypocrite?

Once again, I thought back to the letter Mr. Darcy had given me months ago in Rosings Park. Jane still had not found it among my belongings at Longbourn, but she had written that she would continue her search. I wanted to re-read it, to consider it carefully as I had not taken the time to do so before. I recalled the feelings of mortification I had gone through when first I read it, for I had misjudged Wickham's character entirely. Could it be possible that I now did the same with Mr. Darcy? Or had I been fooled by him, flattered by his attentions, and wooed by the memory of his affection last evening?

That kiss!

Just the memory of his lips upon mine washed over me with such force that in less than a moment my senses yearned for him in the same manner they had last night. I closed my eyes and entered into it, feeling the heat warm my body. And then I was stricken with the almost certain probability that Mr. Darcy had bestowed that same favour on my maid, and I suddenly felt such a chill that I gathered up the rug lying on the seat and wrapped it around me.

You must gain control of yourself and be sensible, I thought.

In this world, it would be unusual for a man of eight and twenty not to have some experience with women before marriage. Why should I expect Mr. Darcy to be different? But to take advantage of an unlearned girl of fifteen — no, that was insufferable! A man who satisfied himself with his servants was unthinkable. Why, he was no better than that lecherous earl who had employed Jane!

Oh, I could not bear to think of it! I summoned all of my strength and searched the byways outside the carriage for distraction, hoping to see an errant rabbit, a flock of sheep, or even farmers ploughing their fields — anything at all that might prove a diversion. When the vista provided no relief, I summoned all of my determination and attempted to think on Mr. Darcy's good qualities — his generosity, his intelligence and good breeding, his affection for his sister — but like a hateful, slimy demon, fear would worm its way back into my head. Thus, around and around my thoughts swirled until without conscious thought, I finally cried aloud, "Enough!"

My outburst awoke Georgiana, but fortunately, she did not comprehend what had disturbed her sleep, and shortly thereafter, we stopped at a village to change horses. I almost bolted from the coach, so anxious was I to interrupt my thoughts and place my attentions on anything else, anything at all. We both were grateful to stretch our limbs and walked around outside for some time before Colonel Fitzwilliam bade us enter the inn for refreshment.

"We have made good time," he said, as we stirred our tea.

"Yes," Georgiana said. "Even yet, I wish that Wills had come with us. If he fears the contagion of disease for us, should we not fear the same for him?"

"Do not worry about him, Sprout. You know Darcy is too fearsome to get sick. Why, there is not an illness in existence that would dare breach his presence."

Georgiana protested his teasing description of her brother. My reaction was somewhat different — I almost bit my tongue in half to keep from adding my own thoughts to the colonel's depiction.

I was thankful that the colonel was our escort, not only for protection, but also because of his amiability with Georgiana. Their good-natured repartee allowed me to remain still. Eventually, I excused myself from their presence and escaped outdoors where I walked up and down in a small wilderness area across from the inn. I revelled in nature and hoped that the trees and grasses might offer respite from the heartache bubbling right below the surface, choking me with its intensity and threatening to erupt in untoward emotion at any time. It was late autumn, however, and now that we travelled northward, I saw the branches almost bare and the grass turned light brown, anticipating winter's approach.

Instead of lifting my spirits, the scene only reinforced the surety that my own hopes and dreams that had sprung to life just last night now belonged in the grave.

IN SPITE OF MY DESPAIR, upon our arrival on the third day, I discovered Pemberley far more than I had ever anticipated, and it did much to distract me and lift my mood. From my first glimpse of the house through the windows of the carriage some distance away, I found myself completely enchanted. Situated on the opposite side of a valley from the surrounding woods and hills, its banks were neither formal nor falsely adorned. I was delighted. I had never seen a place for which nature had done more, or where natural beauty had been so little counteracted by awkward taste.

Although I was tired from the journey, upon entering the place, a new energy possessed me. There was so much to see — so much to take in.

Mrs. Reynolds, the housekeeper, met us at the door, and I liked her immediately. An older woman and obviously efficient, she seemed to genuinely care for my young sister and was enthusiastic in her welcome to me and yet perfectly attuned to her place in the household. I sensed that we would work together with little adjustment, for she seemed willing to have a new mistress about the place.

After serving us tea and at my request, Mrs. Reynolds led me above stairs to my chamber. I was all too ready to shed my travelling clothes and have some time to myself. I was also curious as to the appearance of my room and its placement.

I followed her down a long, vast gallery, magnificent in design. All along the walls, huge portraits of what I assumed were generations of Darcys stared down at me. Toward the end I stopped, my eyes wide, my mouth unconsciously agape at the full-length painting before me —*Mr. Darcy*— and with such a smile over his face as I remembered to have sometimes seen when he looked at me. He was beautiful. There was no other word to describe him.

"Is it not a good likeness, ma'am?" Mrs. Reynolds asked. I nodded, for I did not trust myself to speak. "I am sure I know none so handsome as my master and none so good. I have never had a cross word from him in my life, and I have known him ever since he was four years old."

Indeed! I thought. *Well, then, you must attend some of my conversations with him.*

This was praise most extraordinary, and I listened with increasing astonishment as the housekeeper added, "If I were to go through the world, I could not meet with a better. But I have always observed, that they who are good-natured when children, are good-natured when they grow up; and he was always the sweetest-tempered, most generous-hearted boy in the world."

I began to re-examine my earlier impression of Mrs. Reynolds. I wondered if perhaps with age, she might be slipping into early dementia. I managed to squelch my thoughts, however, and followed her down the hall, all the while listening to even more praise of this man I thought I knew.

"He is the best landlord and the best master that ever lived; not like the wild young men nowadays, who think of nothing but themselves. There is not one of his tenants or servants but what will give him a good name. Some people call him proud, but I am sure I never saw anything of it. To my fancy, it is only because he does not rattle away like other young men."

She opened a door and stepped back so that I might enter. "This shall be your room, ma'am. I hope it meets with your approval."

If I had found my chamber in London charming, this room could only be described as magnificent. I literally could not speak at first, for want of taking it all in. From the pale green and rose colours of the draperies and cushions to the luxuriousness of the bedding, the gleam of the furniture, even the paintings on the walls of hills and dales and nature's glory — all of it seemed far more than I could ever occupy.

As in Town, I had a separate dressing room with a bath, but it was even more spacious and equipped with every necessity a woman could desire. The entire suite was much larger than any bedchamber into which I had entered, and I endeavoured mightily not to run from corner to corner, pulling open drawers and inspecting closets. Such behaviour would not do in front of the housekeeper.

And then I saw the large inner door on the opposite side of the room. *Ah, yes,* I thought, *this time I know to where that leads.* I walked over to it and attempted to disguise my inspection of the doorknob. Sure enough, it did not contain a lock.

"Mrs. Reynolds, did the senior Mr. and Mrs. Darcy occupy these same rooms at one time?"

"No, ma'am, their suites are on the other side of the house. Shortly after your marriage, young Master Darcy wrote and instructed me to prepare these rooms, instead, because there is a fine prospect of the lake from the windows. He wrote to say you were particularly fond of nature, and he personally selected the paintings on these walls."

She smiled as though there was great affection between Mr. Darcy and me, and of course, I did not contradict her. In truth, I was surprised at the thought that he had taken into account my preferences and even rearranged our bedchambers so that I would be pleased. How could he be that accommodating and thoughtful on one hand and yet engage in unforgivable behaviour on the other? No, it did not make sense.

THAT NIGHT AFTER GEORGIANA HAD entertained us for an hour on the pianoforte, she retired and the colonel and I were left alone in the drawing room. He had excused himself several times during the evening and then returned, and I wondered if he had been checking on the extent of our safety. When I asked him, he confirmed my suspicions.

"But do you think that Georgiana is in danger even here?"

"No, but I have been a military officer far too many years not to make certain."

"I still do not understand how anyone could benefit from harming her."

"Harming her would fail to benefit them for certain, but holding her for ransom could prove very profitable."

"Was there a threat of kidnapping, also? Mr. Darcy showed me only the blackmail note."

"No, not as of yet, but if one would attempt blackmail, the thought of kidnapping would not be unreasonable."

"Of course not," I murmured, suddenly ashamed that I had spent the entire day mourning my own loss when the possibility of such a threat hung over my sister-in-law. "Colonel Fitzwilliam, what can I do to assist you to assure Georgiana's safety?"

"Just be in her company. Act as though everything is as it should be. Give her no reason to be afraid, but know where she is throughout the day. If she leaves the house for any reason, go with her, even if it is nothing more than a walk down to the lake."

"How long shall you remain with us?"

"I have taken an indefinite leave from my post as my commander knows the situation, and he has given me leave to stay until the danger has passed. That is, of course, if the Corsican does not expand his present hostilities."

"I am relieved to hear that." I rose and extended my hand. "I shall be glad of your company and your protection. Good-night."

He took my hand and kissed it lightly. "Do not be fearful, Mrs. Darcy. Your husband has the best men on this case, and I think he will get to the bottom of it quickly enough and soon be back by your side."

I nodded and left the room. Well, that answered my question about how much the colonel knew of my marriage arrangement. It was evident he believed Mr. Darcy and I happily married. I wondered if Mr. Darcy had confided the truth to anyone. Did he long for a confidante as much as I? Was he as lonely as I was in this strange marriage we had concocted?

Then a thought struck me, and my heart fell as deeply as an anchor sinks into the sea. He probably did have someone — Mr. Darcy most likely confided in Fiona. If she were his mistress, would he not share the truth of our marriage if only to keep her happy and assure her that she was the one he truly loved? And yet in my presence, she had never let on that she knew. She was skilled at hiding her thoughts, I presumed, with never a hint of jealousy. Well, why should she be jealous? He loved her, did he not?

But did he love Fiona, or did he use her? Mrs. Reynolds' words echoed in my mind: "He is the best master that ever lived."

The *best master* would not avail himself of an innocent young maid in his employ. No, it must be love. Surely, Mr. Darcy loved Fiona, but then why had he professed love to me all those months ago, and why had he come back after my refusal and renewed his attentions to me? He truly must have married me only to provide solace for his sister and to provide a legitimate heir for Pemberley.

I was miserable beyond all telling. If only I had someone in whom I could confide my fears, someone who would advise me, sympathize with me, and tell me what the future held. I thought of writing to Jane and resolved to do so that night so that she would at least know where I was, but even to her I could not reveal my doubts as to Mr. Darcy's character. It would destroy her happiness to learn of my distress, and I wished her to be happy. That was another task I must attend to as soon as Mr. Darcy came. I must make sure he kept his word and told Mr. Bingley of his part in keeping him from my sister. Mr. Bingley must learn that Jane cared for him as much as I was sure he cared for her. One of us deserved to be happily married.

My Aunt Gardiner! I would write to her for advice, for she was the most sensible woman I knew! But then I remembered that I could not bring myself to confide in her when last we met, so how could I do so now?

In my room, I allowed the maid to help me dress for bed and brush out my hair, but after she left, I chose to sit before the fire. I stared into the flames until the logs burned down to ashes, unaware of the passing hours until I began to shiver, suddenly feeling the loss of the blaze.

I wrote to neither Jane nor my aunt. I had no one with whom I could be completely truthful, for I could not bear the shame of admitting that I had married such a man. I was alone — completely alone — and I could see nothing but years of loneliness stretching out before me.

THE NEXT DAY I DESCENDED the stairs to find that Mrs. Reynolds had assembled the entire household staff for my introduction. The number was so great it appeared much like a small army, and as I spoke to each one, I endeavoured to devise some way of remembering their names. There were a number of Marys and several named Thomas, and I was much relieved when it was over and Mrs. Reynolds gave me a detailed list with their names and duties outlined. We then went over the household accounts and menus for the week, and by mid-afternoon, I was gratified to realize that I had not time even once to dwell on my troubles. Running Pemberley was like presiding over a small town, I decided.

I took my cup of tea and settled myself in a small sitting room overlooking the park at the rear of the house. It was not long before the colonel, who had entertained Georgiana outdoors whilst I was engaged with Mrs. Reynolds, walked toward the window at which I sat and waved. I returned his greeting with a wave of my own and then smiled to see Georgiana sneak up behind him and place a wildflower behind his ear.

She acted far differently with him than anyone else. It was as though they were more brother and sister than she and Mr. Darcy. Perhaps she wished he were her brother — but no. It was evident Georgiana loved Mr. Darcy. It appeared hard, however, for her to mature in his mind. She was doing so before our very eyes, for her blossoming figure revealed it all too well.

The colonel entered the sitting room then, and I offered him a cup of tea, which he readily took.

"Is not your young charge with you?" I asked.

"She has gone above stairs to change her shoes. I should do the same with these boots, as we both wandered into mud unawares." He smiled and did not seem overly concerned about the condition of his footwear. "And how has your day gone, Mrs. Darcy? Are you now thoroughly acquainted with all of Pemberley and its retinue of attendants?"

"Goodness, no, Colonel! I fear it may be some time before I am brave enough to address anyone by name other than Mrs. Reynolds. At present, I cannot even remember what my upstairs maid is called."

"Well, when Darcy returns, he will bring Fiona to replace her."

"Yes," I murmured, surprised that he knew her, much less possessed the knowledge that she would come to Pemberley when Mr. Darcy did. "I did not know you were aware of my maid's name."

He looked somewhat embarrassed. "Well, when all of that happened — her predicament — Darcy came to me for advice. I knew how fond Georgiana was of the girl. It was a difficult situation to work out."

"What was a difficult situation?" Georgiana asked, upon entering the room.

"Why, the fact that Mrs. Darcy has so many names to remember here at Pemberley," the Colonel said, covering our conversation with surprising ease. "You will have to assist her, Sprout."

"I shall be glad to, for I know every servant here. Most of them have been in service since before I was born, and now some of their children work for us."

"Thank you, Georgiana. I am sure I will have need to call upon you."

She sat down near me and picked up some embroidery but then laid it aside without interest. "Richard, shall we take Elizabeth riding tomorrow?"

"Do you ride, Mrs. Darcy?"

"A little and ill, indeed, I am certain, compared with the two of you. I had little opportunity or inclination to do so at Longbourn."

"We should take her to see the tenants, Richard. Since Wills is not here, I need to make sure none of the babes or grandmothers is ill, and it will be ample opportunity for Elizabeth to meet them."

"Oh, dear," I said, sighing, "do you mean there are even more names I must learn?"

"Well, yes," Georgiana replied seriously, "and you have not yet been introduced to the stable hands or grooms, the drivers and gardeners."

"As long as you are about it, Missy, I suggest that you demand she memorize the names of all the thoroughbreds in the barn, as well." Not the slightest hint of a smile graced the colonel's face.

"Oh, Richard, how you do tease! Pay him no mind, Elizabeth, for it only encourages him."

We spent the remainder of the evening in good harmony, and upon retiring for the night, we made plans to set out the next day on our ride. I crawled into bed that night, feeling slightly better. I had thought of Mr. Darcy very little, and I truly liked Georgiana. Perhaps we might even become close, as near to sisters as possible in such a situation. I looked forward to the morrow with a somewhat brighter outlook.

THE HORSE COLONEL FITZWILLIAM SELECTED for me was a beautiful roan mare, her red coat sleek and shiny. He assured me she was gentle, and so I allowed the groom to assist me in mounting. Sure enough, she responded easily to my every command, and my confidence grew as the three of us set off on our tour. The countryside abounded in glorious autumnal reds and golds mixed in among the evergreens. I inhaled the aroma of the rich earth in the fields that had been ploughed under since the harvest. Pemberley was a vast estate, larger and grander than the Gardiners had described, and greater than I had ever dreamed.

We rode for most of the day with brief stops at various houses wherein Georgiana amazed me with her ease in greeting the folk. She enquired as to their needs and was gracious in her introduction of me. It was apparent she had done this kind of thing all her life and that her father or brother had trained her well. She genuinely cared for the people; there was no pretence of compassion. Indeed, I had never seen the slightest pretence about the girl since we had first met. My esteem for her blossomed more and more.

We picnicked under a large chestnut tree in the middle of the woods. Mrs. Reynolds made sure that we carried with us a basket of fruit and cheese, a freshly baked loaf of bread, and a bottle of wine. I grew drowsy after eating, and without intent, fell asleep on the rug spread over the grass. How long I slept, I knew not, but I awakened upon hearing voices. I sat up and saw the colonel and Georgiana some distance away, apparently returning from a walk.

"But, Richard, we always have a harvest ball. How can you think that we would not this year?"

"It is well past harvest."

"I know, but we were not here at the right time. Just as the crops were coming in, Wills had to leave unexpectedly for London, and a month later, he sent for me. By the close of September, he travelled to Hertfordshire, and then there was the wedding in early October. We were never able to return to Pemberley until now. Thus, we must remedy the situation and celebrate the harvest even though it is months overdue. The tenants expect it. I think we should hasten our plans before the first snow."

"I only said not to plan on it. Your brother may not return from Town until Christmas. You must not set your heart on it."

"It is not *my* heart that is set, but the hearts of our people. We cannot disappoint them; it is not the Darcy way. I shall write to Wills this evening and urge him to return immediately. Surely his business cannot keep him away that long."

"Georgiana," Colonel Fitzwilliam began, but she marched away from him, evidently determined not to entertain any further discussion of hopelessness. Once again, I was amazed to see her resolute nature. She had displayed little of this fire and spirit in the company of society, but here in her own realm, Georgiana was completely at home and in charge of her opinions. I returned to the house that evening with a new respect for my young sister.

A WEEK LATER, COLONEL FITZWILLIAM had cause to ride into Lambton, the nearest town to the estate, but five miles away. Before leaving, he cautioned me once again to keep Georgiana within sight at all times while he was gone. We spent the morning sewing, and I wrote another short letter to Jane and one to Mamá while she wrote to her brother.

"Shall you not write Wills also," she asked me at the completion of her task, "and we shall have them posted at the same time?"

I rose from the desk at which I worked and walked to the window overlooking the lake, as much to give myself time to think of an excuse as to enjoy the prospect.

"For now, I fear my fingers are cramped from writing. Let us go out and walk about the grounds. I long for fresh air, and the breeze appears to be gentle."

She readily agreed, and after retrieving our shawls, we walked the lane that led down to the lake. I could see trout jump within and marvelled at their antics. Stooping down, I leaned over and trailed my fingers through the cool water. "How beautiful!"

"'Tis," Georgiana agreed, "but far too cold in which to swim."

"Swim? Do you mean to say that you would even consider bathing in this water?"

"Not here." She glanced over her shoulder as though to make sure no one might hear and then whispered, "Follow me. I shall show you a place where the water is much more to my liking."

My curiosity was alive, of course, and I hurriedly caught up with her as we walked a distance through the trees, where we came upon an enchanting small pond. Lily pads encircled a part of it, and a pair of frogs leaped into the water upon noting our intrusion.

"This water is much warmer," Georgiana announced, "and perfect for bathing in the middle of summer."

I looked at her in amazement. "And so you do go swimming here?"

She looked down, a blush covering her pretty cheeks. "I confess I have, many years ago when I was but a child. Fee and I used to sneak down here on late summer afternoons when it was far too hot to play or climb trees." I felt myself stiffen at the mention of Fiona's name, but I tried not to show it. "It is deep out in the middle, but beside the shore one can wade for quite a distance before the water reaches your waist."

"I suppose you have gone sea bathing at the coast. I confess I do not even own a bathing costume, for my family has never undertaken such an excursion," I said, searching for something to say other than speaking of Fiona.

She giggled, leaned close to me and began to whisper once again. "No, I have never gone sea bathing, and neither Fee nor I owned such a garment. We stripped down to our chemises and swam in them."

"Indeed!"

"Do you think me incorrigible?"

I smiled. "Of course not. You were a child."

"Fee suggested it, and back then I so longed for a friend, I believe I would have followed her anywhere."

"And were you successful in not being found out?"

"Almost," she said, and then looked away and said nothing more.

I did not know how to reply. Had this triggered a memory of a time when she was chastened or even punished? Surely, all children had such memories, although I recalled few, as neither my mother nor father paid particular attention to curbing their daughters' pursuits.

Georgiana began to walk around the pond, and I followed her, remaining silent, vowing to give her time if she wanted to confide anything further. On the other side, under a stand of birches, she sat down and began to pull up a wildflower, its bloom now spent. I sat beside her and watched as she plucked each drooping petal, twirled it around in her fingers, and then dropped it into the pond.

"We have never spoken of Mr. Wickham, Elizabeth."

I caught my breath, wondering what she would tell me.

"I know he is now your brother by marriage, but . . . he is a wicked man."

I nodded in agreement.

"He was not always that way. When I was a child, he devoted hours and hours to my amusement."

Her words echoed in my brain. Mr. Wickham had used the same phrase when speaking of her at Hertfordshire.

"And once, he came upon Fee and me right after we had submerged ourselves in this pond. Instead of threatening to tell, he promised to keep our secret, and then he did the strangest thing. He discarded his jacket and waistcoat and even his neckcloth and outer shirt. Fee and I were shocked, and when he began to pull off his boots, I ducked my head under the water, for I feared he might do the same with his trousers! But he did not. Instead, he plunged into the pond and dove and swam all around us. He was as much at home in the water as a fish, and he spent much time that afternoon teaching me how to swim. Fee had already taught me to float on my back, but I had never mastered swimming until George showed me how easy it was."

She stopped her recital and looked directly into my eyes. "Do you think me awful, Elizabeth, confessing this to you?"

I immediately shook my head. "No, my dear. You were a child, obviously enjoying yourself."

"But it was not fitting . . . for us to be so unclothed in George's presence. If my governess or Wills had seen us, they would have been angry. And George cautioned us not to tell, for he feared he might be horsewhipped if discovered!"

I nodded and chewed my lip. What could I say? She was correct in her assessment of the situation, but it was Mr. Wickham who was to blame. He was full-grown, and they were but children — well, Georgiana had been. I could not remain so generous in my opinion of Fiona, for I could not think of her with unbiased judgment.

At last, I took a deep breath and said, "And, I take it, you were not discovered."

She shook her head. "I was frightened, though, and so we did it only once more, but that time we waited until nightfall. George said there would be less chance of being caught, and Fee agreed with him. We came very close, though. One of the grooms walked right over there through those trees, and all three of us stayed under water until we thought our lungs might burst. I was too afraid to dare attempt it again."

She rose and indicated we should return to the house, and I was more than willing, for I had much to think over. I was more shocked than I had let on to Georgiana — not at the childish escapade she had confided, but by the fact that Mr. Wickham knew Fiona. I had always assumed he had left Pemberley before she arrived from Scotland, for I knew that he and Mr. Darcy had both attended Cambridge together, and by that time, Mr. Wickham's want of principle was well known to the son and heir. But now,

Georgiana told me that in actuality he was there, cavorting in the pond with Fiona. My mind whirled with new suspicions, unanswered questions, and the briefest glimmer of hope.

Mrs. Reynolds met us shortly after we entered the house. "The colonel has returned and is in the drawing room, ma'am, and the post has come. Here are letters for both of you."

Georgiana exclaimed with delight when she saw that hers was from her brother and tore it open at once.

"Oh, I hope Wills is coming home and that he approves of the Harvest Ball." She scanned the letter quickly, her face falling at its contents. "He is not coming, but wait — he says we are to go ahead and make plans for the ball — that we are to hold it whether he is here or not. I am glad, but I cannot imagine a harvest ball without Wills."

And I dare not imagine it with him, I thought.

"Who did you hear from, Elizabeth? Did you receive a letter from Wills, too?"

I shook my head in response as I sifted through the mail in my hand, recognizing Kitty's scrawl and a thick parcel addressed in Jane's handwriting. I had not seen Mr. Darcy for over ten days nor heard one word from him. Neither had I written to him. Indeed, I was thankful I had not corresponded when filled with anger, for today's revelation now confused me. I truly did not know what to think. Could it be that all my suspicions were in error, that Mr. Darcy was innocent?

Oh, dear Lord, let it be . . . let it be.

Chapter Ten

That night I walked in my sleep again, and it was no wonder, for if I had ever been troubled before, it could not compare with the condition of my heart when I finally laid down my weary head.

As soon as possible after dinner, I had deserted Georgiana and Colonel Fitzwilliam and escaped to my bedchamber, pleading a headache. I curled up in a large wing-back chair and tore open my parcel from Jane, for I could see that it contained more than a letter.

"Oh, well done, Jane!" I cried aloud when I recognized Mr. Darcy's torn seal on the back of the enclosed pages. My sister had found his letter that I had lost after returning home from Kent. I was anxious to read the words again — it had been so long since I had received it from his hand — and I had read it quickly at the time. I remembered little of what it contained. My father's death three days later had overtaken all other thoughts.

For now, though, I laid it aside, for surely my sisters' letters took precedence in importance. I turned my attention to Jane's correspondence, looking it over hurriedly, pleased to hear that things were going well at Longbourn and that she seemed in good spirits. I then attempted to read Kitty's post, but Meryton's gossip paled considerably when all I truly wished was once again to read the letter Mr. Darcy had given me on the morning after his first disastrous proposal.

I tossed Kitty's news on top of Jane's and picked up the letter. A contrariety of emotion excited me as I made my way through it. I could easily recall how angry I had been when first I received it and how hastily I had put it aside, protesting that I would not regard it — that, in fact, I would never look in it again. Now I wished to weigh with impartiality every circumstance outlined therein and deliberate justly on the probability of each statement. I began with the fact of the senior Mr. Darcy's high regard for Mr. Wickham.

He was his godson, a detail I had overlooked completely the first time I read the letter, and a true marker of how highly Mr. Darcy, Sr. thought of my new brother. Apparently, Mr. Wickham's mother was extravagant, a trait she passed on to her son, which caused her husband's impoverishment. And the elder Mr. Darcy's attachment to Mr. Wickham remained steady to the end of his life.

And then this detail struck me: "My excellent father died about five years ago."

Five years . . . five years.

That phrase played in my head when I first learned that Fiona had a child near that age, but I could not recall where I had heard it before. Now it stood out before me in black and white. I laid the letter down, and moving from the chair to the sofa, I stared into the fire.

Mr. Wickham was a favourite of the deceased. Surely, he would have returned to Pemberley upon learning that Mr. Darcy, Sr. was dying, and he would have stayed for the funeral and the reading of the will. I had no way of knowing how long the gentleman lingered before his demise, but I could well imagine Fiona attempting to distract Georgiana from her grief by engaging in a lark such as swimming in the pond. And knowing Mr. Wickham's corrupt nature, it was not hard to see him steal away from the deathbed to entertain himself with a foolish young lass.

I returned to the letter and saw that it was six months after the death of Mr. Darcy when Mr. Wickham *wrote* that he had resolved against taking orders to become a clergyman and desired three thousand pounds in settlement. That meant he must have left Pemberley sometime during the six months after his benefactor died. If Mr. Wickham had dallied with Fiona and was then confronted with the result of his misdeeds, would it not be consistent with his character to desert her and flee Pemberley?

The letter stated further that Mr. Darcy "was perfectly ready to accede to his proposal. I knew that Mr. Wickham ought not to be a clergyman . . . all connection between us seemed now dissolved."

If Mr. Darcy knew that Wickham was responsible for Fiona's predicament but refused to bear the burden, that would have caused Mr. Darcy to be even more "perfectly ready" to spend three thousand pounds in order to get rid of him. And in the meantime, he had moved Fiona to London, thus removing both bad influences from his impressionable young sister's company.

Suddenly, I began to feel greatly troubled. Astonishment and apprehension flooded my mind. Never, in the whole course of our acquaintance, had I actually seen anything that betrayed Mr. Darcy to be unprincipled or unjust — anything that bespoke him of irreligious or immoral habits. Could it be my own blind vanity that had allowed me to suspect him of such a gross violation of everything right? Among his own connections, he was esteemed and valued — even Wickham had allowed him merit as a brother — and over and over I had seen his repeated concern and protection for his sister. How could I have courted prepossession and ignorance and driven reason away?

Till that moment, I never knew myself.

Angry to discover that I might have been so wrong, I laid the letter aside. Indeed, I resolved to forget all correspondence and prepare myself for bed. So many varied thoughts swirled around my poor brain, it was a wonder I found my way to ring for the maid. I did not wish for any company that night. Thus, as soon as I was undressed, I hurriedly dismissed the girl. It felt good to be free from the constraint of my corset. Perhaps I would be eased in mind as well as body with the change in clothing. I had just shrugged on my robe when I heard a light knock at the door.

Now what?

I opened the door to find Georgiana, who appeared somewhat surprised that I was already dressed for bed. "I came to see how you are feeling. I do hope I did not awaken you."

"No, you did not." I ushered her into the room. "My headache is a little better, and I am certain it will be gone by morning."

When I could see that she did not intend to leave, I invited her to the sofa in front of the fireplace. I scooped up my pile of letters from the end table, intending to place them on the desk, when she stopped me.

"Is that my brother's handwriting? I thought you said he had not written. And what did he say? Did he give you an exact date when he might return to Pemberley?"

"No . . . well, that is," I said, fumbling with the pages, as I attempted to conceal them. In so doing, I managed to drop the outside page of Mr. Darcy's letter that he had given to me in Rosings Park. Georgiana quickly picked it up, saw his opened seal, and observed it addressed to *Miss Elizabeth Bennet.* Her brows knit together as she handed it to me.

"I do not understand. Why should Wills address you in that manner? You are married."

I took the page from her and walked across the room, pulled open a drawer and dropped the entire packet into it before speaking. "There is a simple explanation. This is an old letter your brother wrote to me some months ago. I merely wished to re-read it."

She smiled. "I did not know you and Wills formed an attachment months ago so that you were correspondents."

I returned to the fire, sat down in the chair across from the sofa, and took a deep breath. "Georgiana, did your brother tell you of his proposal to me when we were both in Kent at Easter?"

"Why, no," she said. "Were you betrothed all that time, and I never knew it?"

I shook my head and looked down at my lap. "We were not engaged. I refused him the first time."

Her eyes grew big and round. "I cannot believe it. Did you dislike him so?"

"I confess my opinion of him was somewhat hampered at the time, but it is all in the past and not worth remembrance. Surely, you did not come to question me about distant history. Tell me what I can do for you."

She rose and walked to the fireplace, pressed her lips together several times, clasped and unclasped her hands, and then turned. "Elizabeth, the things I told you this afternoon — the things about Mr. Wickham and Fee and myself — you will keep them in confidence, will you not?"

"Of course, if you wish it."

"I do. I do wish it, especially from Wills. He — well, it is just best that he not know."

"Georgiana, I do not understand. Why must you hide this from your brother? You were only a child; you did nothing wrong. If anyone is to blame, it is Mr. Wickham . . . or — "

"Or Fee?"

I looked away, struggling not to show my loss of composure. "Exactly how old were you and Fiona when all of that occurred?"

"I could not have been more than eleven, and I think Fee had just turned fifteen the previous January."

Five years ago! I almost said it aloud, but caught myself just in time.

"Well then, yes, Fiona should have been more responsible. She was older than you and surely old enough to know it was not fitting to engage in those activities with Mr. Wickham, but as I said before, he is the one truly at blame. And why would you protect Mr. Wickham's name from Mr. Darcy? Surely you know that your brother does not hold him in high regard."

"It is not Mr. Wickham I protect — it is Fee. I would not have Wills think less of her. She has had enough to overcome, and if he thought she had been a poor influence on me — "

"Georgiana, did not your father pass away five years ago?" She nodded. "And Mr. Wickham, I assume, returned to Pemberley for his funeral."

"Actually, I think he came earlier that year, about four or five months before. He stayed until my father died in the middle of summer. I can still remember how miserably hot it was that July."

I swallowed and summoned all of my courage. "And what is the age of Fiona's child? Is he not five years old?"

"He will be next month in December, but why do you ask me this?"

"Georgiana," I took a deep breath, "do you suspect Mr. Wickham is Willie's father?"

She blushed vividly and turned her face away, but nodded in agreement. "I do now. At the time, of course, I was so young I did not even understand what had happened to Fee, but after . . . well, I shall just say certain things happened later that revealed to me the extent of Mr. Wickham's true character. I think it quite likely he could have taken advantage of Fee, but if Wills learns that she had encouraged me to participate in any indiscreet behaviour with George, even as a child, he might remove her from Pemberley altogether."

"Well, as it is, he has not even brought her here, has he?" I said, distaste for the subject evident in the tone of my voice.

Georgiana looked at me intently. "Has Fee displeased you, Elizabeth? Do you want her not to come?"

I coloured, aware that I had revealed my prior suspicions and jealousy by my speech. "I have nothing of which to accuse her, and your brother is the one who decides whether she will serve him in London or Pemberley."

"Serve him? Surely you mean serve *you*, do you not?"

"Yes, of course — I misspoke. Perhaps my headache is worse than I thought."

She rose and started for the door. "I am sorry I intruded. I . . . I hope you will rest well."

After she shut the door, I sighed deeply. I closed my eyes and shuddered when I thought of the circle of secrecy, suspicion and fear that surrounded me. Why did not all of us — Georgiana, Mr. Darcy, and I — just bring everything out into the open and talk of it? Why must Georgiana share confidences with me that I must keep from her brother? Why should Mr. Darcy demand that I not discuss Wickham's attempted elopement with Georgiana with the girl, herself? Why did Mr. Darcy not explain things — important things such as why he had not yet corrected matters between Mr. Bingley and Jane? Who truly was Willie's father? What possible reason did Mr. Darcy have for keeping Fiona in London? And most important — why had he married me and cast me into the middle of all this?

For that matter, why had I not demanded answers? Why had I settled for bits and pieces of information that both brother and sister dispensed in meagre fashion? Where was my own courage and belief that I was entitled to a thorough knowledge of the truth? What had happened to that independent, spirited young woman from Longbourn who was quickly able to form astute judgments and opinions of others?

I did not wish to think on the answer to my last question, for I knew all too well what had transpired. I had fallen in love with Mr. Darcy. It was plain and simple, and no matter how greatly I wished it to be false, it was, indeed, quite true. I now saw his compassion, his integrity, his affection for his sister — in truth, even his kindness in offering marriage to me — composed a man worthy of my love.

Oh, he was arrogant still, even prideful, and sorely lacking in knowledge of how to be a proper husband — yes, these were defects that needed correcting — but in essentials, I had to admit he was as he had ever been . . . a good man.

I returned to the letter, poring over it word by word. At last, even I perceived some truth in Mr. Darcy's view of Jane. I could not deny the justice of his interpretation that her feelings, though fervent, were little displayed. Perhaps he truly did not believe her in love with Mr. Bingley.

When I came to the part of the letter in which he alluded to my family's actions at Netherfield, I was mortified, and my sense of shame was severe because I could recall that their actions did, indeed, merit reproach. I read the compliment to Jane and myself — that he thought we had conducted ourselves so as to avoid any share of the like censure. He thought such praise honourable to the sense and disposition of us both, but it soothed me little, providing modest consolation for the contempt the rest of my family had attracted.

I was struck with the truth that Jane's disappointment, in fact, had been the work of her nearest relations and not merely the influence of Mr. Bingley's family and friend.

By the time the clock chimed two bells, my depression was acute. My head truly did ache. I snuffed the candle and reclined on the sofa pillows. I was too weary even to crawl into bed. I thought I would never sleep, but I did — and the next thing I knew I awakened upon the hardest bed I had ever known. It was freezing, and I was thoroughly chilled. Blinking in the dim, early morning light, I raised myself on one arm and became instantly aware that I was neither in my bed nor on the sofa in my room. I was lying on a cold, hard floor. Although covered with a beautiful rug, the surface remained unyielding, and my back and neck ached as I sat up.

Where was I?

And then I saw him. Looking up, I saw that I had slept in the great gallery beneath the portrait of Mr. Darcy.

FORTUNATELY, I RETREATED TO MY bedchamber without discovery by any of the servants, but later that morning, Colonel Fitzwilliam questioned me as to the state of my health. He was concerned that I did not look rested and wondered if I was still afflicted with the headache from the evening before.

"I am not ill, although I thank you for your concern."

"Truly, Mrs. Darcy, you have shadows beneath your eyes. Was your rest disturbed last night?"

"It was," I admitted, pleased to take advantage of the fact that Georgiana was engaged in the music room, and we were alone. "Georgiana said that Mr. Darcy must remain in London. I do not understand why it should take so long to discover the identity of those engaged in this blackmail scheme.

Have you heard any particulars from him as to the case?"

"Yes, and I can tell you that progress is being made. Unfortunately, two or more servants resigned just prior to the threat, and Darce and his investigator are searching for their whereabouts so that they may question them. London is a labyrinth of hiding places, and so it may be some time before they find the guilty party or parties, but do not fear, they will be caught."

"And is he sure that one or more of the servants is guilty?"

"Well, Darcy has thoroughly questioned everyone still in his service in Town. So far, he has ruled out all of them."

"Do you mean he suspected all of the servants? No one was exempt from suspicion?"

"Mrs. Darcy, your husband takes his responsibilities seriously. If he thinks anyone might harm his sister or you, for that matter, he will not rest until he has uncovered every stone, examined every source. Did you not notice that when we travelled to Pemberley, we used my father's coach and servants? None of Darcy's staff accompanied us. You have spoken the truth. Not one of his servants in London is exempt."

Georgiana joined us then, and naturally, we spoke of other things. I said little, for once again I was struck with how much in error I had been to suspect Mr. Darcy of keeping Fiona in Town for immoral purposes. No matter how much Georgiana loved her, could it be that Mr. Darcy still had not ruled out the possibility of the maid's participation in this scheme?

I ESCAPED THE HOUSE THAT afternoon and the company of my companions, for I longed to be alone. I walked through the woods of Pemberley for more than three hours, lost in thought, floundering in my regret. How I had wronged Mr. Darcy! Overcome with shame and anguish, I stumbled along the path and stopped only long enough to rest now and then.

I now believed there had been nothing between Mr. Darcy and Fiona other than a master showing kindness to an ignorant, unfortunate serving girl. My imagination had conjured the vile attachment that tormented me, and heeding the servants' gossip had stoked the flame. Jealousy allowed it to catch hold in my heart. I was truly wrong, and if I was wrong in my appraisal of his character in that manner, had I been in error about other aspects?

I cast back in my memory to my first association with Mr. Darcy. A year ago, I met him at an assembly ball in Meryton. He had been haughty and rude, but perhaps it was because he was shy. Had he not said at Rosings that he was ill qualified to recommend himself to strangers? No, that was a poor excuse. My first impression had been correct. After all, the man was not perfect — far from it.

I recalled how he had singled me out at the Netherfield Ball. He asked me to dance and then left it up to me to initiate conversation. How exasperated I had felt by the end of the dance, for he revealed so little of himself that conversation was as arduous as manoeuvring a path covered in briars. In truth, I disliked his taciturn disposition, but would I prefer a young man who "rattled about," as Mrs. Reynolds so aptly put it? No, I knew the answer to that question, for when he did speak, Mr. Darcy's words were worthy of attention.

"You must allow me to tell you how ardently I love and admire you."

I closed my eyes as that phrase resounded in my ears. As I thought back to that time when he first asked me to marry, I could still see the earnest expression of tenderness about his countenance. Was it possible he truly had been in love with me?

And to think how I had answered that proposal — with what angry manner I had condemned him — I could not bear to remember it without shame. Was it possible I had employed far too much haste in dismissing his words of love? Had my quick temper destroyed my ability to recognize the prospect that he meant those words? True, his proposal had been unfortunate, far too overconfident, even arrogant, as though he expected me to fall at his feet with thanksgiving for his attention, but still, it did not warrant the hateful mode of my response.

And yet, after all I had said to him, six months later Mr. Darcy travelled to Longbourn unbidden and offered me marriage once again. He had literally saved my family from ruin and had provided the means by which I would have a more than comfortable life as mistress of all this. Why had he done so? Was it for love?

My thoughts turned to the brief time we had been married. I had learned much from him. He was a man of intelligence and breeding. True, he had been abrupt, even demanding at times, and far too obstinate, but had I not provoked him with my angry outbursts, my presumption of how things stood, and my own stubborn questioning of his every action?

And then I was struck with a thought I had failed to ever consider previously. Mr. Darcy took me in marriage and yet allowed me the right to determine when our physical union would be completed, well aware that I would not reach that point at any time in the near future. He had sacrificed his needs for my well-being . . . and still he did so. I knew little of such things, but I had heard enough talk between my mother and aunt to know that a husband could be demanding in those areas, and yet *my* husband continued to exercise patience with me.

I thought of waking up next to him — first, in the inn the morning after our wedding and then, the night I walked in my sleep and awoke in his bed. Both times, I awakened in his embrace, and even now, I felt gooseflesh run up and down my arms as I recalled the pleasure it provoked. If I felt such intoxicating sensations, what must it have done to Mr. Darcy?

I allowed my thoughts to wander to each time we had found ourselves in close proximity since our marriage. I recalled how attractive I found him in his shirtsleeves at the billiards table and how warm I had grown with his arms around me while he taught me the game. I heard his deep voice translate words of love in my ear at the concert. I recalled how our bodies seemed to be perfectly tuned when dancing together at Lord Matlock's ball. And, of course, his lips upon mine the last night I had seen him — that kiss! I shook my head to waken from such musings.

I rose and began to walk back toward the house. It was no little distance, for I had wandered far. I thought that the task of placing one foot in front of the other might distract me from remembering how I responded to my husband's kiss, but it did not. It only caused me to wonder anew at his feelings for me. Could he possibly be in love with me? And if so, why had he not said so again?

Well, I thought, would I risk once more declaring my love to one who had shown every sign of trampling it underfoot? And with the manner of my departure from London, what must he feel now? I watched a squirrel chatter at me from its high perch on the tallest tree.

"Yes," I said aloud, "scold me, for I deserve it."

Oh, I could not bear to think he was alive in the world and thinking ill of me!

THAT EVENING, I NOTICED A definite lack of conversation upon the part of my companions at dinner. Neither Colonel Fitzwilliam nor Georgiana initiated any discussion. They both responded to my remarks with equanimity, but by the close of the meal, I realized they had not spoken a word to each other.

When the colonel excused himself afterwards to have a drink, I examined my sister closely, seeking some reason for her obvious lack of animation.

"Georgiana, are you well?"

"Perfectly." She turned her face away from me.

"Shall you play for me, then?" Music always provoked a favourable response in her demeanour.

"Not tonight, Elizabeth. I am not in the mood."

"Very well. Shall we set up the card table in preparation for a game with the colonel when he joins us?"

"No. I do not care to play cards, either."

"Is something wrong? I have rarely seen you so out of sorts."

She rose and walked to the window but not quickly enough to hide the tears I saw spring to her eyes. I followed and placed my hand on her shoulder. "Georgiana, what is it? Has something happened?"

"Oh, Elizabeth!" She laid her head on my shoulder, clinging to me like a child. "I have made such a dreadful mistake."

"What do you mean? Tell me."

She cried for some time before she could speak, but after I led her to the sofa and gave her my handkerchief, she calmed herself. "I never should have told Richard."

"Told him what?"

"The incident I related to you earlier about swimming with Fee and Mr. Wickham when I was a child." I was surprised at her candour. "I thought I could tell him. I have always been able to tell him things — things I would never reveal to Wills because he is so particular. Richard's manner is more at ease, and he rarely gets upset, but now he is furious! Did you see how he was at dinner? He did not speak to me!"

"But why? Why did you tell Colonel Fitzwilliam of something that happened so long ago?"

"I do not know. I suppose it was because it has been a secret all these years. In this family, there are too many things of which we never speak. When I was able to confide in you and you did not censure me, I felt such relief, and I thought I might take the chance and receive the same response from Richard. But I was mistaken!" She began to cry anew, and I found myself holding her and patting her back, attempting to comfort her.

"Well, what did the colonel say? What were his exact words?"

"Oh, I do not know. At first he did nothing more than become deathly still, but I could see an anger descend upon his countenance, an anger I had only seen once before."

"And when was that?" I ventured to ask although I thought I knew well enough.

She looked at her hands in her lap and began to twist my handkerchief around and around. "I am not supposed to speak of it. It is one more subject forbidden utterance in this house."

"By whom?"

"Wills, of course. He demands I never talk of what happened to me last year."

"Do you mean what happened between you and Mr. Wickham?"

Her eyes flew open, as well as her mouth. "Then you know? You already know how stupid I was, what a blunder I made?" I looked away, my heart full of anguish at her mortification. "But why did you never speak of it, Elizabeth?" I could not look at her but kept my eyes downcast.

"Oh, I see," she said flatly. "Wills told you not to, naturally." She rose and walked to the fireplace, placed her hand upon the mantel and leaned her head against it.

"It was for your benefit, Georgiana, I am sure. Your brother loves you so much, and he thinks, whether correctly or not, that speaking of what happened will add to your distress."

"Why does he persist in blindness? Can he not see that I need to talk about it, that I am tormented with the shame of my mistake? How am I ever to achieve redemption? I am weary of going over this in my own mind and coming up empty. I need to discuss it with someone who will not tell me just to forget it!"

She began to cry and ran toward the door. I called out to her, but as she ran into the hall, her only reply was, "Please, Elizabeth. I must go to my room. I must be alone."

I had achieved only the barest semblance of composure when Colonel Fitzwilliam entered the room. His first remark, naturally, pertained to the whereabouts of his cousin. When I told him she had retired, he frowned slightly.

"So early?"

I took a deep breath and decided to be the first in the family to speak frankly of forbidden subjects. "Georgiana was distraught, and I am afraid much of it has to do with you."

"What did she say?"

"She told me of your reaction when she confessed a childish indiscretion. She said you were furious."

He frowned even more. "Well, I am, but not at her."

"She does not know that, sir."

"But why? Why would Georgiana think I am angry with her? She was, as you say, nothing but a child. It is Wickham I could — " here he broke off, unwilling to voice his angry desire. "Did she say anything else?"

"Indeed, she is angry with her brother because he forbids her to speak of her unfortunate mistake with Mr. Wickham, and she is disappointed that you, as well, responded to this afternoon's revelation much as Mr. Darcy would."

"And have you heard this latest story about Wickham?"

I nodded.

"It pains me to speak ill of your sister's husband in your presence, but I sometimes believe my cousin should have called him out last year. It would have spared many from the damage he wreaks wherever he goes."

"I do not have a good opinion of Mr. Wickham, sir. You may feel free to say what you will."

"When I think of how many people he has grieved, it makes me consider actions unworthy of my character. I feel my anger rise anew each time I am reminded of his lack of honour. And poor Darcy — I thought surely he might kill him when he found him holed up in that miserable room with your young sister! No one would have disputed his right to do so, that I can assure you!"

I was standing beside a chair when the colonel made that last statement, and suddenly I felt the room grow wavy in appearance. What had he said? I sat down immediately and gripped the chair arms with both hands, my knuckles growing white.

"I beg your pardon, sir," I said, my voice quaking slightly, "but did you say it was Mr. Darcy who discovered the exact whereabouts of my sister and Mr. Wickham?"

He looked up quickly, a frown overtaking his brow. "The deuce take it! Has he never told you how it came about?"

When I shook my head, he said, "Well, he must have wished to spare you the sordid parts of the tale, but be assured that Darcy played an essential part in *persuading* Wickham to proceed to the altar. You must know that he would not rest until he had discovered them — " he waved his hand in a dismissive gesture " — but it is just like Darce to forget the days and nights he spent hunting them down through the seedier parts of London until our old friend, Mrs. Younge, led him to them."

"Mrs. Younge," I murmured, although that woman was the least important part of the conversation to me at the moment. I attempted to ask my questions in the most innocuous manner possible, for I did not want to hinder the colonel's narrative in any way. In fact, I was so curious I would have resorted to tricks and stratagems to find it out.

"You know, Colonel Fitzwilliam, my husband is quite modest in relating his good deeds. Shall you not refresh my memory and tell me what you know of the story, for sometimes I think I have not heard all of it even to this day?"

He smiled slightly, acknowledging that Darcy, in fact, was often too reserved in conveying the details of his good works, but the colonel did not suffer from that affliction, especially when it came to praising the unselfishness of his cousin.

"It seems he prefers to do his charitable acts in secret," I murmured.

"For which he will someday be rewarded, I feel certain. Still, I cannot believe he has never confided the entire story to you, his wife. Were you not curious?"

"Exceedingly, but as you know, he is somewhat reticent."

"Well, I am neither bound by restraint nor oath of secrecy! Thus, I have no qualms in laying out the entire story of how Darcy forced Wickham to correct his misdeeds."

Colonel Fitzwilliam then went on to describe in detail how my husband not only had discovered Wickham and Lydia, he had insisted upon bearing the entire expense of insuring Wickham's compliance by paying off his debts and purchasing him a commission in the regulars. He, undoubtedly, afforded him a handsome bribe as well, all so that he might make an honest woman of my youngest sister.

By the time he finished the account, I was so shocked I could hardly speak!

Before I went to bed that night, I spent no little time moving furniture. I tugged and pushed until I had replaced not one chair, but two — one at the door between my room and that of Mr. Darcy, and the other at the door leading to the hall.

If my malady had caused me to spend last night on the cold, hard floor before Mr. Darcy's portrait, I feared this new revelation might cause me to walk all the way to London!

Chapter Eleven

The next day I wrote to Mrs. Gardiner before breakfast. Now that Colonel Fitzwilliam had revealed some of Mr. Darcy's actions regarding Lydia and Mr. Wickham, it was impossible not to know every detail, for to live in ignorance of any part of it was out of the question. I explained to my aunt what the colonel had told me and assured her since the secret was now laid bare, she would not break any promise by telling me the details as she knew them.

"You may readily comprehend," I wrote, "what my curiosity must be to know *how* a person unconnected with any of us at that time and, comparatively speaking, a stranger to our family, should have been amongst you at such a time. Pray write instantly, and let me understand exactly how it all came about."

I had the satisfaction of receiving an answer to my letter within a week. Indeed, my aunt appeared relieved to unburden herself from the confidence imposed upon her. She wrote me the explicit story of how, at Lambton, Mr. Darcy had first learned from her of Lydia's elopement.

He had come to call upon the Gardiners at the inn only a short while after they had just read the letter from me, entreating them to come to Longbourn and assist our family in locating the fleeing couple. My uncle had left the inn to secure their passage on the first available coach, and Mr. Darcy had discovered my aunt alone in a moment of emotion. He had been so kind, so solicitous in his sympathy that she confided the entire tale to him.

Unbeknownst to the Gardiners, Mr. Darcy left for London the next day and scouted out the location of Mr. Wickham and Lydia before calling upon my uncle. He insisted upon bearing the entire cost of Lydia's marriage settlement.

"The motive professed was his conviction of its being owing to himself that Wickham's worthlessness had not been so well known as to make it impossible for any young woman of character to love or confide in him. He generously imputed the whole to his mistaken pride and confessed that he had before thought it beneath him to lay his private actions open to the world. His character was to speak for itself. He called it, therefore, his duty to step forward and endeavour to remedy an evil which had been brought on by himself. If he had another motive, I am sure it would never disgrace him.

"Mr. Darcy and your uncle battled it together for a long time, but our visitor was very obstinate. I fancy, Lizzy, that obstinacy is the real defect of his character, after all."

"Oh yes, Aunt, fancy that, indeed!" I cried aloud.

"Nothing was to be done that he did not do himself, and at last your uncle was forced to yield, and instead of being allowed to be of use to his niece, was forced to put up with only having the probable credit of it.

"In spite of all this, my dear Lizzy, you may rest perfectly assured that your uncle never would have yielded if we had not given him credit for another interest in the affair. I thought him very sly; he hardly ever mentioned your name, but slyness seems the fashion."

Aunt Gardiner wrote that it also gave my uncle pleasure to keep Mr. Darcy's actions hidden from me no longer, but she cautioned me not to tell my family without his permission, as he had been adamant that no one was to know.

The contents of the letter cast me into a flutter of spirits in which it was difficult to determine whether pleasure or pain bore the greater share. I had not yet adjusted to the shock of Mr. Darcy's involvement in Lydia's marriage before I received my aunt's correspondence. Her further revelations only deepened my utter surprise.

Not only had Mr. Darcy acted in a noble, selfless manner, but if my aunt and uncle's suspicions were correct, he might possibly have done so not only for my poor sister's sake but for mine.

Could this be true? And if so, why had he not told me? Why had he not used such a fine example of his character to persuade me to marry him?

"Elizabeth," Georgiana said, "will you join Richard and me in our inspection of Pemberley's back hall?"

Her question and presence startled me from my reverie. I had wandered to a small bench set in a copse not far from the path that led from Pemberley's great lawn to the woods. So intent had I been upon my reading and my own thoughts, I had not even heard the couple's approach.

I rose, quickly folded the letter, and slipped it into my pocket. I was glad to see that the disagreement between them had at last been resolved, and I assumed that Colonel Fitzwilliam had seen to it, for they both appeared in good spirits, a definite change from their terse remarks to each other during the past week.

"I presume this inspection has to do with the Harvest Ball, am I correct?" I asked.

"You are," Georgiana said. "At the rear of the house is a huge open hall, quite adequate to house our tenants and their families. We have always held the Harvest Ball there so that our guests will not feel out of place. Years ago, my father said they would be somewhat intimidated by Pemberley's grand ballroom. I have already assigned tasks to many of the servants as well as planned the decorations, but I wish for your approval of my designs, Elizabeth."

"I am sure whatever you choose will be delightful, for you know much more about harvest balls than I do. I confess I have never attended one."

"Did not your father host a celebration at Longbourn at the end of the season?"

"My dear, Longbourn does not compare to Pemberley in size or tenants. Our harvest consisted of a great deal less; although as a child, I do recall that the workers held a party outside around a huge bonfire. My father allowed Jane and me to accompany him once or twice, but he only put in an appearance and drank a tankard of mead with them before returning to the house."

"Then you shall have a novel experience, Mrs. Darcy," the colonel said, "for at Pemberley's Harvest Ball, the master and his family host the entire evening."

"Oh, yes," Georgiana added, "and there is dancing and singing, more food than can be eaten, and greater amusement than any other night of the year!"

"Indeed!" I remained baffled by the image of Mr. Darcy eating and dancing with his farm workers and their families. Did he not find country society somewhat "confined and unvarying?" And these people would not even qualify as society!

"I learned to dance at a harvest ball," Georgiana announced.

"Now, Georgie," the colonel said, "I happen to know you were instructed in the art by the finest dancing master in London."

"Yes, but that was much later. I had already learned how to dance from the children of our tenants. When I was a child, my father allowed me full rein at the harvest balls to mingle, play, and dance with the other children. They were some of the happiest nights of my youth."

The colonel and I exchanged smiles before he spoke. "Your *youth* is hardly spent."

"Do wait until you come out this spring," I added. "You will dance at many a ball and enjoy numerous happy nights, I trust."

Georgiana shrugged. "Perhaps, but I doubt any of them shall compare with the freedom and pleasure of harvest balls."

I began to anticipate this ball just from listening to my sister. "But has your brother never forbidden your dancing now that you are a young woman?"

She laughed. "Wills shall be at peace. There are no eligible young men for me at such a gathering, Elizabeth. In truth, I rarely remember standing up with boy or man, but rather, I joined the throng of children who danced together at the back of the great hall. None of us truly had partners. As I said, it was more play than real dancing."

"Well, now I take offense because I happen to remember dancing with you myself," Colonel Fitzwilliam said, "at the last Harvest Ball."

Georgiana stopped and looked up at him with a frown. "We did not dance together, for I did not attend last year's ball. In fact, Wills only put in an appearance and then left. It was not a time for dancing."

A shadow covered the colonel's eyes. He took her hand and tucked it inside his arm, patting it as they continued on their way. "Yes, now I remember. Forgive me for even mentioning it, my dear."

I followed them inside the house, saddened that our conversation had turned to an unhappy memory for Georgiana. I had yet to visit that part of the mansion, for it was vast, indeed, and Mrs. Reynolds had not included it in my original tour, possibly because of the amount of time it took to walk there. I listened as Georgiana began to tell me of its history, glad to see her mood grow lighter as she talked.

"This was the original Pemberley, built almost one hundred years before the portion in which we now reside."

Although grand enough in appearance, its age was apparent, being much more rustic, indicative of a far earlier time. I could see it would be perfect for a harvest celebration. Indeed, my young sister had already ordered decorations made from stalks of hay, bits of dried corn, and deep, red berries. Servants now stood on ladders, hanging them on the walls and placing them in the cutout alcoves high above. Enormous long tables lined the perimeter of the room, already covered with pristine white cloths. Several maids fashioned garlands of autumnal grasses and dried flowers intertwined with ribbons, while others looped them along the outside of the tables.

"Ah, it looks quite festive already," I declared.

"Yes, it quite puts me in the mood. Shall we dance now, Sprout?" the colonel said with a laugh.

"Without music? No, you shall just have to wait until Friday night." She then left us standing in the middle of the hall while she joined the maids and corrected the height of the loops.

"It is good to see her happy," the colonel said.

I wished I knew what had transpired between them to restore their good humour, but I did not ask, for I felt it would be intrusive. "Well, I find myself looking forward to this ball, and I shall enjoy seeing you dance with Georgiana again."

He looked at me closely. "Again?"

"I saw you dance together at Eden Park."

"Ah, and all this time I thought we had been successful in our indiscretion."

"As far as I know, you were, for I saw none other observe you, and I have not told anyone."

"Meaning your husband, I assume. I say, Mrs. Darcy, keeping secrets from your lord and master already?"

I made a conscious effort not to roll my eyes at that statement. The colonel had no idea! I chose to change the subject. "Colonel Fitzwilliam, since we are now cousins, I would prefer that you address me by my Christian name. Mrs. Darcy sounds quite formal and distant. Will you not call me Elizabeth?"

"I would be honoured, Elizabeth, if you, in turn, acknowledge that I am Richard. Shall we shake hands on our understanding?"

I laughed and readily agreed, waving to Georgiana when she turned to see our exchange. "I must go and help her if we are to get this hall ready for dancing in less than a week."

"Very well, I shall release you, for I do look forward to dancing with you and with Georgiana once again." There was something wistful about the tone of his voice, and so I delayed my leave taking, surprised by his next statement. "It will most likely be the last time that I do so."

"Why, whatever do you mean? There will be plenty of opportunities for the two of you to dance together once she comes out after Easter. Surely, it will be acceptable, for you are not brother and sister."

He frowned. "Brother and sister? No, indeed, we are not, but I shall be far from England by Easter."

"Where are you going, Richard?"

"I do not know at present, but I have put in for an assignment abroad. If Bonaparte continues his present actions against us in Spain, I shall most likely join our forces there. If not, I have asked to be sent anywhere my commander chooses as long as I am not required to remain on these shores."

My eyes grew wide. "I confess I am surprised, and I am afraid Georgiana will be heartbroken."

"I ask that you do not tell her now, Elizabeth. She will recover well enough once the parties and balls begin."

"Being one of her guardians, do you not deem it essential that you remain in attendance during that time?"

"I did once, but now that Darce has married such a capable woman, I am much assured that the both of you will do all that is necessary to look after her."

I wished that I felt the same assurance. I dreaded Mr. Darcy's reaction when Georgiana began attracting young suitors. "I fear that your genial manner and outlook will be sorely missed at that time, sir. As you know, Mr. Darcy comes close to smothering his sister with protection."

I expected Richard to smile at my exaggeration, but he did not; rather, a pensive, brooding cloud seemed to descend upon his countenance. "You overestimate me, Elizabeth. I am certain Georgiana will enjoy her coming out much more if I am not present."

Just then, the young girl called out, entreating me to join her in looking over the proposed menu for the festivity, and the colonel excused himself to check on the condition of his horse that had recently developed a slight limp. As I walked across the wide floor, I glanced over my shoulder and watched him depart. I had the strangest feeling a greater reason behind Richard's future leave-taking existed, a reason he was not yet ready to reveal.

That evening when I went to my chamber to dress for dinner, I saw that the post had come. Mamá had written as well as Jane, but it was the third envelope that caught my attention. My pulse quickened when I recognized the handwriting of Mr. Darcy.

I sat down and attempted to still my rapid heartbeat. I told myself to be calm, that no need existed for my nervous feeling. It was only a letter and did not appear more than a page. It probably contained little more than a few sentences.

I decided to read my family's correspondence first, beginning with Jane's letter. She seemed unusually happy, but I could not concentrate on her words. I found myself having to re-read the same sentences repeatedly. Instead, my attention insisted upon wandering to the letter that I had laid beneath Mamá's in an attempt to place it in the least order of importance. That did no good — it may as well have been a great, squawking rooster, calling out for my attention! I could not keep my eyes from it.

At last, I rose, took the letter and placed it inside a drawer in my desk. *There!* I thought. *Surely, I can forget it long enough to read my family's correspondence.*

I applied myself with diligence anew and made it through the first missive, losing my way only once or twice. I then attempted to read Mamá's post, but her ramblings made little sense, and I soon gave it up. Returning to the desk, I opened the drawer and retrieved the letter from London that attracted me like intoxicating nectar. It angered me that my fingers trembled when I attempted to break the seal.

"Stop it, Lizzy!" I said aloud, as I unfolded the single sheet of fine, cream-coloured parchment.

Elizabeth,

Progress continues in the matter causing my delay. Our detective successfully followed the man retrieving the blackmail funds, who turned out possibly to be the same "Johnny" you overheard in the garden. He, in turn, led us along the Thames to a house in the lower parts of Town owned by none other than Mrs. Younge. She, apparently, is his aunt and both have been apprehended by the authorities. We are now engaged in determining if any other servant in my service may have aided them in this crime. Please know that your information concerning Johnny has been of invaluable assistance.

Unfortunately, it is highly unlikely I will return to Pemberley in time for the Harvest Ball. Please relay this message to Georgiana.

And now to another matter which I hesitate to write but feel that I must, for I cannot account for the coldness of your manner upon your departure, except to believe that my behaviour of the previous night must have been unwelcome, and for that lapse on my part, I offer my apologies. I would likewise extend my regrets, but in all honesty, I cannot find any such feelings in my heart.

FD

I read the letter through twice and the last sentence over and over. When I could no longer see it through the mist of tears filling my eyes, I traced its outline with my fingers. Did it mean what I thought it might, that Mr. Darcy did not regret kissing me? I cried aloud and began to sob. I had not known how much I needed to hear those words. What release it caused within me to read that simple phrase!

THE DAY OF THE HARVEST Ball arrived before we knew it. A beautiful Friday in late autumn, the weather crisp but not truly cold and with a full moon expected that night, the day could not have been more perfect.

The morning was filled with last minute tasks for both Georgiana and me, but Mrs. Reynolds suggested that both of us take time for a nap that afternoon in anticipation of the evening ahead. I felt quite certain that Georgiana needed little refreshing, for she was aglow with longing for the start of the ball. However, we did heed our housekeeper's motherly admonition and retired to our bedchambers for a few hours.

Slipping off my shoes, I lay upon the bed and pulled up a quilt from the bottom to cover my bare feet. I plumped my pillow and, in so doing, felt Mr. Darcy's letter beneath, where I had kept it since the day of its receipt. I took it out once more, read it again, and then held it close to my heart. I had not answered the letter, for what reason I remain unsure to this very day. What could I say? How could I make him understand all that was in my heart when last I saw him? And, in truth, how could I bear to confess my ugly suspicions about Fiona and him? No, I refused to put all that in a letter, and so I did not write.

Sarah, my maid, tapped at the door some two hours later, and I bade her enter, for I was awake. I had not slept at all, but I had remained upon the bed, attempting to rest. The remainder of the afternoon was spent in my bath, coiffing my hair and donning my dress, a lovely, pale green silk. The deeply scooped neckline flattered my bosom, and I elected to wear only my garnet cross for enhancement. These were simple folk, and I felt no desire to impress them with the black pearl Mr. Darcy had bestowed upon me.

At last, I was ready, and I hurried below stairs to find Georgiana and Richard in the drawing room. She was lovely in a pale cream gown, tiny blooms scattered through her golden hair, and a radiant glow upon her face.

"Elizabeth, look what Richard has just given me," she cried.

I saw the delicate chain of pearls nestled around her slender throat. "They are beautiful. Well done, Richard."

He beamed at her pleasure. "Pearls are for grown-up ladies, Sprout. See that you remember that."

"Oh, Richard, must you spoil my joy with another reprimand?"

"In your brother's absence, I feel compelled to offer the admonition I feel certain he would tender."

"I am no longer a child, you know." She smiled as she said these words, and he bowed in response.

"So I see, my dear. You have become a lovely young woman."

Through the window, I could see carts and wagons approach Pemberley's rear park. I watched as entire families descended. Mothers attempted to curtail their boisterous children, fathers straightened their neckcloths and brushed off their coats, and all of them apparently were excited about the evening awaiting them. The colonel suggested we make our way to the great hall, and so we did.

The room was already filled with people and conversation. The musicians tuned their instruments, and servants scurried here and there with their huge platters of food and pitchers of mead, ale, and wine. Georgiana immediately waded into the throng and welcomed each person, obviously acquainted with them. Again, I was amazed with what ease she served as princess over this kingdom. She was completely at home with Pemberley's tenants.

Colonel Fitzwilliam led me to sit at the centre of the head table where Georgiana eventually joined us. A short while later, he stood and tapped his fork against his glass — a signal that quieted the crowd.

"Neighbours and tenants of Pemberley! On behalf of my cousin, Mr. Darcy, I welcome you to this belated Harvest Ball. He regrets most heartily that he is unable to join you tonight, but he would have me stand in his stead. Miss Darcy and I ask you to raise your glasses in a toast to the new mistress of Pemberley, Mrs. Fitzwilliam Darcy."

"Hear, hear!" The clamour of the crowd was friendly and approving, and I smiled and nodded in response.

"Mr. Darcy bade me assure you that, even though unforeseen events have caused his extended absence from Pemberley for much of this year, all shall remain as it is. He will return. All will be well. All will continue as it ever has. And you are to be commended for your hard work in once again reaping a successful harvest. I offer a toast to each of you."

"Hear, hear!" the crowd rejoined again. "And to Mr. Darcy."

"Now, eat, drink, and dance. Musicians, give us a song!"

There was much cheering and excitement as couples lined up for the first country dance. So many of the tenants approached me in greeting that I entreated Georgiana to take my place and begin the dance with Richard. It did my heart good to see the happiness upon her face. Her eyes sparkled, and a smile graced her countenance for the entire length of the reel, as well as the next, for the colonel led her right back to the floor with the beginning of the following set.

I spent no little time meeting guests and acknowledging their expressions of joy on my marriage. There were naught but friendly faces among the entire throng as far as I could see, and the only damper to my enjoyment was the thought of how much more wonderful the evening might have been if Mr. Darcy stood by my side and we were married in every sense. I missed him more that night than I ever did before.

Richard asked me to dance the next, a tune I thoroughly enjoyed. The dances were much livelier than those conducted at Netherfield or Eden Park with their stiff formality, for these were country folk, after all. I found myself comparing them to the assembly balls held at Meryton, for they were much alike, and I experienced a slight yearning in my heart for those old days now past.

Halfway through the evening, the musicians rested, and the principal meal was served. People had nibbled and drank throughout the night, but they now found seats at the tables and partook of the generous bounty Pemberley provided. Laughter and talk filled the room, and I rejoiced to see Georgiana's continued smiles. Richard sat between us at the head table and teased her persistently, which she bore quite well.

It was just after dinner that he asked me to dance again. I protested and suggested Georgiana take my place, but she begged off. She wished to gather the children into a circle up front near the door and play a game of *Drop the Handkerchief.* And so I accepted the colonel's invitation, and we led the next set, which lasted a good half-hour. By the time the final notes sounded, we found ourselves at the bottom of the line of dancers. I was quite flushed from the exercise but beamed with the joy of it all.

As Richard escorted me from the floor, a commotion broke out across the length of the great room, and a roar of cheering and applause erupted. There was such a company of people blocking my view that I was at a loss to explain its cause, and then I heard Richard's exclamation.

"Why, it's Darcy! He is come after all."

I stood near the end of a long table on the side of the room nearest the servants' entrance, and I was thankful for the sturdiness of the furniture, for I felt an urgent need to lean upon it for support.

Mr. Darcy!

The crowd parted, and I could see him there. Surely, it was my heart that suddenly leaped into my throat and threatened to bar all future breathing. I gasped for air and struggled to still my visibly moving bosom.

Shrugging off his greatcoat and dropping it along with his hat into the hands of a nearby servant, he raised his head and saw me. His gaze was severe. His eyes never wavered from mine, as though we were somehow locked together for all time. A mug of ale was thrust into his hands. He took a brief swallow without giving it a glance and wiped his mouth with the back of his hand, never once taking his eyes from mine. Many men reached out and shook his hand, and I saw him nod without looking at them. Even when Georgiana ran up and kissed his cheek, he put his arm around her shoulder in a brief embrace without breaking his gaze upon me. And all the while he walked toward me, narrowing the distance between us with determined rapidity.

I, unknowingly, began to edge myself backward until there was no longer a table on which to hold, and I found myself at the doorway that led from the hall to the kitchen outside. I clutched the moulding for support, my hands behind me, icy cold.

"Ah, the master sees his bride."

"At last they are to be reunited."

I heard those cries and similar remarks made by the crowd, and from the corner of my eyes, I could see some of them elbow each other and laughing — not coarsely but rather in an approving manner.

"Shall you and Mrs. Darcy lead the next dance, sir?" one of the men called forth with added encouragement from several others.

"Not yet," Mr. Darcy said, advancing toward me all the while, "not until I have greeted my wife in a proper manner."

That produced laughter and knowing looks between the tenants. Still, he walked steadfastly toward me, and I could see the grimness about his mouth and the fire in his eyes. As unobtrusively as possible, I turned and walked through the door, steeling myself to appear perfectly calm and dignified.

"Ah, she wants to greet him in private," I heard someone say. However, the moment I could no longer be seen by our guests, I turned and fled. To this day, I cannot tell you why I ran, only that I did. Sometimes I think I ran not only from Mr. Darcy but also from myself.

I barely missed colliding with a serving girl carrying a huge pitcher and another who walked behind her with a tray of goblets. I quickly stepped to the side and ran out into the night. Frantically, I searched for some place to hide, some provision of escape, when I heard Mr. Darcy's voice call out, "Elizabeth!"

I glanced over my shoulder and saw him almost upon me. I ran faster and faster until I found myself inside the stable, recognizing my whereabouts only by the combined odours of horses, oats, and fresh hay. I darted along the stalls, stumbling over a saddle and harness in the dark. Up ahead I could see the back door of the shelter standing open, and so I ran toward it, hurrying out the other side where I once more felt the coolness of the evening fan my face.

"Elizabeth!" he called my name again, and I knew then that I could not outrun him, for he was right behind me. He reached out and caught my hand, turned me around, and forced me to face him. Bales of hay stacked just outside the stable stood guard like silent sentinels, and I remember my knees giving way and sinking down upon a mound of fresh hay not yet bound, and seeing Mr. Darcy all about me in the moonlight.

He took my face in his hands. Ferocity shone forth from his eyes as he stared into mine. It seemed as though he peered deep enough to see all the way through my heart, down into my innermost being.

"Elizabeth," he said again, this time in a sort of groan, his breath coming short and fast. "Why?"

And then his mouth sought mine with fervent urgency. I welcomed his kiss with all that was within me. I felt his body hard against mine as he gathered me into his arms, and when he pushed my lips apart, my hands encircled his neck, clasping him to me as a dying woman clings to life. I fell back against the hay, and he fell with me. His lips released mine and then claimed them again and grazed hungrily over my cheek, my ear, and down my neck, his hands moving from my face to my shoulders, my arms and back, until at last, he groaned my name again and broke away.

Our breathing came hard and fast. At first, he said nothing, just continued to stare into my eyes, but then he put his hand to his mouth in that manner I knew so well as a signal of agitation, and shaking his head, he stood up.

"Why?" he cried out. "Why, Elizabeth? Tell me why!" He walked away from me and turned his back, obviously striving for composure. "Not one word. Not one word from you in four weeks!"

I made no utterance. In truth, I doubted that I possessed enough sense to form a complete sentence.

"Could you not take pity on me and at least advise me that you had reached Derbyshire safely?"

I looked down at my hands. I opened my mouth to speak, but as I feared, nothing came forth. Finally, I managed to utter something about Georgiana's correspondence, but that would not satisfy him.

"And so you leave your duties to my sister, do you? Well, thank God, she had some compassion on me."

"I . . . I knew that you and Richard also exchanged letters," I said somewhat lamely.

He whirled around then as though I had struck him. "Richard? You now call Fitzwilliam by his given name, do you?"

I swallowed, feeling guilty but not knowing why. "We are cousins, are we not?"

"And what are we, Elizabeth?" he demanded, once more leaning over me, his face so close that I had to shrink away from him in order to focus my eyes. "Are we not husband and wife, married these many weeks, and yet I am still no more to you than 'Mr. Darcy,' while my cousin, it appears, enjoys a closer familiarity with you than I do?"

"No," I said softly, reaching up and placing my hand upon his cheek. "No, he does not. I am *your* wife . . . William."

With those words, I saw the strain in his face begin to melt, and once again I was in his arms, and he began to kiss me anew, our desire for each other impossible to contain. Again and again, we sought each other's lips. My hands roamed from his face to his thick curls, while I felt his arms encircle my waist, the strength of his hands in the middle of my back as he pulled me closer and closer. We continued no little time in this manner until neither of us could breathe. Parting was necessary, at least for a moment, or we would have collapsed for lack of air. At length, he stood and, taking my hands, pulled me to my feet.

"I have so many questions," he said.

"As do I," I whispered.

"This is not the time, however."

"No, we should return. Are we not obliged to our guests?"

When he sighed and nodded, I ran my hand across my mouth, hoping to erase any signs of our passion. I smoothed my skirt before my husband took my hand and led me back through the stable and to the rear entrance of the great hall. He stopped just outside and turned me toward him. I raised my head to see the full moon illuminate part of his face, the other still in shadow.

"You cannot go in like this, Mrs. Darcy."

"Sir?"

He smiled as he reached up and began to pluck bits of hay from my curls. "If you enter the room like this, I fear our guests will know exactly what we have been up to." He then turned me around and brushed off the hay from the back of my gown, a task to which he seemed to apply himself with great relish and which caused my breathing once again to become somewhat laboured.

Inside, we were met with cheers and more knowing winks and comments than I cared to acknowledge. It did not bother me, though, for I was wildly happy as Mr. Darcy escorted me to the head of the line, and we led the next set and the next and the next.

"You have surprised me many times in the past, sir," I said when we finally sat down, "but never like this. I knew you were proficient in a ballroom, but I had not the slightest idea you were such a fine country dancer."

"Every savage can dance," he said, cocking one eyebrow while his eyes rambled from my lips to my neck and below, "even this one."

Chapter Twelve

It was after two in the morning before the Harvest Ball ended. It might as well have been noon on the day before, for I was not tired in the least. No, I was far too exhilarated by the evening's activities and, in truth, by the sheer presence of Mr. Darcy. During the weeks we had been apart, I had almost forgotten how great an effect his appearance wrought upon my emotions. Tonight, however, I had learned in the most beguiling manner that his company ruled my feelings.

At the close of the ball, Colonel Fitzwilliam and Mr. Darcy escorted Georgiana and me to the foot of the great staircase in the centre of the house, whereupon Mr. Darcy suggested that his sister retire.

"I shall never sleep, Wills," she declared, kissing him on the cheek, "for I am still aglow with excitement. And I am so glad you are home and without a sign of London's illness that you feared would ravage Elizabeth and me."

"I told you Darce was far too fierce for any sickness to conquer him," the colonel reiterated.

"Yes," Mr. Darcy said, looking at me, "it takes something much more powerful to take me down. Now, go along, Georgiana. It is late."

She bade each of us goodnight and then reached out and hugged me, an unusual gesture on her part, but one that I welcomed. I watched her climb the stairs and marvelled at how close we had grown in the last month. She had truly become my sister, and I loved her.

As soon as she was out of our hearing, Mr. Darcy indicated that the colonel and I should join him in the drawing room. Upon entering, Richard immediately asked him about the situation in London and the resolution

152

of the crime.

"Is Georgiana no longer in danger?" I asked.

He said that I was correct, the former stable hand had been discovered, and he was in custody along with Mrs. Younge and Johnny. Mr. Darcy's original suspicions had proven true. During a visit to Mrs. Younge by Johnny and his friend from the stable, they had complained to her of Mr. Darcy's unfair treatment and received a sympathetic ear. Johnny then told her how he overheard Lady Catherine's outburst the day she threatened Mr. Darcy, and all three of them had rejoiced to see this breach in his family. Neither of the men had the capacity to consider using such knowledge for profit, but Mrs. Younge, being clever, had looked upon that news as an ideal manner to exact her revenge.

For the first time, I learned that Mrs. Younge was aunt not only to Johnny, but also to Mr. Wickham, being the younger sister of his mother. She had never forgiven Mr. Darcy for foiling Wickham's plans to marry Georgiana. She wrote the blackmail note, Johnny and the stable hand resigned from Mr. Darcy's service, and the plot was in place.

"I shudder to think what might have happened if you had not overheard the servants' gossip, Elizabeth," Mr. Darcy said.

"Yes, that was a most fortunate occurrence," Colonel Fitzwilliam added.

"I am so relieved that it is over," I said. "What will happen to them now?"

"An extended length of incarceration, I would venture," Richard said. "From what I know of judges, they do not look kindly upon riff-raff who attempt to extort gentlemen. Shall we have a glass of brandy in celebration?"

I took that as my cue to depart and bade them goodnight, but I confess my eyes lingered upon Mr. Darcy in particular. All the way to the doorway I could feel his eyes upon me, and glancing back over my shoulder, I was gratified to see it was not my imagination that produced those feelings.

Above stairs, I found my maid had laid out my best gown and robe in obvious anticipation that I would wish to wear them to bed now that my husband had returned. I blushed at the thought but allowed her to help me undress and let down my hair, brushing out my curls.

"Shall I plait it, ma'am?" she asked.

"No, just leave it loose tonight, Sarah."

After she turned down the bed, I dismissed her and sat waiting before the fireplace, a nervous fluttering in the pit of my stomach.

Would he come? And if he did, what should I anticipate?

I rose and stirred the fire, although there was little need. I wandered to the mirror more than once, pulled my hair up off my neck and posed from side to side, then dropped it to curl about my shoulders. Yes, I mused, wearing my hair down is more flattering. I examined the possible beginnings of a blemish on my forehead, but determined it was nothing more than my imagination.

At last, I picked up a novel and attempted to read, but the author seemed to have written utter nonsense, for I could not follow it. Several long sighs escaped before I could stop them, and I walked back and forth to the inner door separating our chambers more times than I cared to count.

Where could he be? Perhaps he would not come after all. I had just reached the door once again and stood there staring at the handle when I heard a knock. I almost cried aloud, and I did jump! Willing myself to be calm, I took a deep breath and forced myself to wait several moments before I reached for the doorknob. It would not do to appear too eager.

There he stood, dressed in a dark, rich robe, his curls damp from obviously having just bathed, and so handsome I thought I could not bear it. I am sure my eyes must have been as large and round as moonbeams when I recognized the hungry expression about his eyes as they moved up and down my form. I do not know how long we stood thus, but to this day, I can recall exactly how he looked and how every nerve in my body sprang to life with longing and yet fear of the unknown.

"May I come in, Elizabeth?" He smiled ever so slightly in that enticing way of his.

I nodded and swallowed. He took my hand and led me to the fireplace, whereupon he raised my fingers to his lips and kissed them with such tenderness I wanted to weep.

"You are very beautiful with your curls loose and flowing. Did you know that?"

"Yes," I said and then realized to what I had just agreed. "I mean, no. I . . . oh, I do not know what I mean!"

He smiled and, taking my other hand, kissed it as well, all the while gazing upon my flustered countenance. "You spoke correctly the first time. You are well aware that you are pretty and that the effect of your beauty is not wasted on me."

He sighed then, released my hands, and turned away. I felt the loss of his touch acutely, almost painfully. Just in time, I stopped myself from reaching out to him. He walked away, placing the sofa between us.

"And in that robe you are disturbingly hard to resist . . . but I must." Confusion must have shown in my eyes, for he added, "It would be unfair of me to proceed any further this night."

"I do not understand, sir," I managed to say.

"I want you, Elizabeth. That is obvious. And the manner of your greeting tonight gave me hope that you feel the same. Am I correct, or have I misinterpreted your response once again?"

I blushed, not only at the fact that my desire for him was plain to see but also at the memory of how I had taken leave of him in London. "You have not," I murmured.

He swallowed, and I could see how he struggled to maintain his composure. "There are things that exist between us, however, that need to be made straight before we come together as husband and wife — things of great importance, matters I would not lay aside for the mere heat of passion, only to have them separate us once passion is spent. Do you understand me, Elizabeth?"

I nodded slightly.

"It is far too late to begin such a discussion tonight. You can see that it is best for me to return to my chamber and you to remain here, can you not?"

With great reluctance, I nodded again.

"And do you agree?"

"Yes, except — "

"Except?"

"Except there is no lock upon the door between us and I — well, you know of my affliction."

He smiled broadly then, his dimples winking at me in the most exquisite manner. "And have you been affected by such since you have come to Pemberley?"

"Once."

"And did it cause you to climb into my bed?"

I shook my head.

"Then where?"

I blushed anew and cast my eyes upon the carpet. I hated to confess to him the insupportable destination of my last sleepwalking adventure.

"Elizabeth?" He covered the distance between us and joined me at the fireplace. Placing his hand upon my chin, he raised my face to meet his eyes. "Tell me."

"I awoke in the gallery, having slept on the floor . . . beneath your portrait."

The light in his eyes kindled anew, and I saw him fight to keep himself from taking me into his arms, for I knew what I said pleasured him and, in truth, did more than pleasure him. His voice came out deep and hoarse when he spoke.

"You cannot know what that means to me."

Taking my hands, he kissed the palm and inside of each wrist and then, with a determined air, walked toward the door, where he turned one last time that night. "I must bid you good-night, Elizabeth, for although I consider myself a strong man, the hold you have over me tonight leaves me utterly weak."

Once the door closed behind him, I sighed deeply and sank down into a chair, for my knees had grown uncommonly wobbly. Little doubt existed in my mind as to which of us was the weaker. Was I relieved at his forbearance? Yes, somewhat, and yet another part of me wished that he had swept me off my feet and had his way with me, for I could still taste his fervent kisses when he had greeted me with unbridled emotion a few hours earlier. If kissing had thrilled me so, what greater pleasure must lie in store?

I did not walk in my sleep that night. Unfortunately.

I awoke in my own bed, quite alone and fairly late in the morning. I rang for Sarah, and she aided me in putting on a pale yellow morning dress. While she fixed my hair, she mentioned that the servants' coach from London was to arrive that afternoon.

"Do you mean they did not come with Mr. Darcy last night?"

"No, ma'am, Mrs. Reynolds said the master rode on horseback the entire way."

I did not know why that relieved me, but it did. Even though I felt certain there was nothing between Mr. Darcy and Fiona, my own diffidence wanted to hear it from his lips. That thought, naturally, led me to consider that he, in turn, would most likely demand an explanation from me as to why I had left him in such a cold manner in London. What could I say? I knew that he would be angry if I confessed my earlier suspicions, and I was now quite ashamed of them, but on the other hand, he must take some of the blame. If he had been forthright with me and answered my questions about the maid and her child, I never would never have given any credence to servants' gossip nor would I have suffered such anguish all these weeks.

No, I resolved, he was as much to blame as I.

I fled the room as soon as the last pin left Sarah's hand and secured my curls. At that moment, I cared not whether my hair fell down around me. I wanted to see Mr. Darcy. Upon reaching the breakfast room, however, I hesitated, suddenly shy and wary of what I might encounter. I knew there was someone present, for I heard the sounds of a teacup placed on a saucer. I closed my eyes, took a deep breath, and summoned my courage before entering. My fears were groundless; there was no one to greet me except Georgiana.

"Good morning, Elizabeth. Did you sleep well?"

I nodded and seated myself, accepting the cup of coffee placed before me. I strove not to show my impatience or burning curiosity and forced my voice and actions to appear perfectly ordinary.

"And where might the colonel and Mr. Darcy be off to this fine morning?" I asked.

"Wills was holed up with his steward for some time, but he has now joined Richard, and they have gone shooting."

"Shooting," I murmured, as though it was the most natural thing in the world for my husband to do. Well, why not? Why should he do what I *expected* him to do? This was Mr. Darcy, after all. But how could he have greeted me with such passion last evening, danced with obvious abandonment and joy, appeared in my chamber clearly struggling to control his desire, and now avoid my presence? What enabled him to go about the day as if nothing had happened between us, while I was reduced to a puddle of confusion and nerves, wanting nothing more than to see him?

Whatever it might be, it served him well, for neither he nor the colonel made an appearance until late afternoon. By that time, I had knotted my embroidery into a helpless tangle, read the opening page of a new novel at least fifteen times, paced the floor in the drawing room until I feared I would wear out the rug, and practiced the same sonata on the pianoforte repeatedly, missing the exact chords each time until Georgiana suggested that I rest my fingers, although I think she actually wished to rest her ears.

"Shall we not go for a long walk?" I finally suggested, rising from the piano stool. "I have been indoors far too long."

She readily agreed, and after donning our bonnets and buttoning our spencers, we had just walked across the great lawn to the path leading into the woods when we met Richard and William returning with the servants and dogs.

"We are just off for a long walk," Georgiana announced.

"A long walk?" Richard said. "Shall we join them, Darce?"

"Why not?"

They handed their guns to the servants and fell into step with us. Brother and sister soon walked ahead, and the colonel and I were left to converse.

"Were you successful in your hunting?" I asked.

"A little. And have you recovered from last night's festivities?"

"A little." *A very little*, if I was entirely truthful.

We soon came to an opening in the trees where we could see a still somewhat verdant meadow up ahead, rare for that late in the year. Georgiana pointed it out, and she and her brother soon climbed the stile and safely waited on the other side. The colonel indicated that I should go before him, but Mr. Darcy called out for him to come ahead, that he would help me across. He took my hand as I climbed the steps, and I felt a quickening in the pit of my stomach when his hands went up around my waist and he lifted me down. He did not immediately release me, even though I stood safely on the ground. Instead, he gazed into my eyes, his expression unreadable until I saw his eyes travel downward to my lips and then back again.

"Thank you," I murmured.

We continued a short distance behind the others, but it was not long before they had far outdistanced us. Whether it was due to their speed or our lack thereof, I could not say.

We said nothing to each other, but walked in perfect silence as though there were not at least fifty pertinent subjects waiting to be discussed between us. At last, I summoned my courage.

"Did you sleep well?"

He looked away, beginning to twist the ring he wore on his smallest finger. "No. I slept little and not well at all."

"I am sorry."

"You should be."

"Sir?"

"I find that I can no longer sleep with just a wall and an unlocked door between us, Elizabeth. For now, I shall remove myself to another chamber farther away from yours."

I frowned. "Is that truly necessary?"

"For your sake, it is. I no longer trust myself to sleep so close to you, not until we have talked things out. I cannot bear another night of lying awake, every part of my senses listening in hopes that you will somehow find your way into my bed whether conscious or unconscious, and if you do, knowing that I shall be unable to restrain myself."

That familiar quickening now grabbed me, almost causing me to gasp aloud. I looked away, unable to face him. We walked thus for some time, each of us in silence with so much to say hanging heavily between us. We reached the shade of a huge, spreading oak tree before he stopped.

"Elizabeth, I dare not push too hard, tread too quickly, for I recall our leave-taking in London the morning after I first kissed you."

I closed my eyes and sighed deeply, wishing I could take back that awful morning and those terrible accusations I had imagined. "Oh, do not remind me of my actions then. I cannot think of them without abhorrence."

"I want an explanation, Elizabeth. I need to know why you appeared so angry — why you never wrote to me. Had I offended you that greatly the night before?"

"No," I cried out immediately, "a thousand times no, William." I raised my hand to touch his cheek. "Your kiss did not offend me. Believe me, it never will."

I saw the light kindle in his eyes and relief significantly ease the lines of worry on his face, as he drew me to him. Slowly and deliberately, he untied the ribbons to my bonnet and tossed it aside. With one hand upon my waist and the other holding the back of my head, he bent down, his dear face coming ever nearer and his mouth almost upon mine.

"Wills," Georgiana interrupted us. "Clouds are gathering, and it looks like rain. Richard says we must return. Are you coming with us?"

Immediately, we both drew apart and I looked away as William attempted to answer her. The colonel, however — bless his heart! — quickly said, "Come, Sprout. Do you not see that we are intruding?"

"Oh, I am sorry!"

We both said, "No, no, it is nothing," or something similarly inane as they passed us, heading back toward the house.

"I will escort Georgiana home, Darcy," the colonel said, trying his best not to laugh. "Carry on."

We watched their retreat until they could no longer be seen. Georgiana turned around to look at us at least once while Colonel Fitzwilliam took her by the shoulders and turned her back toward their goal.

"Should we return with them?" I asked, noting the dark clouds gathering.

Mr. Darcy shook his head. "First, we must talk, and surely this is far enough away to afford us privacy." He took my hands in his, but I pulled away and took several steps from him.

"If we are truly to talk, William, then you must stand there and I over here, for I cannot think clearly when you are so near and . . . especially when you touch me."

He smiled and nodded. "Handsome and wise."

I blushed and felt my heart begin to beat erratically once again. "And you must not say things like that."

"Like what?"

"That I am handsome."

"Would you have me lie?" He cut his eyes at me in a way that threatened to reduce me to a helpless muddle.

"No, of course not. But you must not look at me in that manner, either."

"Shall I turn my back?"

"Perhaps." I acknowledged silently that from either side, his presence was handsome enough to tempt me. "Oh, I cannot set it right. I shall just not look at you!"

Neither of us said anything for a few moments, and even though I did not face him, I could feel his eyes upon me, almost as caressing as his hands. I wondered how I would ever keep my wits about me when his mere presence filled me with such yearning.

I began walking farther afield, but he would not let me go alone. "Are we truly to go for a long walk?" he asked.

"I think it is best to walk while we talk." How utterly stupid! I thought. Now I was speaking in rhymes. I would soon be reduced to spouting gibberish!

We had reached the crest of a small hill by that time. It overlooked a tenant farmer's house below, and I could see a woman hurriedly collecting the wash she had set out, the wind whipping the sheets about. A young boy carried small stacks of firewood into the cottage, and a babe toddled in and out the doorway. Old, petrified tree stumps remained directly at the spot where we stood, and I sat down to rest upon one of them. Mr. Darcy broke off a dried reed and swished it back and forth between the remaining stalks, an action he appeared to engage in with absence of mind.

"Shall you tell me now, Elizabeth, why you never wrote since we have been apart? Am I correct to assume it has something to do with the manner of your leave-taking from London?"

I looked away. My pulse began to race. How could I confess my hateful suspicions? There was no escape, I knew. I took a deep breath.

"I did not write because I knew not how to say what I must — and because I knew that it would cause you distress. Before I walked downstairs that last morning, Fiona had just told me she was not to travel with us — that she was to remain in Town with you and go to Pemberley when you did. This surprised me and, in truth, made me angry."

"But why — "

I raised my hand to silence him. "Let me continue, for if I do not say it all, I never shall. I thought — I feared the servants' gossip might possibly be true, that you loved her, that she was your mistress, and that Willie . . . might be your child."

He was deadly silent, the only sound his sharp intake of breath.

"The night before when you kissed me, I had convinced myself I was wrong, that I never should have listened to such ugly talk, but when you kept her with you, all those old doubts swept over me, and I allowed jealousy to cloud my thinking. I misjudged you as unworthy and Fiona along with you. I know now I was wrong, completely wrong. I learned that during the weeks we were apart. I now strongly suspect that Mr. Wickham is responsible for the birth of Willie, but my return to sanity does nothing to justify my prior thoughts."

When I ceased to speak and he said nothing, I ventured a look in his direction. His face was dark, and his chest moved visibly, a clear indication of how I had wounded him. When he turned to meet my gaze, I almost gasped aloud to see the depth of anger in his eyes.

"You truly thought that, Elizabeth?" His voice sounded hard as stone. "You had no greater understanding of my character than to think me capable of such despicable behaviour?"

I barely nodded. "I did not wish to do so, sir. In truth, I wonder that I ever believed it in my heart, but at the time I was angry, confused, and unable to see past the fact that you were sending me off to Derbyshire while keeping Fiona in Town with you."

"I kept her there to help me! Fiona knew which of the menservants had made overtures to her. She was necessary to help solve the case. I was ready to consider using her as bait in order to lure them out of their miserable holes, if necessary. I would have done anything to protect Georgiana."

"I can see that now, and I acknowledge that my suspicions were groundless, but you must remember that when I asked, you refused to tell me the name of Willie's father. You said it was 'your responsibility.' Why did you not reveal that it was Mr. Wickham? What possible reason could you have had not to inform me?"

"Wickham is your brother by marriage. I did not wish to paint him in a worse light. I knew you regretted the necessity for your sister's union with him, and I hoped to spare you any greater pain on her behalf. I see that I was wrong to have done so."

"You were wrong. You should have answered my question, William. You should — oh, what is the use of discussing it? What is done is done, and now we must bear the consequences."

"I see." His speech was clipped and abrupt. "We should return to the house."

He began to walk with such speed that I almost had to run to keep up with his long legs. He made no further conversation. I could see I had injured him with a wound so deep I feared it might not heal. Oh, why could I not have invented some silly story to account for my prior behaviour? Why had I been so brutally honest? I knew the answer full well. I wished with all my heart for this marriage to become one of mutual trust, and if it were to be, we could not proceed on a bed of lies. We had to tell each other the truth from that day forward.

The storm broke long before we reached the house, soaking us through. Mr. Darcy removed his greatcoat and without touching me, placed it about my shoulders. He did not take my hand or assist me in slogging through the mud. The only time he offered his assistance occurred at the stile when he briefly took my hand as I climbed over it. There were no hands about my waist or long looks in my eyes.

It seemed that not only had the storm broken, but our brief spell of happiness as well.

A hot bath helped me recover physically from the long walk in the rain. Emotionally, I remained devastated. My mind replayed statements I had made and then heard the angry words Mr. Darcy had spoken, back and forth, over and over. I soaked for no little time, oblivious to the aroma of the salts added to the steaming water.

Afterwards, Sarah dried my hair before the fire, and I lay down upon the bed while she tidied the room and took the remains of my wet clothing and towels below stairs to the laundry. When she returned, I asked that she have a tray sent up with supper and that she inform Mr. Darcy I would not join the family that evening.

Less than a quarter-hour later, a forceful knock at the door caused me to sit up. When I called out to enter, my husband strode into my chamber, his curls still damp from his own bath.

"Are you ill?" he asked immediately.

I shook my head, suddenly aware that he was fully dressed while I wore only my robe.

"Then why will you not leave your chamber?"

"I — I thought it best."

"Best? In what way?"

"Perhaps we have seen enough of each other for today, sir."

He pressed his lips together and looked away, obviously still angry. "Very well, if that is your wish." He stalked out of the room, closing the door behind him.

Oh, William, it is not my wish, I wanted to cry aloud! Why had I not spoken? Why did his presence reduce me to a tongue-tied simpleton? I picked up a pillow, threw it at the door, and then buried my face in another, giving way to tears.

Sometime later when Sarah brought up my tray, I told her to take it away, that I was not hungry. She frowned, and I knew she could see the tearstains on my face, but I had not the means to hide them. As she turned to leave, I heard another sound in the hall, and hoping it was Mr. Darcy,

I hastily wiped my eyes and rose from the bed. It was not. Instead, Fiona entered the room and curtseyed before me.

"Begging your pardon, Mistress, I just wanted you to know that I have arrived."

"Come in. Was your journey uneventful?"

"Yes, ma'am, except my Willie got sick from the jostling of the coach. He's never ridden in one before."

"I hope his illness will be of short duration."

"Oh, yes, ma'am. He's better now that we're here. If it's agreeable to you, ma'am, I'll be up to serve you in the morning. The master said I might be excused for tonight to get Willie settled and all."

So she has already seen the master, I thought. "Of course. Tomorrow will be fine."

She thanked me but did not move to vacate the room, and so I added, "Is there anything else?"

She smiled. "Just that it's grand to see you again, ma'am, and to be back here at Pemberley."

I nodded and with another curtsey, she left my chamber. Why had I not been more welcoming? The girl had done nothing to harm me, and yet I still resented her, resented that she had come between my husband and me. She had done nothing of the sort, of course, but it was much easier to be angry with her than with myself. I had made a mess of things, and Mr. Darcy had done precious little to help me out of it. I wondered if we would ever sort it all out.

Chapter Thirteen

That night I could not sleep. I tossed to and fro until my sheets were in a hopeless tangle. Finally, I arose and poked at the fire enough to cause it to blaze up a little. The room having grown cold, I put on my robe and slippers, sat before the fire and pondered upon what I should do. My first impulse was to flee.

Yes, I would escape to Longbourn, to Jane's welcoming arms and understanding heart. I would even endure Mamá's endless harangues just to be once again where I was loved, for home was a place where they would take me in, no matter the reason. Not like Pemberley where the master of the house now looked upon me with evident distaste. How could I endure living there under such circumstances? For now, how would I endure the night, wondering how much Mr. Darcy regretted having married me?

The small clock on the mantel chimed three times. I sighed again and wondered what I should do. And then my anger began anew. I was not the only one at fault. Mr. Darcy could have prevented my fears and distrust if he had been forthright, if he, in turn, had trusted me with the truth. I became so angry I began to pace, and not long after that I decided to confront him even though it was but three o'clock in the morning.

Very quietly, I tapped at the door separating us, and when I heard no answer from within, I slowly turned the knob and peered inside. The room lay in total darkness. Not even the remains of a fire existed in the fireplace. I ventured in and felt my way to his bed. When I bumped into the bedpost, I called out his name but heard no answer. I ran my hands along the bed and could tell that it was made up, that he was not there. He had decided to sleep elsewhere after all. Was it because of his ill temper, or might he still consider me a temptation? I could not rest until I knew the answer.

I returned to my room, and after lighting a candle, I walked out into the great hall. I knew the location of Georgiana's chamber and the colonel's, as well. That left only the two suites that had belonged to Mr. Darcy's parents and one William had used years before on the floor.

I padded along the carpet close to the south end of the hall where I knew the prior master suites were placed. I tapped lightly at the door that Mrs. Reynolds had told me belonged to Mr. Darcy's father and that William himself had used since becoming master. When I did not hear an answer, I quietly turned the knob and lifted the candle, but to my dismay, I found it empty.

I then proceeded to look in Mrs. Darcy's former room, and not finding my husband there either, I considered giving over and returning to my own bed, deciding he had possibly removed himself to another wing.

He must want to get as far away from me as possible, I thought.

The only room remaining on the hall was one William had used as a young man, long before becoming master of Pemberley. It was situated at the farthest end of the hall, and Mrs. Reynolds had told me it was rarely even used as a guest room, as it still contained numerous items William had saved from childhood and others he had brought home from his days at Cambridge. I knew that I would not rest if I did not check it too, so I softly pushed open the great door, and in the dim candlelight, I caught my breath when I saw him asleep in his old bed.

Quietly closing the door behind me, I walked inside and cleared my throat. It proved a vain attempt, for he did not awaken. I held the candle closer. He slept soundly, his beautiful, dark curls tousled, his face softened by slumber with neither sign of anger nor anguish about it. My heart melted at the sight.

Upon impulse, I placed the candle on the small table beside the bed, blew it out, and stood there chewing my lip. I shivered in the coolness of the night, took a deep breath . . . and crawled into his bed. He roused slightly and turned over. Now thoroughly chilled from my walk in the hall, I cuddled up to his back and placed my arms around him, hugging his body close to me to feel its familiar warmth. If I had to leave tomorrow, I would at least have the memory of this night.

It was not long before I fell into deep slumber.

I awoke to the sensation of a finger running lightly along my cheek and then across my bottom lip. Slowly, I opened my eyes, shocked at the sight of Mr. Darcy's face so close to mine. Momentarily, I forgot how I had come to lie in his bed, but then the knowledge of my daring act flooded my consciousness.

"Good morning, Elizabeth," he said.

"Good morning," I managed to murmur.

"Do you know where you are?"

I nodded.

He raised an eyebrow.

"It seems that you have been stricken by your affliction, forcing you into my bed once again."

Slowly, I shook my head back and forth.

He frowned and raised himself up on one elbow. "Then how — "

"I came willingly," I said softly.

His smile turned somewhat tenuous. "Truly? But why?"

"I needed to be with you one last time."

"Last time? Of what are you speaking?"

A heavy sigh escaped before I could suppress it. Then summoning my courage, I spoke quickly. I did not even pause to take a breath until I ran out of air. "I know, sir, that my previous mistrust of you has destroyed your faith in me, and you told me some time ago that once your good opinion is lost, it is lost forever so, yes, I think it best that I leave Pemberley today, for I cannot see how we are to ever make a marriage out of this jumble."

"Well, we certainly cannot if you are to run off at the first sign of trouble." He lay back on the pillow.

"First sign?" I was incredulous at his understatement. "Sir, we have been in trouble since the beginning."

"How do you mean?"

"Our marriage began as nothing more than a practical arrangement. Distrust on both our parts has been rampant."

He sat up once again and looked directly at me. "I cannot answer for your feelings, Elizabeth, but you speak in error as to mine. I have never distrusted you. Not ever."

"Then why have you not confided in me? Why have you avoided telling me the truth whenever I have asked certain questions?"

"I take offense at that!" Anger resounded in his voice. "I abhor deceit and have never lied to you."

"You have not lied, but you have refused to answer my questions."

"Only when I deemed it best."

"Well, it is not best," I said with as much force as possible. "Have you ever slightly considered, sir, that you might not always know what is best for others?"

For some reason he seemed to relax then and spoke almost lazily, while that tantalizing smile of his played about his mouth, "Hmm . . . you think that, do you? And so your solution is to leave. Well, just where do you propose to go?"

"To Longbourn. And you may rest assured I shall release you from your obligation."

"Release me? And may I ask how you presume to do that?"

"I do not know. Surely, your barrister can work out the legalities whereby you may be free to marry again."

He laid his head back upon the pillow and once again began to run his finger along my cheek and across my lips. "And if I do not wish to be free?"

"But you must. You were angry and hurt by my distrust. I saw it in your eyes, William, and I heard it from your lips."

"True. But my anger and your distrust can be overcome."

I found it most difficult to think clearly when he persisted in caressing my lips, and I became aware that we lay very close together; in fact, we were practically lying in each other's arms.

"How?" I managed to whisper.

"Well, you have made a good beginning by coming to me. But if you run off now, I cannot see how that will help sort things out at all. Much better to stay and face the music."

"I am afraid, sir, that I do not know the song."

"Oh, but I do, my dear. I know it well."

He began to kiss me slowly, deliberately, caressing my lips with his in such a delightfully tender manner that I felt my whole body catch fire. I longed for more, and when he persisted in only teasing me with the barest of strokes, my arms tightened around his neck and pulled him down, down, until his lips parted and became truly mine to possess.

After a few moments, he pulled away, breathing heavily. "You are irresistible in the morning. Did you know that? Completely irresistible."

He began to kiss me again, our passion growing with each touch. When I thought I would not — could not — deny him any part of myself, he released me and sat up in bed, rubbed his hand against his mouth, and shook his head.

"This will not do, Elizabeth. It will not do."

I did not know what to think or say. "Shall I leave, sir?"

He turned and looked at me over his shoulder, cutting his eyes at me in the most intoxicating manner. Early morning sleepiness still softened his expression. His nightshirt stood open at the neck, revealing the beginnings of his beautiful chest. "No, you shall not leave. Not now, not ever. You shall stay at Pemberley, and you shall stay in my bed until we have talked this out."

"That might take some time."

"I have nothing more important in my life, Elizabeth. Do you?"

I shook my head, so thrilled that he did not want to banish me that I could hardly think straight. We then began to discuss our differences, a list of which would exhaust the reader, but which we made a valiant attempt to assail. He bade me tell him every reason I had distrusted him and dared to believe the ugly tale about Fiona. For his part, I must admit that he listened well and did not interrupt me even when it was evident by the fire in his eyes that he would have preferred to stifle me. When I finished, I sat quietly, waiting for the onslaught of his temper.

Instead, he asked a simple question. "And do you now admit you were in the wrong?"

"Utterly and completely. And will you admit you should have been more direct and forthcoming in answer to my questions?"

"I will. And so this part of our misunderstanding is now behind us, am I correct? You do believe that there is nothing between your maid and myself."

"Yes," I replied.

"Then we must seal it with a kiss and never speak of it again. Agreed?"

I am sure my eyes widened at his suggestion, but I was quick to nod in agreement. I sat up as he took my hands and pulled me to him. His lips closed upon mine, and I can only say that he kissed me quite thoroughly, so much so, that when he released me, I felt both the room and bed begin to spin. He steadied me with his hands and told me to lean against the headboard, while he reclined against the foot.

"For we must now move on to the next item on your agenda," he said firmly.

I wondered how he could kiss me with such abandon and then move right on to thinking sensibly, when my head was in such a muddle, but I strove mightily to think clearly and determined that the next words I spoke would be sensible.

"Sir, I must say this, for it is another example of how you keep things from me, although on the other hand, I must admit it is the most generous thing you could ever do, so I suppose I am not actually complaining, and yet I am in a way because you should have told me so that I would have known and afforded you the appreciation that you deserve most — "

"Elizabeth, you confuse me."

"I am somewhat confused, myself. I shall begin anew by thanking you for your kindness to my poor sister, Lydia. Ever since I have known it, I have been most anxious to acknowledge to you how grateful I feel. Were it known to the rest of my family, I should not have merely my own gratitude to express."

I looked up to see how he met my declaration and noted the look of surprise on his face, and then a forbidding frown settled about his eyes. "I am sorry, exceedingly sorry, that you have ever been informed of what may, in a mistaken light, have given you uneasiness. I did not think Mrs. Gardiner was so little to be trusted."

"You must not blame my aunt, for it was Richard — Colonel Fitzwilliam — who revealed it to me and, of course, I could not rest until I knew the particulars. Let me thank you again in the name of my family for that generous compassion which induced you to take so much trouble and bear so many mortifications for the sake of discovering them."

"If you *will* thank me, let it be for yourself alone. Your family owes me nothing. Much as I respect them, I thought only of you."

Not trusting myself to look directly at him, I stared at the rumpled sheets and counterpane, thrilled at his words. He had done it all for me — and me alone.

"But Fitzwilliam!" he said, angry disbelief in his voice. "I cannot believe he told you."

"Had you sworn him to secrecy in the matter?"

"I had not. I did not think it necessary, for at the time of its occurrence, I did not envision him ever crossing your path again. And here, I have thrown you together daily these past weeks. What else has my cousin revealed about me?"

"I can think of nothing other than sharing bits of your correspondence about that shabby business in London." When he made no further comment, I took a deep breath and made a bold suggestion. "Now that this mystery is out in the open, shall we seal it with a kiss as well?"

He smiled, his eyes darkening. "Agreed."

I scrambled into his arms before he could change his mind, and this time I kissed him with an utter lack of restraint until I could feel the muscles in his arms begin to quiver. When I drew back slightly, his voice came out quite roughly, as did his breathing. "And . . . the next item . . . might be?"

I drew back, but I did not retreat to my former place at the head of the bed. Slowly, we removed our hands from each other's arms, and I began to play with the pleat in my gown, rubbing it back and forth between my fingers to keep my hands occupied and thus refrain from touching him.

"Have you kept your promise to me about Mr. Bingley and Jane? From my sister's correspondence, it does not appear that you have."

He frowned, grabbed a pillow and punched it with such force that I expected to see feathers fly, before placing it at his back. "I have not."

"And why not, may I ask? It was agreed upon before our marriage."

"That is correct, but at present I have serious doubts as to the wisdom of such action."

I straightened, pulling my shoulders back, for I could feel that familiar ire rising within me. In doing so, my gown slipped off one shoulder, but I ignored it. Why should he insist on being stubborn about this? What possible reason could he have? I struggled to keep my voice even. "Then you must tell me why. You certainly owe me that much, Mr. Darcy."

He looked directly at me. "We are back to *Mr. Darcy*, are we? You sit in my bed clad only in your gown, which is falling down in the most fetching manner, and yet address me as Mr. Darcy." I immediately replaced the errant part of my gown, but he reached over and aided it in exposing my bare shoulder once more. "I like it better like that," he said, his voice a low growl.

"Sir, you avoid the subject."

He smiled, which almost made me forget the subject myself.

"Very well. I have not spoken to Bingley because I fail to see in him what you do. You profess that he is in love with Miss Bennet and that her feelings are the same. I will not argue with you as to her state of mind. When in her presence, I saw no apparent proclivity in her manner toward Bingley, but I shall accept the fact you possess a thorough knowledge of your sister's wishes, and I bow to your thinking in that regard. However, I now wonder whether Bingley is truly in love with Miss Bennet."

"How can you doubt it?" I demanded. "At Hertfordshire, he showed every inclination of a man besotted. Why, the entire county talked of it! We all expected an announcement of their betrothal by last Christmas until you and his sisters persuaded him otherwise and whisked him off to Town."

"And just exactly how did you come by that intelligence? Who told you that Miss Bingley and Mrs. Hurst and I spoke of such things with him? I have wondered that ever since you accused me thus in the vicar's parsonage last April."

"Richard told me that very afternoon before you . . . visited me."

"Fitzwilliam again? What is he now, an old woman? I never knew him to have such a loose tongue! Or do you possess a particular talent in extracting information from him?"

I glared at him and then saw the smile playing about his mouth. "Oh, no, William! You will not distract me by changing the subject and ridiculing your cousin, no matter how clever you are. I want an answer. How can you not believe that Mr. Bingley was unduly influenced by you and that your interference has kept him from declaring himself to Jane?"

"That is precisely why I have reservations."

"I do not understand."

"If Bingley truly loved your sister enough to marry her, neither his sisters nor I could have pressed him into rethinking his decision."

"But he thinks very highly of you. It is evident he looks to you for guidance, and you have caused him to doubt her preference for him."

"Elizabeth, if I loved a woman as you think Bingley loves Miss Bennet, *nothing* could keep me from her, neither her impertinent remarks, nor her teasing manner, nor accusations of defects in my character — not even her reluctance to accept my invitation to dance would deter me."

I realized we no longer spoke of Mr. Bingley and Jane. He lifted my chin, forcing me to meet his gaze. "Not even when I proposed and she refused me, declaring that I acted in an ungentlemanlike manner and that I was the last man she would ever marry . . . not even that would keep me from pursuing her, from doing everything in my power to make her mine."

"Pray," I pleaded, attempting to turn my face from his, "do not remind me of what I said then, of how terribly I abused you."

"What did you say of me that I did not deserve? Though your accusations were ill founded and formed on mistaken premises, my behaviour to you at the time merited the severest reproof. It was unpardonable. My conduct, my manners, my expressions during the whole of it is now, and has been many months, inexpressibly painful to me, though it was some time, I confess, before I was reasonable enough to allow their justice."

"I had not the smallest idea of my words being taken in such a way."

"I can well believe it. I have been a selfish being all my life. As a child, I was given good principles but left to follow them in pride and conceit. Such I was from eight to eight and twenty, and such I would remain except for brief episodes, episodes that will only reoccur and change me into a more worthwhile person with your influence, dearest, loveliest Elizabeth!"

Oh, I felt all the anger I ever directed toward him dissolve at the words coming from his mouth and the look in his eyes. If I had taken the time to glance down, I would not have been at all surprised to find myself reduced to nothing less than a pool of mush.

"We both have many questions one for the other," he said. "That we have acknowledged, but truly, there is only one that matters. At Hunsford cottage last Easter, I told you that I greatly admired and loved you. I still do."

My heart stood still. I swear that it refused to beat!

"I tried to conquer my desire for you — I tried most desperately — but it was a hopeless case," he said. "At Longbourn in October, you asked me why I wanted to marry you, and I refused to tell you, but I will tell you now. The sole reason is that I love you more than life itself. I loved you more on the day of my second proposal than I did at Kent. I love you more today than I did yesterday, and I know without a doubt that I shall love you even more tomorrow. I will love you, Elizabeth, until I no longer draw breath, and that is God's truth."

I reached up and took his face in my hands. Slowly I pulled his mouth toward mine, while I felt his hands go around my waist, gathering me into his arms. Our lips touched, and that exquisite taste of heaven washed over me once again, drawing me in with its enticing flavour, setting every nerve within me on fire. His essence captivated me, and I welcomed it, surrendering to the joy of being loved.

Sometime later, he released my mouth and simply held me in his arms. With his hand, he cradled my head against his strong shoulder, binding me to him in the closest of embraces.

"You must answer this question, though," he said.

"Oh, William, no more questions. I am spent."

He cleared his throat. "I believe I am the one who answered the most questions. You have escaped with naught but one."

"Very well, but you are merciless."

He raised me so that he could look into my eyes. "May I dare to hope you are beginning to love me . . . perhaps just a little?"

I could not help myself. I rolled my eyes. "A little? How can you doubt it? Have I not behaved like a shameless hussy each time you kissed me? I even crawled into your bed this very night!"

He smiled. "Such description is false, Elizabeth. After all, we are married. I would say you have responded like a tender-hearted wife who takes pity on her drowning husband."

"Ah, William, you mistake my motives. I have never pitied you, not even once."

"Then will you say the words?"

I gazed into his eyes, willing myself not to weep. "I love you, William, from this day forward, for better or worse, for richer or poorer, in sickness and in health. I will love, cherish — and try to obey you — till death us do part, according to God's holy ordinance, and thereto I give thee my troth."

My vision blurred as tears filled my eyes. Laying my head against his chest, I slipped my arms around his waist. His heart beat rapidly in my ear, and his breathing grew laboured. His voice was deep and ragged when he spoke. "This time I believe you."

"This time I spoke the truth." I raised my face to his and sought his lips. What began as a gentle caress soon deepened into a long, intoxicating kiss that threatened to blaze into a conflagration as he stroked my back, holding me closer and closer. It took a huge clap of thunder to bring us to our senses. We both drew apart, looking at the windows as if to ask what had happened. Surely, God in heaven must have laughed to see such surprise on the faces of two of his silliest creatures.

"More rain," William said, pulling me back against his chest. "Did not you once say that you loved to be in bed when it rains?"

"I believe I said I love to sleep when it is raining."

"Hmm, well, I do not anticipate that you will sleep any time soon."

I trembled at the thought of what he suggested, but instead of proceeding to kiss me, he said, "Tell me, when did you first love me?"

I laughed. "Oh, no, William, no more questions!"

"Tell me the answer. When did you first love me?"

"I hardly know. It has come on so gradually, that I do not know when it began. I was in the middle before I knew that I had begun."

"I must know this, Elizabeth, and you must give me a truthful answer. Did you fall in love with me *after* Fitzwilliam told you of my actions toward Wickham and your sister?"

I could hear the emotion in his voice, and I knew I must not tease him anymore. I shook my head. "No. I cannot fix on the hour, or the spot, or the look, or the words which laid the foundation, but I was already in love with you long before I heard his revelation."

He pulled me to him once again and held me tightly, so tightly I could hear our hearts beat as one. "You know not how much that means to me," he said, his voice almost hoarse.

"But why? What is so important about *when* I began loving you?"

"I would not have you love me out of gratitude."

So that was why he had not told me and why he had sworn the Gardiners to secrecy. He would not use that example of his fine character to cause me to marry him. He would rather force me into an arranged marriage and endure my anger and hostility for months on end — possibly forever— without any certainty I would ever become an agreeable wife.

Oh William, I thought, do you never do things the easy way?

And then I discovered that at least one time he did just that, for it was exceedingly easy for him to teach me how a husband and wife please each other. I decided he was correct in his first statement after all. I loved being in bed when it rained . . . as long as he was there, too.

By the time we awoke the second time, the storm had passed, and the sun now blazed far up in the heavens. I sat up, wondering at the hour, but the only clock in the room had not been set for some time since no one had occupied the chamber for several months. William stirred, and opening his eyes, he reached for me and pulled me back into his arms.

"Where are you going, my pretty wife?" He caressed my cheek with the back of his hand.

"Wherever you wish, my good sir." I smiled and stroked the curls back from his forehead.

"Hmm, I can think of some interesting places."

"Mr. Darcy!" I pretended to be shocked.

"No, no, my dearest, you can no longer play the innocent with me, for I know the truth about you." He began to nuzzle my neck, and I could not suppress my giggles.

Just then, we heard a noise out in the great hall. "What was that?" I said.

He looked up briefly and shrugged. "Probably one of the servants lighting the candles."

"William, there is no need for candles. Look! The sun is far above the house. It must be quite late in the day."

He sat up then, looked around, and acknowledged I was probably correct.

"It appears to be mid-afternoon," he said.

"Everyone must have risen hours ago. Should not we do the same?"

He sighed as he smiled at me and then reached down and kissed me. "Yes, but it does seem a shame to leave the room where I have known the greatest happiness of my life."

My heart skipped a beat to hear those words, to know that I was the cause of the great joy that shone forth from his eyes. "Oh, William, I feel the same."

"Do you, my darling? Have I made you happy? Truly happy?"

"How can you doubt it?" I kissed him in return, and we were soon swept away by a new wave of passion when an even louder noise from outside the door interrupted us.

"Blast!" He raised his head. "I must see to this as much as I hate to leave you."

"Wait! If you open the door, whoever is there will see that I am here in your room."

176

He smiled. "Well, it is not as though you should not be, my dear. You are my wife." He rose from the bed and grabbed his robe.

"Pray, let me put on my robe, first."

"Very well." He handed me the garment and waited while I slipped it on.

"William, does it show?"

"Does what show?"

"You know . . . what we were . . . well, you know."

He struggled in earnest not to laugh openly. "Only if I cannot cease smiling." He reached over and kissed the tip of my nose. "Do not worry, sweetest wife, it is not written on your forehead. Our secret is concealed."

Still, I quickly climbed out of the bed, wrapped my robe securely about me, and tried to smooth my wayward curls before he opened the door. Attempting the most serene and dignified expression that I could muster, I stood beside the bed. William opened the door to find in the hall not only his valet, Fiona and Sarah along with Mrs. Reynolds, but Colonel Fitzwilliam and Georgiana, as well. They were all in earnest conversation, the servants out of breath, seemingly having hurried down the hall.

"Wills!" Georgiana cried when he opened the door. She immediately ran to him and embraced him. "We thought something had happened to you. And where is Elizabeth? She is not in her room, and no one has seen her. Richard has combed the grounds, and he could not find her or you. I am afraid something has hap — " And then she saw me. "Oh, there she is! Why, did you and Elizabeth sleep in your old chamber last night?"

"Georgiana," Colonel Fitzwilliam quickly moved to her side and took her arm. "Come with me."

"Were you showing Elizabeth some of your things from Cambridge?"

"Georgiana," Richard said again.

"Richard, what is it?"

"Come along," he said forcefully, "now!"

"But why?"

"Never you mind." He raised his eyebrows at William, and I could see the nerve in his cheek quivering as he struggled not to laugh. Taking Georgiana by the arm, he prodded her down the hall to the stairs and then below. The servants had all immediately scattered, averting their faces as they were well trained to do. William turned to me, and I could see his efforts to repress his feelings reflected on his face.

I sighed and walked past him through the door that he held open.

"So much for concealment," I said under my breath.

We both stole a glance at each other from the corner of our eyes, and although our shoulders shook as we walked down that long hall to our separate chambers, I am proud to say we did maintain some manner of dignity and successfully refrained from bursting out in laughter until we were safely hid behind closed doors.

Chapter Fourteen

hat evening at dinner, Colonel Fitzwilliam announced he would leave the next morning to return to his regiment in Town. His words were met with disappointment and regret from all of us, especially Georgiana. She pleaded with him to stay until her brother reminded her that their cousin did have responsibilities other than her entertainment.

She sighed and pouted. "I have grown accustomed to your being here all the time, Richard. Shall you not resign your commission and buy a house in Derbyshire?"

"A very inviting suggestion, Sprout, but hardly practical."

"You will return and spend Christmas with us, will you not?" I asked.

"Thank you, Elizabeth. I should love to, but as the holiday is but a few weeks from now, I think not. My duties will require my continued presence, I am sure, since I have taken such an extended leave."

"But no one works at Christmas. Surely, you can slip away," my sister said.

"Georgiana," William said, "Fitz knows what he can and cannot do."

She said nothing more for a while, but I could see her spirits turn melancholy. William surprised me with his next statement, although it was anything but unwelcome.

"I suggest we invite Mrs. Bennet and Elizabeth's sisters to come from Longbourn and join us for Christmas, as well as the Gardiners."

My face lit up at the idea of seeing my family once again. "Oh, William, that is generous of you!"

"I shall write to them this evening," he said. "And what say you to extending the invitation to Mr. Bingley?"

I would have kissed him then and there if we had been alone! At last, he would make good on his promise to correct things between Jane and Mr. Bingley. I nodded vigorously, and our eyes locked in loving accord.

"I suppose that means you will invite his sisters, as well," Georgiana said somewhat half-heartedly.

William frowned, and I struggled not to sigh, but I rose to the occasion and summoned every gracious bone in my body. "Of course, we should ask them, should we not?"

"If you think best, my dear," William said somewhat grimly.

"Where shall you spend Christmas Eve, Richard?" Georgiana asked.

"Most likely with my parents unless they invite Lady Catherine to visit them. If she is there, then I should prefer the company of my junior officers on post. Surely we lonely fellows can produce more holiday cheer among ourselves than I would experience at Eden Park."

We all smiled in agreement although Georgiana's smile did not last. "I cannot bear the thought of your being alone at such a festive time of year."

"Then you must provide me with a happy memory to recall when I am far away. Might you favour me with yuletide selections on the pianoforte after dinner?"

She readily agreed, and we spent a portion of the evening listening to her play. Mr. Darcy prevailed upon me to join her in a duet, and we sang several old tunes. At the end of our pleasant interlude, William walked his sister to the stairs after she bade us good-night, leaving Colonel Fitzwilliam and me alone in the music room. I took advantage of our privacy to speak to him.

"Will you call again at Pemberley before leaving for your post abroad?"

The look on his face was pensive. "I am not sure exactly when I shall leave, but I hope to visit again."

"Perhaps you might come for Georgiana's birthday in January. Have you told her of your plans to leave England?"

"No, I shall remain silent in that regard as long as possible, for I cannot bear to see her unhappy, although I know she will forget all about me before long. She is young and has so much ahead of her."

"She does, but I cannot believe she will forget you easily."

I watched him walk to the mantel and stare at the flames. Then he reached in his pocket and drew forth a miniature. Running his thumb back and forth over the tiny portrait, his normally superb posture weakened as his shoulders fell into a slump. I drew nearer and observed that it was Georgiana's likeness that he caressed.

"Forgive my intrusion, but I cannot help but feel it is because of Georgiana that you make plans to depart these shores. Am I wrong?"

He turned, and I was surprised at the pain I saw reflected in his eyes. "I wish that you were, Elizabeth."

"But why? I know I should not ask, but is it possible you are in love with Georgiana?"

He replaced the portrait in his pocket and turned his face away, but not before I saw the truth wash over his face. "If I am, it is my cross to bear and mine alone."

"Can you not tell her?"

He shook his head. "She is still a child. I am like an older brother to her — a comfortable, old friend she has loved since childhood. No, I cannot inflict my burden upon her. 'Tis better to leave things as they are and for me to remove myself from her life."

"I do not agree," I said forcefully.

"To what do you not agree?" Mr. Darcy said, entering the room just then.

"Whether Mrs. Hurst is more tiresome than Miss Bingley," Richard said smoothly but with a knowing look in my direction. I marvelled at how well he concealed his strong emotion. It was evident he did not wish to share our conversation with his cousin.

Mr. Darcy laughed and said he thought it probably a draw. "Sometimes I wonder whether Charles Bingley is truly their brother. Perhaps he is a foundling, for surely he is their complete opposite in manner and disposition."

"Siblings are not always alike," I said. "Some of my sisters are nothing akin to each other except in name."

"Quite right, my dear." He sat in the chair closest to me. "And you are completely different from all of them — the very best of the lot, I declare. Would not you agree, Fitzwilliam?"

"Absolutely. You have won the prize, Darce. There can be no doubt. And now I shall retire and leave the two of you, as I feel certain my absence will not be missed."

I blushed, remembering how we had exposed our affection more than once in front of the colonel since my husband had returned to Pemberley.

William did nothing more than raise an eyebrow at him, however, as we bade him good-night.

After he had left the room, William said, "Come here, my love."

I rose, took a step toward him and laughed when he pulled me down onto his lap and began to kiss my neck.

"William! What if the servants come in?"

"They will leave immediately. Pemberley's servants are discreet."

He began to work his way around the bodice of my dress, leaving a trail of kisses that interfered greatly with my ability to breathe. When I could stand his teasing no longer, I took his face in my hands and sought his mouth, kissing him until he, too, had difficulty drawing breath.

"Do you know how happy you have made me tonight?" I asked, drawing away at last.

"Give me time, and I can make you happier." He reached for me to capture my lips once again.

I laughed softly but held myself away. "I have no doubt, but I refer to what you said at the table. Thank you for asking both Jane and Mr. Bingley to Pemberley for Christmas. I can only assume that you intend to make things right between them."

He sighed deeply. "I shall do what I can even though I still have reservations that Bingley is worthy of your sister."

"She loves him, William. Is it not up to her to decide his worth?"

"I suppose, although I would much rather see her with someone who is more self-assured, more settled and mature. How would it suit you if we were to arrange for her and Fitzwilliam to become reacquainted? Now, there is a man who knows what he wants. If he spent much time with Miss Bennet, is it not possible they might fall in love?"

I rose from his lap and turned away, not wishing to reveal my thoughts.

"Where are you going?" he demanded.

"Not far." I looked back at him over my shoulder and smiled. "Just far enough to be able to think clearly and to make a sensible statement. You know Jane prefers Mr. Bingley, and as to Colonel Fitzwilliam, has he not made it clear that he must marry a woman of fortune? Surely, Jane's lack of means would hamper any such alliance."

"Fitz is not poor by any means. He would provide for your sister very well, and with the dowry I have arranged for her, they could live comfortably."

"I have never seen an inclination for each other on the part of either of them."

"They have been in the same company but a short while. Perhaps I can prevail upon Fitz to change his plans and join us during the holiday after all."

I walked back to him and knelt at his feet, taking his hands in mine. "William, I do not think we should play matchmaker in all of this."

"Why not? You are perfectly willing for me to prod Bingley towards your sister."

"She loves him," I said softly, laying my head upon his knee. "Believe me, I know my sister's heart, and she does not love Colonel Fitzwilliam. Jane will never care for anyone as she does Mr. Bingley."

"Very well, my dear." He began to stroke my curls. "It shall be as you wish. I can deny you nothing."

I raised my head and smiled as he leaned down to kiss me. "Then shall we go above stairs?"

"Gladly!"

We rose and exited the room, my hand tucked inside his arm. As we climbed the great staircase, I asked, "Whose bed shall we sleep in tonight, William?"

"Mine," he announced without the slightest hesitation.

"And why not mine?" I was unable to keep from teasing him.

"Because I have dreamt of having you in my bed far too many nights. You have to admit that I have been much more than patient, and now I demand my rights."

"Perhaps I have dreamed the same dream, only in my bed," I persisted.

"Then let us be fair. Who has dreamt the longest? There is no question about it. I win without question, for I have loved you much, much longer than you have loved me."

I could do nothing more than smile and lean my head against his shoulder as we continued on our way, savouring the pleasure I anticipated. How delightful to know I should never have to sleep alone again.

Light snow fell as Colonel Fitzwilliam left the next morning. It covered the grounds of Pemberley like fairy dust, glistening each time the sun peeked through the clouds and lit up the landscape. I hoped it might lighten Georgiana's mood, but it was not to be. She moped around for most of the day, and in truth, her countenance did not change much for the next ten days until my sisters and mother arrived from Longbourn and the Gardiners a day later. They, of course, had accepted the invitation with alacrity. Jane wrote the response, and one line in her letter had piqued my curiosity as well as William's.

"I have something of great importance to tell you, Lizzy, but I shall wait until we are face-to-face before doing so."

I could not imagine what it might be, and my only fear was that she had accepted the proposal of some kind gentleman from the county, as she had threatened to do when I last saw her at Longbourn. Neither William nor I had written her to expect Mr. Bingley's attendance at Pemberley, as we had not yet heard from him. William said his friend was a poor correspondent and that we would probably hear from his sisters before he wrote, and sure enough, Mr. Bingley proved quite late in sending his acceptance.

Miss Bingley and Mrs. Hurst responded that neither would be able to take advantage of our hospitality. It seemed Mr. Hurst's brother had already asked them to spend Christmas at his house in Surrey, and they were invited to a Christmas ball to be held at the home of Lady Jersey's nephew, who resided in the same neighbourhood. One can imagine what severe disappointment that caused our household, but we bore it as best we could.

I had much to do to prepare Pemberley for the onslaught of visitors and thus did not spend much time alone with Georgiana. William persuaded her to accompany him into the woods with a few servants to select the Yule log and holly bough, but that excursion did little to lift her spirits. He complained to me about her lack of holiday cheer and asked if I knew why her low mood persisted. I told him the truth — that Georgiana had not confided any reason to me, but in my heart I felt guilty in keeping silent as to what I thought lay at the base of it. Whether she knew it or not, I thought Georgiana as much in love with Colonel Fitzwilliam as he with her. And yet, I feared that William would not wish to hear that.

So it was a great relief to have Mamá, Jane, Mary, and Kitty arrive and meet her. They provided a noisy, welcome diversion, and I was glad to see my family claim much of my young sister's attention. She and Mary shared a delight in music, and when at the instrument, they were quite compatible. Kitty's natural exuberance could not help but aid Georgiana to emerge from her natural reticence, and I hoped my new sister's decorum in turn might influence Kitty.

Of course, Mamá was in awe of Pemberley — in truth, all of my sisters were impressed — but she fell speechless the first day of her visit when I took her on an extensive tour of the house. The rest of us took advantage of the muted respite and found ourselves longing for it once her vocal abilities returned. She blessed Mr. Darcy again and again for marrying me and then played the coquette with him in the evenings after tasting a glass of wine. He bore it all with a tolerable spirit, and I tried my best to console him when we were alone in his chamber at the end of each day — a tiresome duty, but one I felt compelled to endure.

We were truly surprised by one of Mamá's statements, which she bestowed upon us as soon as her ability to speak returned.

"Lizzy! Has Jane told you the news?"

"What news is that?"

"Mr. Bingley has returned to Netherfield!"

I looked at Jane in amazement and observed her blush and attempt to conceal her smile. "No, she did not tell me." I stole a glance at Mr. Darcy, who appeared as surprised as I.

"Then let me tell you all about it. He came with a company of gentlemen a fortnight ago. I had it from Mrs. Long, and then Mrs. Philips confirmed the fact. It was a shooting party, and no ladies accompanied them. But, oh, Lizzy, we were in such a state, for Mr. Bingley resided three days in the neighbourhood and still he did not call! Well, I said it was all your father's fault. If he had not gone and died, he would be there where he belonged and could have called on Mr. Bingley. Yes, yes, it was all his fault!" She paced back and forth in the drawing room waving her handkerchief around to punctuate her speech.

"Mamá!" Jane remonstrated, for all the good it accomplished. I shook my head, and with a meaningful look at my sister, I attempted to return my mother to the point of her conversation.

"And so Mr. Bingley did not call upon any of you?"

"Oh, but he did, Lizzy! On the fourth day of his sojourn, Kitty looked out the window, and what do you think she saw? None other than Mr. Bingley riding up the path to Longbourn on his dappled mare! Oh, he was so pleased to see Jane again! It was as plain as day. No one could mistake his preference for her."

"Mamá!" Once again Jane wore an imploring expression.

I watched Mr. Darcy retreat to the window, that shell of disapprobation descending upon his countenance. Why could my mother not learn to curb her tongue?

The arrival of the Gardiners that afternoon provided not only welcome guests but also distractions for both Mamá and Mr. Darcy. He spent no little time reacquainting my uncle with Pemberley's grounds, and if it had not been snowing, I think they would have fished the lake dry just to be outdoors and away from a house filled with women.

It was the third day of my family's visit before Jane and I found time alone. That afternoon, Georgiana and Mary practiced a duet, Mamá listed Mr. Darcy's assets to Mrs. Gardiner once again and planned Jane's upcoming nuptials, even though she had not yet received a proposal, while Kitty entertained the younger Gardiners outdoors in the snowy garden. I tucked Jane's hand in my arm and whisked her off to a parlour in the east wing. From the window, we could see my husband and uncle walking the path that led to the pond.

"Oh, Lizzy, are you truly as happy as you appear?" Jane asked.

My face was wreathed in smiles. "Truly. It is just as you hoped. I have come to love Mr. Darcy, and wondrous thought, he loves me in return."

"Of course, he does! I knew he did the moment he asked for your hand at Longbourn."

"I confess that I did not. And I am afraid I behaved badly and made him miserable for quite some time."

"I cannot believe it!"

"Come, Jane, you know what a reluctant bride I was. Indeed, I acted terribly to him for no little time. It is a wonder he did not return to Longbourn and dump me on Mamá's doorstep with a list of complaints hung 'round my neck."

"Lizzy!"

I could not help smiling. "But he is too good, absolutely too good a man to do such a thing. He has borne my anger and suspicion and bad temper and won me over. He is truly the best of men."

"Oh, Lizzy, I am so happy for you," she said, but I could not mistake the wistful sound of her voice.

"And you? Your last letter made me alive with curiosity. What is this news you have to tell? Does it have to do with Mr. Bingley?"

She blushed and looked down at her hands in her lap. "He has not made a declaration to me, if that is what you mean. But I am happier than I have been in a long time."

"Because?"

"Because even though we were separated close to a year, when he did call upon us, it was like he had never gone away. I still believe I have never met a more amiable man in my life."

"And is he yet at Netherfield?"

"No, he returned to London last week, but he promised to come back to Hertfordshire with the new year."

"Oh, I cannot wait any longer. I must tell you this! Mr. Darcy has invited Mr. Bingley to spend Christmas with us. He comes to Pemberley tomorrow!"

The colour drained from Jane's face, and her eyes grew larger and bluer than usual. "He is coming here?" she repeated.

I took her hands in mine. "You shall spend every day in each other's company for the next fortnight."

"Oh, Lizzy, do you think that best? What about Mamá?"

I sighed and closed my eyes for a moment. "If Mr. Bingley loves you, he will have to accept your family. Mr. Darcy has learned that, and if he of all men can tolerate the Bennets, surely Mr. Bingley can."

We both laughed, and I was grateful I could laugh, for three months ago, I never would have believed it possible.

MR. BINGLEY DID ARRIVE THE next day, along with a new snowstorm. He walked into the great hall, his hat and coat dusted white within the short distance from his carriage to the door. A bitter wind blew in with him, causing the candles to flare. Mr. Darcy and I had just left the breakfast room and crossed the hall when the door opened upon him. We were exceedingly pleased to see him and ushered him into the salon where my family had gathered after eating.

I thought Mamá would suffer apoplexy upon first sight of Mr. Bingley — her mouth hung agape a full five minutes. Neither Jane nor I had warned her he was coming for fear it would only encourage her inappropriate remarks in the presence of Mr. Darcy.

I paid particular attention to the reaction of both Jane and Mr. Bingley upon seeing each other and was most gratified to see their eyes light up and to witness the difficulty both of them had in tearing their gazes from each other.

Unfortunately, Mamá recovered her voice all too soon. "Mr. Bingley, you sly thing! You planned to follow Jane all the way to Derbyshire and never a word of it when last we visited."

"Mamá!" Jane and I both said in unison.

"How nice to see you again, Mr. Bingley," Mrs. Gardiner interjected smoothly, drawing him into the room.

Her husband quickly stepped in as well and engaged him in a discussion of the road conditions. From then on, it was as though an unspoken agreement arose between my aunt and uncle, Mr. Darcy, Jane, and me to spare Mr. Bingley further conversation with my mother, a task most arduous, indeed.

The inclement weather forced the men to spend most of the coming days indoors, whereupon they made frequent use of Mr. Darcy's library and billiards room. Georgiana and I prevailed upon our female guests to assist us in trimming the Yule log with greenery in anticipation of its being lit on Christmas Eve. We also strung apples, twigs, and ribbons to decorate the holly bough so that it would be ready to hang from the ceiling in the main drawing room. We spent much time in the stillroom selecting holly, ivy, bay and rosemary with which to adorn the house, and soon the fragrant herbal aromas permeated Pemberley in a most pleasing manner.

Mamá insisted upon adding mistletoe to the holly bough even though it had been long considered a "kissing bough" without that accessory.

"It will not hurt to provide added encouragement to the holiday tradition," she said, winking and raising her eyebrows in Jane's direction.

I simply closed my eyes and shook my head, embarrassed for Jane's mortification and yet helpless to control my mother. We would be fortunate if we got through the holidays without Mamá proposing to Mr. Bingley upon Jane's behalf!

EACH EVENING IN THE PRIVACY of our bedchambers, I asked my husband if he had yet spoken to Mr. Bingley, and each evening he replied that he had not. After three days of this, his recalcitrant manner began to grate on my nerves, and my nightly nagging did little to endear me to him.

"Elizabeth," he said quite forcefully on the third night, "do not ask me about this again. I shall speak to Bingley when the time is right."

"But when shall that be? You have put this off for months, and now you have been in daily contact with him, and still you remain silent." I had just climbed into his bed, and he blew out the candles before joining me.

"I promised you I would do it. Will you now trust me to keep my word?"

The anger in his voice was unmistakable, his tone sharp. I knew I needed to yield and that I had pushed far enough. I said nothing, but the look I gave him before he extinguished the final light was full of fire.

I lay down and turned on my side away from him, biting my tongue when he reclined beside me. I resolved to remain silent. If he forbade me to speak on the subject again, I simply would not speak at all! Righteous anger caused me to swell up like a toad, and when I think back upon it now, I am grateful we lay in darkness, for I am certain I was not a pretty sight.

We remained in silence for some time. I was far too angry to go to sleep, and I sensed he encountered similar difficulty. Pulling the cover over my shoulders, I tossed about several times, attempting to find a comfortable position, and made certain my disgruntled sighs were quite audible. He did not move, but his breathing revealed he was awake. After none of my obviously incensed actions provoked the desired apology from him, I wriggled as close to the edge of the bed as possible. I lay there miserable for some time. Finally, I sat up, turned back the cover and threw my legs over the side.

"Elizabeth, what are you doing?" He immediately sat up.

"Returning to my chamber," I said evenly.

"Is there something you need from your room? Shall I light a candle?"

"The only thing I need is my own bed."

"Whatever for?"

"How can you ask that, sir? I shall never go to sleep in this mood, and neither shall you. I think it best that we sleep apart tonight."

"I do not agree. I wish for you to remain in my bed, and I ask you to respect my wishes."

Oh, how superior he sounds! I thought. I sat there, beginning to fume

189

and willing my voice not to betray my feelings. "I suppose you consider this an excellent opportunity for me to *obey* you."

"You may choose to perceive it in that manner, but I see it as an opportunity for you to be gracious and indulge my preference."

"And am I to remain awake throughout the night just to be deemed gracious and indulgent in your sight?"

"I said nothing about remaining awake, Elizabeth. I want you to lie down and sleep beside me as you have done ever since we truly became husband and wife."

The reminder of our union was not lost on me. I had revelled in our oneness, thrilled that he loved me and gave me such pleasure, for he was a patient, generous lover. That night, however, it was not enough to erase the harsh words that had passed between us.

"I fail to see how I shall ever sleep tonight if I remain here."

He rose from bed and lit a candle on a nearby table. "I find a good book helps me fall asleep, and I know you have employed a similar habit in the past. Let me read to you."

Read to me? What was he thinking?

With great curiosity, I watched him walk across the room and select a book from among the myriad assortment on his shelves. When he returned to the bed, I was shocked to see that he held a Bible in his hands.

Was it his intent to preach to me? Oh, happy thought, indeed!

William took his time finding the passage he sought, and then he laid it aside and looked into my eyes with a look that no longer contained anger. I turned away from his gaze, unwilling to let my wrath be so easily appeased.

"Have I ever told you of when my mother died?"

That new subject took me completely by surprise. I shook my head slightly.

"I had just turned fourteen years of age, and Georgiana was very young. My mother had been ill since my sister's birth and enjoyed scant days of good health from that time on. It was as though she had been dying for more than two years.

"That last week my father bade me go in to see her alone at her request. She told me she loved me and how proud of me she was, and then — " his voice almost broke, "she told me she would not be here to see me grow up, and that was one thing she regretted most about leaving this world. She said she longed to see me a bridegroom and meet the woman who would be my wife. Then she had me retrieve her Bible, and she instructed me to turn to several passages she knew by heart.

"First, she warned me to look for a good woman, for she impressed upon me that marriage is for life. She said I would find myself miserable if I did not heed the words of King Solomon."

He handed me the book and pointed out two verses in Proverbs. I read aloud:

The contentions of a wife are a continual dropping . . . It is better to dwell in a corner of the housetop, than with a brawling woman in a wide house.

I glared at him. "Perhaps you should have paid closer attention to your mother's admonition."

Taking the Bible from me, he smiled. "No, I listened well, for she told me to turn to the final chapter of that same book. There she showed me the type of woman I should seek, and I found her.

Who can find a virtuous woman, for her price is far above rubies? The heart of her husband doth safely trust in her, so that he shall have no need of spoil.

"My heart trusts in you, Elizabeth. Will you not allow your heart to trust in me?"

I looked away, moved by both the passage he read and the tenderness of his own declaration. Stubbornness still reigned in my heart, however, and so I spoke in a somewhat flippant manner. "I did not know you were a biblical scholar, sir."

"Hardly, although I have read the book at my mother's insistence. I am no sermon-maker, Elizabeth — just a simple man trying to learn how to be a husband to the only woman in this world I shall ever love."

I caught my breath when I looked up and saw the look in his eyes. "William, that is not fair."

"What is not fair?" he said lazily, taking my hand in his.

"How can I remain angry when you say such words and look at me in that way?"

He smiled again. "That is my intent, dearest little wife."

I looked away and sighed, knowing I would warm to his charms like butter melts in the noonday sun. I resolved, however, not to make it easy for him and searched my brain for something neutral upon which to speak, delaying his victory as long as possible. "I should have liked to have known your mother."

"She would have loved you."

"She gave you dissimilar advice about marriage than my mother gave me."

"Oh? And what did your mother tell you, or do I want to know?"

"She told me to do anything and everything you asked, to never refuse you, to keep you happy, and that way I would be sure to receive a generous amount of pin money."

He laughed aloud, his dimples gracing his face in that boyish way that always made me smile. "I believe I quite like your mother's advice, and it is not as dissimilar as you might think, for she referenced the Bible, as well."

"Now there you are mistaken, sir. I know for a fact my mother knows but little of the book, and she has absorbed even less from the vicar's sermons, for I have watched her struggle in vain to stay awake each Sunday morn."

"But in her own way she quotes St. Paul." William took the Bible from me and turned the pages. "Listen to this from the Corinthian letter.

The wife hath not power of her own body, but the husband . . . defraud ye not one the other.

"Yes, I do like your mother's advice."

"Let me see that," I demanded, reaching for the book.

He held it up out of my reach. "What? Do you not *trust* me, good wife?"

I rose up on my knees and reached for it again, but his arms were much longer than mine, and I consequently fell against him and into his lap. "William, let me read it, for I believe you have concocted that verse."

He held me close to him with one arm and we tussled together, now laughing until I was too weak to keep trying.

"Let me see it, I pray you," I finally said, but in a much more gentle voice.

He continued to hold it aloft. "Only if you take back what you just said. You must say that you believe me, that you will always believe your lord and master as befits an *obedient* wife."

I lunged for the book again, but he proved faster and stronger. "Very well, I believe you. Now will you let me see it?"

"What is the need? You said you believed me."

"William, I wish to read it for myself."

He smiled again and began to kiss my cheek, working his way down to my ear and that spot on my neck just below that he knew pleasured me greatly. In doing so, he lowered his hand, and I grabbed the Bible. Although it was difficult to concentrate when he continued to trail kisses up and down my neck, I lay back on his pillow and held the book close to the candle until I found the passage he had read.

"Aha! Just as I thought, Husband, you neglected to read *all* of St. Paul's sermon. Listen to this.

Let the husband render unto the wife due benevolence . . . and like-wise also the husband hath not power of his own body, but the wife!

"There, I knew there was more to it than you read. What say you to that?"

"Far be it from me to quarrel with St. Paul." He now lay beside me, his voice soft and low. "I give you complete power over my body, and I shall be glad to render due benevolence unto you, my dearest, darling little wife."

I closed the book and placed it on the table. Who was I to argue with a saint?

Chapter Fifteen

Christmas Eve arrived before we knew it. The day was spent in a flurry of activities. The decorated holly bough was hung from the ceiling in the main drawing room, and that evening Mr. Darcy and Mr. Bingley carried in the huge, gaily trimmed Yule log as our guests and I applauded its arrival.

The youngest of the Gardiners' sons ran and sat upon it before anyone else could, and so he was commended for his efforts by assurances of much good luck awaiting him in the coming new year. Mr. Darcy gave him a gold coin to begin the cycle, and his brother and sisters crowded around him, exclaiming over it. My husband then lit the new log with the saved end of last year's Yule log that he and Georgiana had burned at Pemberley, and our roaring Christmas fire blazed.

Merriment and joyous cries of "Happy Christmas" could be heard all around. Georgiana carried in the Christmas candle and, after lighting it, placed it upon the mantel. It was an exceptionally large taper in order to burn through the night. The adults filled their glasses from the wassail bowl, and the children were provided with cups of hot cider. When all had been served, Mr. Darcy stood before the fireplace and asked for our attention.

"My friends and family, I wish you all a Happy Christmas. May the new year bring each of us joy, prosperity, and happiness. I drink to your health." He downed his glass.

"And to yours, Mr. Darcy!" Mr. Gardiner said.

Mr. Bingley chimed in, "Hear, hear!"

As we sipped from our glasses, I rejoiced that we were all together in

that beautiful home at the dearest time of the year. I also rejoiced to hear
Mr. Bingley echo his support of my husband, for I had noticed a definite
chill between them the last two days.

William had told me that he at last informed Mr. Bingley of his part
in concealing Jane's presence in Town last winter, and he apologized for
ever attempting to dissuade him from courting her. Mr. Bingley was quite
angry when he learned the truth, and there had been little conversation
between the two friends since their talk.

"In truth, my dear," William said to me, "I know not whether Bingley
is angrier with me about my concealment or because I took him to task
regarding his lack of ardour toward Miss Bennet. I told him he needed
to stand up and be a man. If he truly loves your sister, he should not let
anything his sisters or I said keep him from declaring his intentions. He
does not need my blessing."

"And what did he say to that?" I asked.

"He became somewhat defensive and placed the blame on my shoulders,
for he said I had convinced him Jane Bennet did not care for him. I, in turn,
told him he should be strong enough to keep his own counsel and discover
the truth for himself. I believe he had already reached that conclusion before
we spoke, for he did travel to Netherfield last month without asking my
opinion. Perhaps his feelings for your sister will be the making of Bingley."

By Christmas Eve, all seemed mended as Mr. Bingley's endearing amiability had returned. With respectful forbearance, he endured Mamá's
pointed remarks whenever Jane strayed within five feet of the kissing bough,
and I noted he was rarely far from her side.

The Gardiners' young daughters each stood below the bough and were
promptly bussed by their father, who then lifted them up to retrieve a
berry from the decorative holly. This was met with laughter and frivolity
and much teasing by their brothers that "no *other* man will ever kiss them."
Kitty caused them to cease their torment by standing beneath the holly
bough herself, whereupon each of the little boys was goaded into claiming
a kiss, one on either of her cheeks. Mortification reigned supreme upon
their blushing young faces, but it served its purpose, as they no longer
beleaguered their sisters.

We played games with the children and gave each of them a small gift,
and the room was soon littered with tiny scraps of gold paper. At last, their

nanny ushered them off to bed, having fed them earlier. That was the signal for the adults to enter the dining room and sit down to our Christmas Eve dinner, only the beginning of many feasts we would partake of during the twelve days of Christmastide.

After dinner, Mr. Darcy surprised me by asking Georgiana and Mary to take turns playing for us so that we might dance. The servants pushed back the chairs in the music room, and we soon began a rollicking reel. Each time we passed beneath the mistletoe, Mr. Darcy would steal a quick kiss from me, to the delight of my younger sisters. I could not believe with what ease he entered into the gaiety of the season. Mr. Gardiner did the same with his wife, and we laughed at how she blushed.

"Bingley, it is now your turn," Mr. Darcy called as his friend danced my oldest sister down the row. I caught my breath, shocked at my husband's rare audacity, and wondered if Mr. Bingley would carry through on his suggestion. He did! And I could not say who was pinker, Jane, Mr. Bingley, or my mother, for she laughed and cheered so much so that her cheeks turned positively rosy.

Suddenly, I had the strongest yearning for my father's presence. Oh, he would have sat by the fire, shaking his head at the "silliest young women in England," but he would smile that smile of his, and I would see the light in his eyes when he gazed upon my mother. That night I could see what attracted her to him all those years ago, for she appeared as much of a girl as any of her daughters. I sensed that her laughter and light-hearted spirit had attracted the cynical nature of my father, adding a dimension to his life he had never experienced before.

The next morning we rose early to attend Christmas church services. The small sanctuary was filled with people I had come to know since moving to Derbyshire, and our neighbours hailed us with smiles and greetings of "Happy Christmas!"

As I sat in the pew between my husband and Georgiana and listened to the vicar read the old familiar story, a stream of sunlight beamed through the stained glass windows and bathed our family in its warmth. I was extremely grateful for how good God had been to me that year — a year in which I had known the greatest heartache in my life and yet the greatest happiness.

ON BOXING DAY, GEORGIANA AND I had just completed wrapping the last of the servants' boxes when I heard a shriek echo from above stairs, a familiar sound I recognized as my mother's voice. Georgiana's eyes widened in wonder, and we both ran up the stairs.

"Mamá!" I cried, upon entering her sitting room. "What is wrong?"

"Wrong? Oh, Lizzy, nothing is wrong! Everything is right in the world!" She reclined upon a chaise, and Jane sat beside her, fanning her with a handkerchief. From the looks on their faces, I had little doubt of what had transpired.

"Jane?" I asked, stretching out her name.

She jumped up and embraced me. "Oh, Lizzy, he loves me! Mr. Bingley loves me!"

"Well, of course he does!"

"Oh, I cannot believe it! He wants to marry me! He has gone to my uncle this very moment."

By that time Mary, Kitty, and Mrs. Gardiner had rushed into the room, and there was such a commotion that some of the servants put in an appearance to see what was the matter.

"When did he ask you?" Kitty asked.

"Did he kneel down?" Georgiana wanted to know.

"When is the wedding?" Mary added.

Jane tried her best to answer each of their questions, but they came with such haste, it was nigh impossible. Mrs. Gardiner eventually managed to shush everyone and allowed Jane to tell us the details.

"He asked me this morning, only a short time ago."

"I knew it would happen!" Mamá interrupted. "I was sure you could not be so beautiful for nothing!"

"Where did it happen?" I asked.

"We took a stroll around your garden, Lizzy. Yesterday's sun melted some of the snow, and the wind died, so it was quite pleasant out-of-doors."

"And that is possibly the only place you could be alone, am I not correct?" I asked, laughing.

She smiled and nodded. "He said he has loved me ever since he first came to Netherfield. He did not know I was in Town last winter, Aunt. That is why he never called at Gracechurch Street. I do not understand why Caroline or Mrs. Hurst did not tell him, but it is no matter now. All is made right, for he wants us to be married as soon as possible, Mamá."

"Oh, yes, you must be married by special licence, my dear. I am sure Mr. Bingley can see to it, and we will hold the wedding in Longbourn Church. How about in April when the first lilies begin to bloom?"

"How about in February before anything blooms?" I interjected. "That way Jane will be the most beautiful flower in the county."

"February!" Mamá cried. "Oh, no! I cannot possibly plan a wedding by February. We shall have to travel to London for gowns, for that is where all the best warehouses are, and with the inclement weather this time of year, we cannot depend upon getting it all done that soon."

"Why not meet in the middle," Mrs. Gardiner suggested, "and marry in March?"

Jane's eyes lit up, and Mamá was soon persuaded to agree. The remainder of the morning was spent in countless re-telling of the entire proposal scene and my mother's endless wedding plans.

THAT EVENING, GEORGIANA AND I joined Mr. Darcy in the great old hall where we had held the Harvest Ball. All of the servants assembled, and after enjoying a feast of venison and turkey, we handed out their gifts. The majority of the boxes held money, of course, the most prized contribution we could give them, but I had selected a singular gift for Fiona.

Before our guests arrived to spend Christmas with us, Mr. Darcy and I had spent a day shopping in a neighbouring town. There I had chosen a small gift for Georgiana and others for my sisters and mother, when I came across a shawl trimmed with a lovely piece of Irish lace. For some reason it made me think of Fiona — delicate, pretty, and yet serviceable, exactly like her. I resolved to purchase it for her then and there. We had already prepared a box of money for her, and Georgiana previously found a small toy for Willie, but I wanted to give the maid something special, something just from me.

I now drew her aside in the great hall and offered her the wrapped parcel.

"But Mistress, the master's already given me my box."

"I know, but this is from me."

Her eyes grew big with wonder as she undid the string and opened the package. "Oh, ma'am, it's beautiful, truly beautiful!" she said, as she held the lace in her hands. "I've never had anything so fine. Thank you, ma'am, oh, thank you!"

"You are welcome, Fiona. I believe it was made for you."

She reached out and took my hands in hers, squeezing them, a bold move for a servant, but one I welcomed. I had wronged the girl within my mind, and even though this gift did not make right what I had done, it gave her pleasure, and I sincerely wanted her to have it. As she curtseyed and walked away to join Betty and Willie and show them her treasure, I looked up and caught Mr. Darcy watching us. Our eyes met, and I could feel the warmth of his approbation.

We enjoyed mutual approval of each other and nary a discordant word between us during the remaining days of Christmastide, a marvellous feat in which I rejoiced since we endured a house full of company for close to three weeks.

Our festivities culminated with the celebration of Twelfth Night. Our closest neighbours, the Darnleys and Ashtons, joined our guests that evening. It was an evening in which we donned masks, and the children engaged in playacting, events that required I use all of my powers of persuasion on my dear husband to cause it to come about.

"Elizabeth," he said, "we have not observed Twelfth Night in such a manner since I was a child."

"All the more reason to do so this year."

He did not agree with my argument, protesting the masks in particular, but he allowed it, perhaps because of my gentle persuasion. Slowly, I was learning the man could be more easily swayed by honey than vinegar.

Mamá was almost as excited as Kitty and Georgiana about the thought of a masked evening, and she questioned Mr. Darcy thoroughly as to whether either of his neighbours had eligible sons among their family. He thrilled her by announcing that Edward Darnley was an excellent young man as was his older brother, and they would be in attendance that evening. She was not quite as thrilled to learn that Mr. Ashton had a pretty daughter whom young Edward was courting.

"But you say there is an elder brother," Mamá said, pursing her lips. "Even better. We shall make what we can of the opportunity."

She then went in search of Kitty and Mary to oversee their gowns and masks for the evening. Even this blatant vulgarity on my mother's part did not dissuade Mr. Darcy's good mood, however, and I marvelled each day at how tolerant of my family's foibles he had grown.

I made several trips to the kitchen before the party, personally overseeing the décor of the Twelfth Night cake. I was glad to see that Cook had not disappointed me. The sugar for the frosting was tinted red in colour, and decorations of gilded paper transformed it into a wondrous sight.

"And did you remember to include a bean and pea within before baking?" I asked.

"Yes, ma'am," Cook replied. "It is just as you ordered."

The old custom had not been observed at Pemberley for many years, but I wished to reinstate it, and as I was now mistress of the house, I made that decision on my own. The beautiful cake was brought in and placed on the dining table for all to behold.

That night, after music and a clumsy but hilarious theatrical of *A Midsummer Night's Dream* playacted by the younger members of the family, we sat down to a lavish dinner of boar's head and turkey, plum pudding, and gingerbread. Then the cake was cut and everyone served a piece.

It seemed quite fitting that Mr. Darcy found the bean contained in his slice of cake and thus served as king for the night. However, we were all in uproar when Mamá discovered the pea in her serving, and she was proclaimed queen for the evening. They took their "thrones," chairs that Georgiana and Kitty had decorated with garlands of white paper flowers, into the smaller ballroom. From there we were obliged to do any and everything they commanded.

I knew Mr. Darcy was born for the role, but he had his hands full when Mamá ordered him around along with everyone else. Her natural proclivity for being in command only added to his dismay. She decreed that Mary should play a jig, and Mr. Darcy and I should lead the dance. She then paired the remaining unmarried couples, beginning with Jane and Mr. Bingley, of course, and ending with Kitty and the Darnley's older son. Dancing a jig was not to Mr. Darcy's liking and certainly not in front of his neighbours, but he carried through nonetheless. After it was over, flushed from the exercise, he made his own law.

"I decree that the king shall not be commanded to dance again this night!" He retired to his throne and welcomed a glass of punch Georgiana fetched for him.

By the time our guests departed at the end of the evening and we retired to our chambers, my husband was only too glad to be alone with me behind closed doors. I commended him for his forbearance during the party and throughout the extended visit from my family and Mr. Bingley.

"Do not praise me too highly, Elizabeth, for if truth be known, I look forward to the morrow when they shall leave Pemberley, and we shall have our house to ourselves."

I fingered the chain of perfect emeralds around my neck, the Christmas gift he had given me, and thought how truly generous a man I had married. Earlier, Fiona helped me change into my nightgown and robe and brushed out my hair, but I told her to leave the necklace, that I would take it off myself, for I knew the colour flattered my eyes. Now, I joined him before the fireplace in his chamber and slipped my arms around his neck.

"Praise does not exist high enough for you, William. You are truly the best of men."

He smiled and gazed into my eyes, took me into his arms, and kissed me tenderly before speaking. "I am far from that, my love, but I believe I do deserve some commendation. This Christmastide has been, by far, the liveliest either Pemberley or I have experienced. I truly hope for a quieter time the remainder of January."

"My poor darling!" I rested my head against his chest. "I am afraid you shall rue the day you ever brought me into your house."

"How can you say that?" He held me at arms' length where we could face each other.

"You must admit I have disrupted your life entirely. And when you married me, you acquired a number of relations whom I know have tried you sorely and shall continue to do so."

He shook his head. "You are wrong. My life was not one of contentment before you came into it but rather loneliness and tedium. Oh, I had friends enough — my home, my place in society — but it meant nothing nor could it ever mean anything to me again without you. And yes, your family is *interesting*, but I now take them as they are, and I am grateful."

"Grateful? Jane, perhaps, and Mr. and Mrs. Gardiner, but surely you are not grateful for all of them."

"I am," he said, pulling me onto his lap as he sat on the sofa before the fire. "For without them, there would be no Elizabeth, no dearest, prettiest Elizabeth. You are a part of them and they of you, and I would not have it any other way."

I began to kiss him then, softly at first, tenderly caressing his lips until our passion caught fire and soon blazed brighter and higher than the flames before which we sat.

Chapter Sixteen

If I said that Mr. Darcy and I never had another cross word between us, it would be false, for as married couples throughout time have known, it is impossible to live with someone and always agree. And because we were of different temperaments, we still had much to overcome in a relatively new marriage. The next such difficulty arrived a short time after Georgiana's seventeenth birthday.

She had been much cheered with a house full of guests during the holidays, but once they left, her spirits dampened. She spent many hours at the pianoforte or reading. The only time I saw her countenance brighten was when she or Mr. Darcy received a letter from Colonel Fitzwilliam. Upon receipt of a personal letter addressed to her, Georgiana would vanish to read it in private, but when a missive arrived for her brother, she would search for him throughout the house and urge him to read it aloud immediately. I grew more and more anxious about what her reaction might be when Richard revealed his plans to leave the country.

My foreboding was not in vain.

The colonel arrived on the last day of January, the day before Georgiana's birthday, and he spent ten days with us, days in which the weather turned bitterly cold and forced us to keep to the house the majority of time. The day before he was to return to his regiment, however, we were blessed with a beautiful, sunny morning. The wind stilled, the temperature rose, and the warmth of the sun felt like heaven's kiss shining upon my face.

After breakfast, Mr. Darcy suggested he and the colonel go riding, and when Georgiana asked to be included, he agreed. I begged off, as I had not felt well the past few days. I assured my husband I would be content to curl up by the fire with a new novel he recently brought me from the bookstore in Lambton. They were gone for much of the day, and I found myself enjoying the unusual solitude. I slept a while, and by the time they returned, I felt better, a fortunate turn of events, for I needed all my resources to deal with the tempest that blew into our house with the arrival of my sister.

"I cannot believe this! I refuse to believe it!" she cried.

"Georgie, pray listen to me." The colonel pleaded to no avail, for she ran past the drawing room and up the staircase to her room, her sobs evident for all to hear.

I rose from my chair before the fire and walked to the doorway. "Richard? What has happened? Is someone hurt?"

He started up the stairs, but stopped at my words and the addition of Mr. Darcy, who walked in from outside. I had never seen such a look of concern in the colonel's expression before and feared that some calamity had transpired. I was relieved to see that the three of them were not injured as far as I could tell.

"Her behaviour is insupportable!" William exclaimed. "Why should she be so distressed?"

"Will someone tell me what the matter is?" I asked again.

Both gentlemen accompanied me into the drawing room so that we would no longer discuss matters in front of the servants. William threw his gloves and hat on a small table and began to pace back and forth. "I must go to her. I shall tell her she is acting like a child."

"Will one of you please tell me what is wrong with Georgiana?"

Colonel Fitzwilliam sighed and gave me a long look. "I told her I would leave for Spain next week."

"Oh, Richard, that soon?"

He nodded, and William stopped pacing. "I fail to see why this upsets my sister so. She knows you are an officer, and the army is sent abroad from time to time. Does she expect you to be exempt from your duties? Why, you were in France a few years ago, and I do not remember Georgiana having a strong reaction."

"Perhaps she was not old enough then to think of the danger," I said. "She now is aware that the colonel will face the enemy when he goes to Spain."

"There is little chance that I will see battle. In my position, I usually remain with other commanding officers, overseeing things from a safe distance. Georgie need have little worry for my safety."

"Should you not go up and reassure her?" I suggested.

"No," William announced. "I shall deal with Georgiana. I will not have her behave in this manner." He began to walk toward the door.

"William," I said quickly, "why not let me go to her? A woman's touch may be what she requires right now."

He looked at me just long enough to listen, but shook his head. "You may go after I am done, Elizabeth. For now, I want to know what is at the bottom of all this." With that, he walked out the door, and we could hear his rapid ascent up the stairs.

"Oh, I do wish he had listened to me." I sank down upon the sofa. "Colonel, must you truly go? Cannot you see that Georgiana will be lost without you?"

"I cannot stay. Once orders are given, there is no going back, and besides, I still think it best that I leave."

"But why? I confess I do not truly understand your reasoning."

"Elizabeth, I have thought about this for a long time — dwelt upon it, in fact. I am sixteen years Georgiana's senior. I remember holding her as a babe. She was the most beautiful child I had ever seen. That is all she was to me for the longest time, my dearest little cousin, and then when her father died and his will named me guardian along with Darcy, I felt even closer to her and, I suppose, more protective if that is possible. She has always been like a little bird, tiny and fragile. Like Darce, I, too, longed to keep her locked up somewhere — somewhere no one could ever hurt her. But we failed. We both failed." He walked to the window and stared out through the trees at the sunlight now fading.

"You cannot hold yourself responsible for what happened to Georgiana with George Wickham. You and William did all you could to provide a safe world for her. It is neither your fault nor his that all of you were deceived."

"I acknowledge the truth of your statement in my mind, but somehow my heart refuses to accept it. All I know is that, when she was recovered and brought back, Georgiana was no longer a child in my eyes. Oh, I still tease her. I think I call her 'Sprout' to cover my own feelings, to try to convince myself she is still but a girl and has not blossomed into a young woman. I confess I have seldom seen a face or figure more pleasing to me than hers, but I am a partial old friend. I love to look at her . . . indeed, I could look at her forever, for I have fallen in love with her." He stood half in shadow. The fading sunlight was just enough that I could see the anguish upon his face.

I rose and joined him at the window. "And is it inconceivable that she may love you as well?"

He pressed his lips together and shook his head. "Of course, she loves me! We have loved each other as cousins all our lives, but no, she is not old enough to know what mature love is, to return the measure of devotion I feel. Do you not see, Elizabeth, that I cannot place that burden upon her? She needs time — *her time in the sun* — and with you as her sister, I know she will have it.

"Oh, Darce will fight you left and right, but you must be strong for her. Work your charm on him, and make him see that he must let her go. When she comes out in the spring, he must not discourage the young men who call — only make certain they are worthy. I am not courageous enough for the task, and that is why I must leave. But you can, Elizabeth, and you can make Darcy accept it. Let Georgiana have her chance."

"Do you not fear the possibility she may accept a suitor and marry?"

He stared at the floor but not before I saw him wince. "I do," he said, his voice barely audible. "Perchance that would be best. I want her to fall in love, to know the ecstasy and misery such feelings cause, and yet I cannot bring myself to witness it. You and Darcy must sustain her through this."

I put my hand on his arm, for I longed to comfort him somehow. If my heart broke to witness this sacrifice, what must he feel?

"I shall do what I can, Richard," I said softly, but I did not think it would be nearly enough.

William walked into the room just then. "Elizabeth, she wants you."

I nodded and left them, wondering what had transpired between brother and sister. Upstairs I found a subdued, chastened young girl with tear stains still on her face. I poured some water into a basin, moistened a cloth and gently bathed her cheeks.

"Can I help you, Georgiana?"

She shook her head and sighed. "Wills says I act like a spoilt child, and I know he is right. I do not understand why I am so upset. Richard has gone away time and again, and he has always come back. He will return, will he not?"

"Of course," I said quickly. I did not want to bring up the chances a soldier takes in war, no matter how lightly Richard dismissed them, and I hoped she would not think of them.

"It is just that I am so afraid to face my debut in Town without him."

"Your brother and I will be with you, as well as Lord and Lady Matlock. You do not have to do it alone."

"I know that, but Wills cannot dance with me. Richard could, and he is a divine dancer."

I turned away and closed my eyes, acknowledging then that the colonel was correct. In many ways, Georgiana was still so young; her greatest worry was with whom she would dance. "There will be many young men who will dance with you."

"Will there? What if no one asks me?"

I smiled. "You worry in vain. I am sure you will be vastly popular."

"Oh, no, I do not wish to be popular. The thought of making conversation with all those strangers frightens me exceedingly. With Richard there, I should always have someone at my side. If I felt alarmed by one who asked for a set, I could dance with him instead. Elizabeth, I do not know why I say all this or why his leaving upsets me so. I am confused."

"You are growing up, my dear." I patted her hand.

"I thought confusion never plagued adults, that they always knew what is best."

"In truth? Hardly ever. That is a myth we tell children. Now that I am grown, I know it only too well."

The faint semblance of a smile played about her lips, and I embraced her. "All will be well, Georgiana. I truly believe that."

She rose from the bed then and, after drying her face, accompanied me down the stairs. The evening progressed without further unpleasantness, although both Georgiana and the colonel remained unusually subdued. She agreed to play his favourite selections on the pianoforte, and I noticed the wistful, yearning expression in his eyes as he watched her performance.

LATER THAT NIGHT IN THE drawing room after Richard and Georgiana had retired, Mr. Darcy returned to the earlier incident. "Elizabeth, did you learn what was behind Georgiana's ill temper this afternoon? She made little sense to me."

I closed my eyes and prayed for wisdom. I desired to be honest with my husband, and yet I did not want to betray Richard's confidence.

"I think Georgiana is simply afraid of the future. She expressed qualms regarding her coming out in the spring and especially without Richard by her side. She relies on him more than we know."

"They have always enjoyed a close companionship, but surely she understands he cannot entirely shield her from society's scrutiny. And does she not consider me adequate protection against any rogues or rakes that come calling?"

"Oh, I am certain you will do all that is necessary in that regard. Perhaps even more than is necessary," I added under my breath.

Unfortunately, he heard me. "Do I detect a complaint in that last remark?"

"Not a complaint, sir, just a statement of fact."

"I do not understand."

"William, you know you are far too protective of Georgiana. I fear the coming Season shall prove difficult for you."

"How can you say that? After what happened with Wickham, how can I be *too* protective?"

"I was fifteen when that happened, Wills," Georgiana said, startling both of us by her return.

"We thought you had retired, dear," I said quickly.

"I came back for the book I left over there." She crossed the room to the chair in which she had sat earlier. "And Wills, I am no longer that same girl. Must I suffer for it the rest of my life?"

"Georgiana," he said forcefully, "I did not mean to infer in any way that you were responsible. Let us say no more on the subject."

"But I *was* responsible. When will you or Richard ever accept that? *I* listened to Mr. Wickham's flattery. *I* allowed myself to be seduced by his pretty words. *I* knew that elopement was not the proper way in which to marry, and yet *I* agreed to it. He is not the only one at fault."

"Georgiana!" Mr. Darcy's voice rose. "We shall not discuss this further. You know my wishes on the subject."

"Yes, I do," she replied in a barely audible voice, obviously chastened, "but do you know mine, Wills? Has anyone other than Elizabeth ever asked me about my feelings?"

"Elizabeth?" He turned to glare at me. "Have you discussed that unforgivable occurrence with my sister in direct contradiction to my orders?"

I opened my mouth to speak, but Georgiana interrupted. "Only when I brought it up. Do not blame Elizabeth."

"I do not want the incident spoken of again. Do I make myself clear?" His tone sounded deadly.

Georgiana nodded, and keeping her eyes on the floor, she sat down on the sofa and began to cry quietly. I started toward her when Mr. Darcy spoke again. "Elizabeth, do you understand me?"

I turned and glared at him and wanted to cry, *Only too well, sir! And do you understand that you are the most obstinate man who ever lived?* But I swallowed my ire and nodded. We both turned our faces from each other, and I bit my tongue until I could taste blood.

Remember, *a soft answer turneth away wrath*, I repeated to myself, for I had begun spending time in the Old Testament book of Proverbs since learning it had been a favourite of Mr. Darcy's mother. I walked to the sofa and sat beside Georgiana, taking her hand in mine. By that time, I had regulated my breathing, and I lowered my tone before I spoke.

"William, I pray you will hear what I say. Neither Georgiana nor I set out to go against your wishes."

"Oh, no," his sister added. "We would never do that. It is just that — "

"Just what?" he demanded.

"Sometimes I think Richard may be leaving because of what . . . you will not allow me to speak."

"My dear," I said, "that misfortune has nothing to do with Richard leaving."

"It may. After I returned from Ramsgate, I sensed a difference in him. Oh, he is the same in his affection and care, but at times, I find him looking at me in an unusual manner, as though I am no longer myself. I feel damaged, that I shall never be good enough again in either Richard's or William's eyes, so how can I be good enough to face society?"

"Oh, no." I put my arms around her, as she began to cry anew. "You are wrong, dearest. William, tell her she is wrong."

He joined us immediately and took her into his arms, cradling her head upon his chest. "Georgiana, do not cry. Elizabeth is correct. You are not damaged. You are as beautiful and whole and innocent as before it ever happened."

"I am not innocent, Wills," she said between sobs. "I allowed Mr. Wickham to . . . to kiss me and more than once."

William's eyes met mine, and I saw greater anger flash within his. I tried desperately to signal him not to react in that manner by slightly shaking my head. When he remained silent, I knew that he could not voice his thoughts without saying more than he should, and so I spoke in his place. "Georgiana, is that all? Is a kiss all you shared with Mr. Wickham?"

"Why, yes, of course, but is that not bad enough?"

"It is enough." I met William's relieved expression with my own. "But no real harm has occurred. And you are mistaken in taking the blame. Compared to Mr. Wickham, you were an innocent child, and he took advantage of your naivety, he and Mrs. Younge. I know of Mr. Wickham's charm only too well, for I, too, was fooled by it in the past."

She turned away from her brother to look at me. "You, Elizabeth?"

When I nodded, he interrupted. "There is no need to speak of that. I want this conversation to end."

"Wills, I pray you," Georgiana said, and I was surprised at the depth of pleading in her tone. "I need to know how Mr. Wickham prevailed upon Elizabeth — that is, if she is willing to tell me."

"But why?" He looked totally bewildered. "Why must you speak of a subject that evokes nothing but pain?"

"To be heard," I said gently. "To know we are not alone in our foolishness. Sir, this is what women do. It is, perhaps, our fate rather than our merit. We cannot help ourselves. We live at home, quiet, confined, and our feelings prey upon us. You are forced on exertion. You have always pursuits, business of some sort or other to take you back into the world immediately, and continual occupation and change soon weaken impressions. You need not talk of such things, but you must allow us."

William looked at me as though I spoke a foreign language. To his credit, however, he made no further demand, but simply stalked across the room. I took Georgiana's hand and began to tell her the story of when I first met Mr. Wickham in Meryton and of how I, as well as most of the folk in Hertfordshire, believed the false story he spread about her brother. She was horrified, of course.

"When did you learn the truth?"

"Last Easter when I visited in Kent. William wrote me a letter and told me of Mr. Wickham's true nature."

"Was that the letter I saw you re-reading in your chamber when Wills was in London?"

I nodded and saw Mr. Darcy turn directly toward me, a question in his eyes. He did not interrupt us, though, and I continued relating how Mr. Wickham had seduced my youngest sister last summer and how he never would have married her if not for Mr. Darcy's generous intervention. She looked at her brother with new admiration. "So that is what caused you to leave Pemberley with such haste last August."

He did not reply and turned to the window, but I nodded in agreement with her statement.

"Can you now understand, Georgiana, that you were not at fault to believe Mr. Wickham? The man is a master at deception, and your admiration was based on falsehoods, but perfectly understandable."

"Do you think Richard shares your acquittal of me?"

"Of course, he does," William said quickly. "You must never believe that you were to blame again, Georgiana, not in my or Elizabeth's eyes, and certainly not in Fitzwilliam's. Shall we now let the incident die once and for all?"

He had left the window and come to stand before us. Taking Georgiana's hands, he lifted her to meet his gaze.

"Yes, Wills," she said, "but please allow Elizabeth and me to sort things out from now on. If you truly want us to be sisters, grant us this comfort and no longer declare that certain matters will not be mentioned in this house."

Mr. Darcy sighed and nodded ever so slightly in agreement, but after his sister left the room, I watched his brows pull together in a frown, and I could see how he struggled to repress his emotions.

"William, you refrain from stating your true sentiments. Will you tell me why your countenance continues to be downcast?"

"Is it not obvious? Georgiana's request goes against all that I have ever known. I have spent my entire life avoiding discussion of unpleasant personal subjects, as my father did before me. She is correct. We grew up in a house where private matters remained private. And all this talk about feelings! My father never would think to ask such disturbing questions.

Now my sister demands independence from that censure."

And, I thought, he was only too aware that Georgiana dared to challenge him because of my company.

With a somewhat weary gesture, he sat down in a large chair before the fire, leaned back, his hand upon his mouth, while he stared at the flames. I knelt before him and took his other hand in mine.

"Are you angry with me?"

He shook his head, but his expression did not change, and he continued to gaze at the fire.

"You do believe I have had undue influence upon your sister, do you not?" When he made no response, I continued. "I might remind you that is the reason you married me. You asked that my lively ways might somehow affect her spirits."

He met my eyes. "That was the reason I gave for marrying you, but we both now know the truth."

I smiled, aware that his voice had grown deeper and less troubled. "Yes, and do not think that I am ungrateful for your love, but still I take my obligation seriously. I know I have caused you unhappiness by forcing this issue to come to light."

He sighed again. "I do not blame you. If there was force, it came about because of my sister's distress, and although I hate to admit it, probably for the best. Forthright discussion of hurtful occurrences will never be easy for me, Elizabeth, but if my carrying forward the pattern I learned from my father harms Georgiana, then I must change, no matter how painful that change is to me."

"You are exceptionally brave, my love." I took his face in my hands.

"No, I am not, and I am in dire need of comfort at this moment."

I began to kiss his lips tenderly. "Does this help?" I murmured.

"Hmm, I cannot tell for sure. You must do it again."

He gathered me onto his lap then, and I proceeded to comfort him in such a way that we both derived great benefit.

We bade Colonel Fitzwilliam adieu the next morning. Georgiana tried her best, but she could not halt the tears spilling from her eyes. As Mr. Darcy gave last minute orders to the driver, Richard kissed my young sister's hand.

"Oh, Richard!" She flung herself into his arms. "Promise me you will return soon."

His arms embraced her tenderly, and his eyes met mine as he kissed her hair. "There is no need to fret, Sprout. I shall be back before you know it. After all, I cannot miss dancing at your wedding."

Although he spoke the words in jest, the pain in his eyes was unmistakable. Mr. Darcy and I stood beside her as she waved until the departing carriage could no longer be seen in the distance.

"Surely, he will not be gone too long." Georgiana's voice broke.

"No," her brother said. "You know Fitzwilliam. He makes an appearance when you least expect him. I would not be surprised at all to see him return within six months or less."

My husband's prediction was in error, however. We did not see Colonel Fitzwilliam for four long years, and a great many things can happen in that length of time.

Chapter Seventeen

We travelled to Hertfordshire in early March for Jane's wedding to Mr. Bingley. It had been an exceptionally cold winter, and I thrilled now to see indications of spring begin to appear in the countryside. We were to stay at Netherfield, for that great house contained much more room than Longbourn for Georgiana, Mr. Darcy, and me, along with our maids, valet, and other servants.

As we climbed the stone steps leading to the entryway, vivid memories washed over me, transporting me back to an earlier year. The last time I entered that house, I danced with Mr. Darcy and deemed him the best dancer I had ever encountered, but surely the most difficult man to understand upon the face of the earth. My, how much my opinion had altered in little more than a year!

Mr. and Mrs. Hurst as well as Miss Bingley were also in attendance at the estate, and thus, Georgiana and I oft times found ourselves spending much of the day at Longbourn. My young sister much preferred the noisy uproar of my old home to the stilted, hypocritical remarks Mr. Bingley's sisters inflicted upon the general conversation. Back and forth, their talk would swing from gushing over "dear Jane" to thinly veiled, sniping remarks aimed at my mother and younger sisters. It was evident they lamented the fact their only brother was marrying down in the world. Mr. Darcy and Mr. Bingley, along with Mr. Hurst, escaped as early as possible each morning to their retreat of sport, and so the Superior Sisters found themselves in the sole company of each other for most of the days preceding the wedding.

Mamá, naturally, was almost hysterical in her preparations for the nuptials. I did my best to relieve Jane of her oppression and welcomed my Aunt Philips' daily attendance, as it at least gave Jane and me some respite and a chance to be alone with each other. Of course, Mrs. Philips had returned to her tiresome habit of quoting proverbs, and I vowed to Jane that I might engage in a desperate act if I heard *"Happy is the bride that the sun shines on"* one more time.

One morning, after she glanced outside at the approaching clouds and then uttered it for the fifteenth time, I finally spoke up.

"I would not put much stock in that old saying, Aunt, for I can testify it takes more than sunshine to make a happy bride."

"Now, Lizzy," she replied, "these *old sayings,* as you call them, have stood me in good stead for many a year, and I will have you know I have been proved false on nary a one."

"But surely you must recall, it poured on my wedding day, and yet I find myself quite cheerful."

She tsked-tsked over my rebuttal and tried to think of another appropriate adage with which to salvage her opinion, but I conveniently remembered a task calling me to another room and made my escape. In fact, I had endured all of the close family contact I could for the present, and seeing that Georgiana was happily trimming bonnets with Kitty, I grabbed my shawl and bonnet and skipped out the back door.

I longed for a walk in the old, familiar woods, and the weather was mild enough to accommodate me. I revelled in the beginning buds popping out on trees and shrubs and the touch of purple the crocuses provided as they peeked out for a look at the new season.

I walked no little way that afternoon, and after a while, seeing the sun begin to lower in the sky, I observed that I should begin to make my way back to my mother's house. Before I returned, though, I climbed the small hill behind Longbourn Church and walked through the gates fronting the cemetery where my father was buried.

I could not walk those lanes and woods without thinking of him, without recalling how I lost him at almost that very time only a year ago. Finding his grave, I knelt and placed upon it the small bouquet of wild blooms I had gathered. I ran my fingers across the roughly carved letters of his name and the dates of his birth and death below.

"Oh, Papá," I whispered, as a tear escaped down my cheek, "I miss you so."

I allowed myself to cry a bit and then blew my nose and began to recall happier times. I could still see the twinkle in his eye and that sly, unreadable expression about his face when he made one of his droll statements, usually at my mother's expense, the meaning of which she never seemed to grasp. I remembered the talks we enjoyed in his study or walking about the grounds at Longbourn and how he could not wait for me to share a new book he received and enter into a long debate of its merits. Although neither a perfect man nor parent, he had been a very dear father, and I missed him most heartily.

I began to speak to him aloud in that way people have spoken to their departed loved ones for centuries, longing to feel a bit of communion with one another again.

"How I wish you were here to see Jane marry, Papá. She will make a beautiful bride, but of course, you have always known that. Mr. Gardiner shall escort her down the aisle, but do not think he can replace you, for that is impossible. You need not worry about her, though, for I believe she and Mr. Bingley will be happily settled. Their tempers are by no means unlike, each of them so complying that nothing will ever be resolved on, so easy that every servant will cheat them, and so generous that they will always exceed their income."

I could not help but smile to think that my father would most probably have uttered that statement, had he been there. Our minds had been much alike, and we had enjoyed a compatibility of temper and humour unlike anyone else in our family.

I sat back upon the damp ground, looking up as the light wind rustled the new leaves on the trees, now causing my curls to blow slightly. I felt cheered my father was buried there, for it was a lovely spot, and if one looked but a short distance, the spire of Longbourn Church could be seen through the trees.

As I lowered my gaze, I was surprised to see a man's figure emerge from the wood, growing ever closer as he walked toward me. I smiled upon recognition of William's familiar gait and long legs. Hastily, I tried to brush aside the tears from my cheeks and began to rise. He put out his hand, motioning me to stay where I was sitting.

"Do not get up, dearest, unless the ground is uncomfortable for you," he said, as he knelt beside me and with one finger under my chin, tipped my face up to meet his. "You have been weeping." He gently rubbed his thumb across my cheek.

"How did you know to find me here?"

"I did not. I have combed those woods behind us for a good half-hour, looking for you. This place was my final quest before returning to Longbourn. Are you cold? Shall I give you my coat?"

I shook my head. "I am not chilled, William. Do not worry so. After several hours of Mamá's endless fluttering and Mrs. Philips' proverbs, I was desperate to find a peaceful spot."

He smiled. "I see you have picked flowers for your father."

"Yes, and I told him of Jane's wedding. Oh, how I wish he could be here!"

"As do I." He put his arm around me and held me close. "Have you told him of our news?"

"Not yet," I said softly and then placed my hand upon the gravestone. "Papá, come next autumn, Mr. Darcy and I shall make you a grandfather."

"Surely, he would want a granddaughter the image of you."

"I am not so certain of that. After spending his life amongst scads of women, my father might now prefer the addition of a man-child to his family."

"Either way, as long as the babe looks like you, I shall be happy."

"A short, scrawny boy will not do, William. Let us hope that any son we have will inherit your good looks and my excellent temper." I spoke in a cheeky manner, took his hand, and placed it upon my stomach. "I fear I shall not be slim for long. I hope I can hide it until after Jane's wedding."

"So you have told neither your mother nor sisters?"

I shook my head. "It shall be our secret for now — yours, mine and my father's."

He smiled, and kissing my nose, he hugged me even closer. "And if it is a boy, shall we name him for your father and mine?"

"I would love that."

"Are you ready to leave, my love? You should not sit on damp ground too long, and the sun is beginning to set."

I nodded and allowed him to help me rise. I ran my hand over my father's stone once more and stooped to place a kiss upon it, but I did not cry again. Instead, I tucked my hand in my husband's arm and allowed him to lead me down the hill, leaning upon him for my support.

A WEEK AFTER THE WEDDING, we travelled from Netherfield to London. Arriving a bit early for the Season but having much to do to insure Georgiana's debut, it was only practical that we do so. In spite of her misgivings and nerves, she made a lovely appearance upon society, and just as the good colonel had predicted, young men lined up not only to dance with her but also to call upon her from then on. I spent my days advising her on pertinent topics of conversation, serving as chaperone, and consoling my husband's distraught nerves at the number of beaus now filling our townhouse.

More and more, I hoped our child would be a boy, for if William was this particular about his sister, how would his daughter ever survive?

Surprisingly, I made it through the four months of balls and parties without physically showing that I was with child until near the close of the Season, mainly because I suffered nausea from morning till night and gained little weight. Fiona proved invaluable, for she not only could commiserate with my plight, but she knew several old Scottish remedies that relieved my suffering for short periods.

By the time we returned to Pemberley in July, my sickness vanished as quickly as it appeared, and I soon began to put on weight and achieve that glow that surrounds expectant mothers.

My confinement proceeded without incident, and our first son, George Thomas, was born on the twenty-eighth day of October at four o'clock in the morning, barely more than a year after Mr. Darcy and I had entered into our arranged marriage. I elected to nurse him myself rather than secure the services of a wet nurse, and I gloried in motherhood, marvelling daily that this beautiful little person had come into my life.

He was the image of his father, and I laughed often, seeing exactly how William would have looked as a babe. When he screwed up his tiny brows into a frown, I could see a miniature Mr. Darcy tuning up to wail, and when I coaxed him into a smile, I delighted in a glimpse of his father's dimples lighting up his little face.

Fiona surprised us six months later by announcing she was leaving Pemberley's service. It seemed that one of Mr. Darcy's tenants, a Mr. Martin MacAdams, had courted her right beneath our noses, and she at last agreed to marry him. I hated to see her leave, for I had grown to rely upon her excellent services, but at the same time, I rejoiced to see her find someone who loved her and Willie and would give them a home of their own. We attended their wedding in the small village church, and I smiled when Fiona entered, wearing the lace-trimmed shawl I had given her the year before at Christmastide.

That next summer, news came from Longbourn that Kitty was to marry the local curate, Mr. James Morris. She had spent much time at Netherfield, and under Jane's gentle tutelage, she had matured into a quieter, more dignified young woman. Mamá was upset at first, for she still desired a more advantageous match for her, but with Jane and Mr. Bingley's influence, she was soon made to see the wisdom of the union, for the young man was truly in love with Kitty and she with him.

I wish I could say that Mary made a like marriage, but it was not to be. Instead, once she remained the only daughter at Longbourn, she began to write. Like water bubbling forth from a spring, words poured from her pen. She sent her stories to my aunt in Town for her enjoyment, and Mr. Gardiner was actually able to find a London agent who wished to publish them.

I confess I was speechless after reading the first edition, for I fully expected a spinsterish version of *Fordyce's Sermons* aimed at warning young women of the perils of attending too many balls, unchecked flirting, and the dangers of the opposite sex. Instead, Mary wrote witty, satiric romances based on thinly veiled characterizations of my mother and younger sisters, and she oftentimes fashioned a heroine who appeared to be a composite of Jane and myself. The books became so popular she eventually took a house in London where she enjoyed the company of many cultured and erudite persons of the arts. I wonder that Papá did not turn over in his grave to see such an unexpected change in his quietest daughter.

Lydia, as expected, lived the sort of life all of us feared she would. Mr. Wickham's enchantment with her soon evaporated, and we heard rumours of his seeking excitement elsewhere. She, however, continued to enjoy the advantages of being a married woman and carved out an existence among military society in Newcastle, enjoying the favour and attention of officers and their wives because of her effervescent personality. Jane and I were both asked for frequent monetary assistance, and we, of course, helped our youngest sister whenever we could.

Jane and Mr. Bingley left Hertfordshire two years after their marriage and bought a house in a neighbouring county near Derbyshire, a mere thirty miles from Pemberley. This, of course, pleased my sister and me excessively, and we enjoyed raising our families together. Jane gave birth to two daughters in quick succession, and I am happy to say they not only inherited their mother's pretty blonde curls but their father's sunny disposition as well.

As for Georgiana, it was evident she was to marry someone from our own neighbourhood in Derbyshire — Mr. Darnley's eldest son. Of all the young men paying her attentions, he impressed Mr. Darcy as the only one qualified to be her husband. He asked and was granted permission to court her and did so for some length of time. Georgiana seemed to care for him — when questioned, she said she did not find him unattractive — but after several months, when he asked for her hand, she turned him down.

My husband and I both were surprised at this turn of events, but as William said, "She is still very young — not quite one and twenty."

At that time, I had given birth to Edward, our second son, some two months earlier, and the doctor had just granted me permission to walk in the gardens at Pemberley. The day after Mr. Darnley's refusal, I came upon my sister sitting on a bench among the rhododendrons. She seemed oblivious to her surroundings, a far-away look in her eyes, a wistful expression playing about her countenance.

"Georgiana, may I intrude? I hope you do not grow melancholy about your decision regarding Mr. Darnley."

She looked up quickly and returned to the present. "Of course, you may join me, Elizabeth, and no, although I hated to hurt the gentleman's feelings, I have no regrets."

Her presence of mind impressed me. Indeed, Georgiana's growth into a mature, self-assured young woman pleased me greatly. I could only hope that my influence had helped this to come about.

"You look well," she said.

"I am well, now that I am allowed out of doors."

"It must be difficult for you to be confined, loving to walk as much as you do. I recall a day years ago when Richard and I came upon you on that bench hidden away over there at the edge of the lawn. You were reading a letter. I believe it was not long after you and William married and only a few days before the Harvest Ball."

"Mmm, I think you are correct, and I recall that letter being very important to me."

"You seem so much happier now than you were those first months of your marriage."

"I am, but why should I not be with two fine sons and the love of your brother?"

Georgiana smiled and looked away. "I am glad you and William made a love match, but your example makes it difficult for me to even think of marriage."

"Why, whatever causes you to say that?"

"I look upon your marriage as ideal. I want the same for myself."

"My dear, your brother and I do not live perfect lives. You are well aware we often disagree and even argue."

"Yes, but it never lasts for long. You may quarrel one day, but by the next morning, all is made right. I desire that kind of union."

"And you shall have it," I said, emphatically. "Mr. Darnley may not be the right man for you, but you are still very young, Georgiana. There will be other men to court you. In truth, once word gets out that you have refused him, I am certain a steady stream of gentlemen callers will plague your brother once again."

She frowned and looking away, remained silent for a while. I rose and began to snip a bouquet of marguerites and daisies, placing them in the basket I carried on my arm. It was not long before she took the basket from me, offering to carry it while I made the cuttings.

"Has Wills heard from Richard lately? It seems as though he has been gone forever. He has not written to me in more than six months. I sometimes fear he has forgotten me."

I pressed my lips together. I dreaded to relate the news we had received the evening before.

"Elizabeth?" She walked in front of me so that she could see my expression. "What is it? Has something happened to him?"

I took her hand and led her back to the bench. "A letter came from Lord Matlock late last evening. Colonel Fitzwilliam is in London, staying at Eden Park."

"Eden Park!" she exclaimed, her eyes aglow. "He has returned to England at last! It has been four years. Do you realize he has been out of the country that long?" I nodded and could not help but see that those four years had not diminished Georgiana's feelings for her cousin. I wondered, though, what had happened to him.

"I shall go in and write to him immediately, asking him to visit us here at Pemberley," she announced as she rose from the bench and turned in the direction of the house.

I put my hand on her arm. "Georgiana, a moment, please. There is something you must know."

"What is it?"

"The colonel has been injured in the war."

"Injured! In what way?" she cried, sinking down onto the bench beside me.

"A sword wound to his leg."

She made a small cry, much like an animal caught in a snare. "But he will be well, will he not?"

"Aye, the earl said he would survive, but it will take time for the leg to mend, and he will certainly walk with a limp the remainder of his life."

Tears formed in her lovely blue eyes and threatened to spill over at any moment. "Oh, my dear Richard! I cannot bear to think of him being hurt. I must go to him! We must all go to him immediately." She jumped up and ran toward the house. "Where is Wills? He must make plans for us to leave this very day!"

William, of course, made no such plans. He was unwilling to leave our new son and me, and since I was unable to travel yet, a great argument arose between brother and sister. Back and forth they volleyed reasons for and against the trip, but Georgiana would not be dissuaded.

Eventually, William conceded to her pleading and agreed she could travel to Town, but only if her former companion, Mrs. Annesley, would leave her house in Lambton, where she had retired some years ago, and accompany her. Georgiana was such a favourite of the older lady that she was easily persuaded to make the trip.

The next day the ladies and their maids, Mr. Darcy's most trusted footmen, and his most careful driver transported his sister to Eden Park. Against her brother's will and truly against any reasoning he put forth, she had insisted she would go.

As we watched the carriage drive out of the park, William sighed and swore once again. "Blast, this stubborn streak in Georgiana is most unattractive. I know not from where it comes!"

I held my breath to keep from laughing aloud. The two of them grew more alike in temperament each day, but neither of them could see it.

Our annual Harvest Ball took place at the end of September that year, an event William and I both relished because of the special memories it evoked between us. I was somewhat surprised that Georgiana had not returned by that time, since it still remained her favourite party of the year.

As I attempted to read through the lines of her sporadic letters, I could only hope that her relationship with the colonel progressed. It appeared that Richard was in low spirits, since his injury had necessitated his retirement from the military. I wondered if he would now consider himself even less qualified to ask for Georgiana's hand or, for that matter, whether he still cared for her in that manner. After all, they had been apart over four years, and none of us had seen him during that time. I felt certain my sister cared deeply for him, else why would she turn down every eligible young man who attempted to court her. Perchance, however, I was playing the romantic, and it would not turn out as I hoped after all.

William, of course, knew nothing of all this. He was as hopelessly blind as always to his sister's feelings, although he had learned to allow her to express them. We had made some little progress during the years.

I was not, however, the sole romantic in the house. Among the numerous surprises I had encountered from my husband since our marriage, his tender, nostalgic sensibility was one that I never expected. He seemed to recall each and every time we had done something for the first time.

One evening before Mr. Bingley's wedding to Jane at Netherfield, Mr. Darcy had summoned two musicians and asked them to play the very song to which we had first danced. The only dancers in the ballroom, he led me through the steps as though we were at a fancy dress ball. I attempted to stifle my laughter, but it was impossible when at the end of the song, we caught Caroline and Mrs. Hurst standing in the doorway with shocked, but obviously envious expressions upon their faces.

At the townhouse in London, the adjoining door between our chambers stood open permanently. It might as well have been removed, for it no longer barred either of us from the other. My sleepwalking adventures ceased as quickly as they had appeared, once I spent every night in my husband's bed.

In a private moment, Mr. Darcy even admitted that the night he surprised me in my bath, he had seen me, indeed, stretch my leg up in the air and run warm water down it. That sight had caused him to stand transfixed, unable to turn away as he should have done. By the time he made that confession, of course, all I could do was smile, for the shock and anger I felt that night had vanished forever.

Many evenings when Georgiana was away, Mr. Darcy would lead me into the billiards room after dinner, where he continued to instruct me in the proper way to play the game. I must confess I proved a slow learner, and it took much patience and intimate demonstrations before either of us felt I had mastered the game. I never did understand the point of the sport, unless it was to allow lovers the opportunity for close proximity while being tutored.

In like manner, I had yet to learn the Italian language and even still required my husband to translate the words of particularly romantic arias in my ear when we attended recitals and concerts. He must have thought me quite thick to make such slow advancement in my studies of the foreign tongue, but he never complained, patient soul that he is.

Upon more occasions than I can remember, when rainstorms struck Pemberley at night, William and I would slip away to spend the evening in his old chamber at the end of the hall. I had never allowed Mrs. Reynolds to transform it into a guest room. It remained our secret haven where we had first allowed fulfilment of our great need and passionate love for each other.

THAT NIGHT AT THE BALL, as we had done every year, Mr. Darcy and I stole away for a few moments, deserting our guests to return to the stable and the haystack just outside its back door. A full moon shone once again, as though we had ordered it, when William and I dropped upon the mound of hay and he began to kiss me.

The years had not diminished the thrill of his touch, nor had I grown immune to the delicious taste of his kisses. If anything, I was more putty in his hands than ever, for I knew full well the pleasure he could give me, and I could see the joy in his eyes when he provoked that response in me that pleaded for more.

"Can you still recall that moment when first we kissed on this spot?" he asked.

"How can I not?" I raked my hands through his curls.

"Why did you run from me? I have always wanted to know."

I shook my head. "I still do not have an answer, William. Perhaps I wanted to know whether you would come after me, whether you truly wanted me."

"I was born wanting you. I may not have known it at the time, but I believe I searched for you all of my life."

Those words and the tender look in his eyes reduced me to a helpless muddle once again, and we struggled desperately to contain our passion. After many kisses and close embraces, we rose to return to our guests. He, of course, brushed the hay from my person, but I, in turn, spent no little time in doing the same to his backside, a task I deliberately took time to accomplish.

So, stealing away from the Harvest Ball to the haystack retreat outside had become a yearly recurrence and, I confess, one that made the entire night that much sweeter.

We had just returned to the great hall and the party, when I looked across the room and saw none other than Colonel Fitzwilliam enter the room with Georgiana on his arm and Mrs. Annesley following close behind them. The older lady quickly joined acquaintances who greeted her, and our cousin and sister moved further into the room.

Richard appeared thinner and older than we saw him last, and he now relied upon a cane to assist him in walking. However, his experience had only added a distinguished air and done little to mar his looks.

We quickly crossed the room to greet them and from the sparkle in their eyes, I surmised that all was well. They joined us at the head table and partook of the sumptuous feast laid before us. Following dinner, the colonel asked Georgiana to dance, but she protested, saying she was perfectly happy sitting beside him. He insisted, however, and led her to the floor. I know not how much pain he endured to go down the line of that dance, for he hid it well with the smile upon his face. Afterwards, though, he did not dance again, and Georgiana, who enjoyed the art more than anything, was content to remain seated by his side for the remainder of the evening.

Two days later, I came upon Mr. Darcy sitting at his desk, his face turned toward the window, so deep in contemplation he did not hear me enter the study. When I called his name, he appeared startled, as though he had returned from a great distance. I, of course, immediately questioned his inattentiveness. He said Colonel Fitzwilliam had just asked his blessing on his engagement to Georgiana. Needless to say, I was thrilled, but I attempted to temper my reaction until I knew William's response.

"It seems that Lord and Lady Matlock are settling the bulk of *her* fortune upon him immediately. His father's title and majority of wealth will go to his elder brother, of course, but because of his mother's generous endowment, my cousin feels he can provide for my sister more than adequately."

"And did you give your approval?"

"Yes, of course, if Fitzwilliam is Georgiana's choice."

"Oh, he is, I am sure."

He looked at me curiously. "Elizabeth, something tells me this announcement is not news to you. Am I correct?"

I looked away, searching for the right words. "I have long suspected Georgiana cares for him."

"Of course, she cares for him — we all do. I have the feeling, however, you have known for some time that she loves him not only as a cousin but as a man. Am I wrong?" I shook my head slightly and he pressed on. "What do you know of the matter?"

"I guessed that Colonel Fitzwilliam was in love with Georgiana before he left England. When I asked him, he confessed it, but he requested I keep it in confidence. I feared he might never declare his intentions, for he insisted she have time to mature, time to reach her own conclusions as to her feelings for him. He left without expressing his desires to her. He was too much of a gentleman to do that."

"And yet he told *you*," William said, a slight frown crossing his face. "What other secrets do you harbour that you have kept from me?"

"None. Believe me, this is the only one. I am much relieved that it is out in the open and that it has turned out well."

Just then, the colonel and Georgiana entered the room, and she ran to embrace first her brother and then me. "Oh, Elizabeth, did you ever think I could be so happy?"

"I did, and I rejoice with you!"

When William did not add his felicitations, I nudged him slightly with my elbow, and he immediately gave voice to them.

Well, I thought, *we are an old married couple after all, for here I am elbowing my husband, an action I thought I would never employ!*

Georgiana returned to Richard's side and tucked her hand inside his arm, her face wreathed in smiles as she looked up at him.

"Richard," I said, offering my hand, "let me congratulate you! You have won the prize."

"I have, indeed, Elizabeth. I have won the fairest flower in all of England, for my little Sprout has blossomed into the loveliest rose!"

Some five weeks later, Mr. Darcy and I set out for London to attend Richard and Georgiana's wedding. It was a short engagement, to be sure, but they both declared they had been apart far too long. When Mr. Darcy voiced some objection, I reminded him that we had been engaged less than a fortnight before our wedding took place.

Our sister elected to be married from the majestic sanctuary in which we worshiped when we lived in Town. I was somewhat surprised, thinking she would choose the small church at Derbyshire, but both bride and groom preferred London. Once again, Mrs. Annesley had aided us by travelling to London with Georgiana some weeks earlier to shop for her trousseau and wedding clothes, remaining with her at the townhouse until we joined them. That enabled us to refrain from taking the little ones into Town with its stale air and disease. We left the children with Jane and Mr. Bingley, as she was expecting her third child and, upon doctor's orders, could not travel. Although I had weaned my babe by that time, it was difficult to leave him and his brother, but William promised we would return within a week.

Unfortunately, it began to rain the day we set out, and the farther we travelled, the harder it rained. The roads soon vanished, becoming soggy, muddy ruts, and we bounced around inside the carriage much as we had done on our own wedding day. When we stopped at a small village to change horses on the second day of our trip, we were dismayed to learn that the river up ahead had risen sharply, and the bridge was now four foot deep in swiftly rushing water. The local villagers warned us not to proceed until the rain let up and the water receded. By that time, evening reigned, the storm causing us to make poor time.

As I entered the small, rustic inn with Mr. Darcy, a sudden wave of familiarity brushed over me, and I looked around, wondering when I ever could have been there. Mr. Darcy and I rarely stayed at an inn, for he much preferred the comfort and luxury of our own homes or that of our friends and family. We had spent the previous night on the road at the home of Mr. Darnley's brother.

"You are in luck, sir," the innkeeper said, bustling about in anticipation of entertaining paying guests for the night. "The best suite — the only suite — in the house is free. Two connectin' rooms, sir, right up these stairs. Just follow me."

That voice!

I turned to look upon our host, and yes, it was the same little man who had ushered us up those stairs years ago. We had entered the very place in which we had spent our wedding night. As I reached for the handrail, I remembered the burnished chocolate colour, and when I looked down, I saw those same wooden steps worn to an even duller shine.

At the head of the stairs, the man led us past a closed door to the so-called suite at the end of the hall. Inside, Mr. Darcy walked around inspecting the two rooms, an impatient, displeased air about him.

"Is this the best you can offer, man?" he asked.

When the innkeeper nodded, William looked at me with an apologetic expression. "Well, we have no choice. I suppose we shall have to make the best of it."

"Yes, sir." The man hurried to the grate to lay a fire. "Let me get a good blaze started, and then I'll have the wife carry up what's needed."

"Before you do that," I said, "did I not see another room at the head of the stairs? Is it vacant?"

"Oh, yes, ma'am, but it's only a single room, not near so nice as this 'un."

"Could we see it?" I asked. Mr. Darcy frowned at me. "It is my particular wish."

"Yes, ma'am," the innkeeper said, a look of confusion about his face, as he led us down the hall and opened the door.

We walked into the room, and immediately a rush of memories flooded my senses. Had it not been only yesterday that I followed my new husband into that chamber, a most reluctant bride, fearful and vexed that I had been forced into an arranged marriage?

The same lumpy old chaise sat to one side, its middle sagging even more, if possible. The furnishings had not been altered in the slightest during the years; even the same worn quilt covered the bed. I walked around the room, running my fingers lightly across the small table set before the cold fireplace.

"I should like to stay in this room, Mr. Darcy." I turned to observe his reaction. I was not disappointed, for I could see the shock of recognition in his eyes, as well.

"Here, ma'am?" The owner of the inn's voice was incredulous. "But the other rooms be far more grand."

"We will take this room," my husband said. "Light the fire, and see that our things are brought up, if you please."

The man shook his head in wonderment, but he did as he was told. When he finished, his wife and serving girl furnished the room with clean towels and poured fresh water into the ewer. Upon their departure, Mr. Darcy took my hands and brought them to his lips.

"What are the chances we should find ourselves in this room once again?"

"And after all this time?" I replied.

"The very room in which we spent our wedding night." He shook his head. "A poor beginning, you must admit."

I smiled and walked over to the bed, running my hand across the quilt. "A very poor beginning. But I must confess the room holds an appeal for me."

"In what way?"

"This was the first bed in which we slept together."

"A pity that neither of us was conscious of it."

"Yes," I said, turning to him, "a very great pity."

He ran his finger along the side of my face and under my chin. "I can still see the fire in your eyes that greeted me that next morning. My, but you were angry!"

"And why not?" I retorted. "You promised to sleep on that lumpy old chaise, as I recall."

He looked at the referenced piece of furniture and then at the bed. "I did, but something drew me to your bed, Elizabeth."

"Nothing drew you, William. In truth, you were somewhat the worse for wear from drink, and you stumbled into bed with me by mistake."

He slipped his arms around my waist and pulled me closer. "I think not, my love. I may have been inebriated, but it was not a mistake — never a mistake. I think an unseen force drew me to you as clearly as though we were somehow tied together. It was that same force that took me to the assembly at Meryton where I first laid eyes on you, that caused you to find your way into my bed when walking in your sleep, and that led you to lie beneath my portrait at Pemberley when I was still in London. We were meant to be together, to love each other, to be drawn one to the other forever. It is a force that will not be denied."

I opened my mouth to speak, but he covered it with his own sweet lips. That delicious taste of heaven caused a familiar quickening deep within me.

"Do not deny it, Elizabeth," he managed to mumble between kisses. "Do you hear me? Do not deny it."

In truth, I had no intention of denying it, but if he thought that I was and insisted on kissing me to prevent my doing so, I saw no reason to tell him otherwise. I simply surrendered to his love, an action I continue to enjoy to this day.

The End